SACRAMENTO PUBLIC LIBRARY
828 "I" Street
Sacramento, CA 95814
01/14

BETWEEN A RAKE AND A HARD PLACE

CONNIE MASON
AND MIA MARLOWE

D0973196

Copyright © 2014 by Novel Ideas, Inc.
Cover and internal design © 2014 by Sourcebooks, Inc.
Cover image by Judy York

Sourcebooks and the colophon are registered trademarks of
Sourcebooks, Inc.

All rights reserved. No part of this book may be reproduced in any
form or by any electronic or mechanical means including information storage and retrieval systems—except in the case of brief
quotations embodied in critical articles or reviews—without permission in writing from its publisher, Sourcebooks, Inc.

The characters and events portrayed in this book are fictitious or
are used fictitiously. Any similarity to real persons, living or dead,
is purely coincidental and not intended by the author.

Published by Sourcebooks Casablanca, an imprint of Sourcebooks,
Inc.
P.O. Box 4410, Naperville, Illinois 60567-4410
(630) 961-3900
Fax: (630) 961-2168
www.sourcebooks.com

Printed and bound in the United States of America.
VP 10 9 8 7 6 5 4 3 2 1

To everyone who wants to make a list of secret pleasures.

One

London, March 1818

Every English heart mourns the loss of Princess Charlotte and her stillborn son last November. But the royal succession is in question, so it's tallyho and off to the "Hymen Race Terrific" for King George's three unmarried sons. No stakes could be higher for Their Highnesses, the Dukes of Clarence, Cambridge, and Kent. Which royal duke will be the first to wed, bed, and breed? Whose offspring will one day wear the crown?

Only time and a lady's consent will tell.

From Le Dernier Mot,
The Final Word on News That Everyone
Who Is Anyone Should Know

LADY SERENA OSBOURNE UNCROSSED HER LEGS AND barely resisted the urge to rub her burning inner thighs.

Drat these trousers!

She'd planned this exploit for weeks. She committed the map of London in her father's study to memory so she could walk to Boodles, exclusive haunt of the country squire and horse set, without asking for directions. She commissioned the beautifully tailored masculine ensemble she was wearing, though bribing her *modiste* to do it secretly had cost the earth. She determined the right time for slipping away from the watchful eyes of her footman.

But she hadn't counted on chafing.

Men must have cast-iron undergarments.

Unfortunately, Serena couldn't wear her usual pantalets beneath the blasted gray wool without spoiling the line of the trousers.

But other than the chafing, she found wearing men's clothing as exciting an adventure as she'd hoped. When she walked down the male dominated section of St. James Street to the gentlemen's club, she reveled in a newborn sense of freedom. Ordinarily, a woman walking without an escort on that block would be castigated as a wanton, but she strolled it freely, albeit itchily, in her trousers, waistcoat, tailcoat, and great-coat. Plenty of layers to conceal her true form.

There'd been a moment of panic at the ornate door of Boodles when she wasn't sure her disguise as her cousin Rowland would hold. They favored one another strongly, being blessed with fashionable coloring as blue-eyed blondes, and had the same delicately chiseled features, down to the small dimple on their chins. She and Rowland were both Osbournes to the bone.

Rowland was not gifted with unusual stature or broad shoulders, so that made the disguise easier to pull off. But if the doorkeeper at the club had looked too closely when Serena removed her topper, he'd have seen that her blond hair was bound by a pale ribbon and secreted down her back beneath the stiff collar and cravat. Evidently, Rowland hadn't put in an appearance at the club recently enough for the differences between them to be noted, and she was admitted readily.

Now Serena was ensconced before a cozy fire with a cup of fine Arabica bean coffee on the small table beside her wing chair, a freshly ironed copy of the *Times* on her lap, and the low hum of masculine conversation all around her. She relished being surrounded by the rich mahogany paneling, brass fittings, and undeniably masculine scent that was a combination of damp tweed—for it had rained early on—spicy bergamot, and old leather.

She'd done it. She was the first woman to invade Boodles since its establishment in 1762. All Serena wanted was a taste of Boodles' brew and the chance to flout the rules while she could. Once she became the royal duke's bride, her life would no longer be her own. She'd be hard-pressed to have any sorts of adventures then.

Now all she had to do was drink her coffee and make good her escape without engaging anyone in conversation and she'd be—

"Osbourne, isn't it?"

Serena gulped and looked up into a pair of speculatively narrowed green eyes. They belonged to Sir Jonah Sharp.

Her friend Lysandra always had plenty of gossip to share about this particular gentleman, and none of it the least complimentary. The raw-boned, wickedly handsome fellow was said to be a rake of the first water. With the face of a vengeful archangel and the broad shoulders of a dock worker, Sir Jonah was destined by nature to turn feminine heads everywhere he went.

There were more than a few evil rumors floating around about his less than exemplary military service, though he was reputedly lethal with a sword. He didn't wear one now, but Serena wondered if his thick cherry walking stick might conceal a blade.

Something about the man made her insides quiver like a plate of aspic. She realized with a start that he'd asked her a question. "Yes," she said, pitching her voice as low as she possibly could. "I'm Osbourne."

It was no lie. As Lady Serena, the only child of the Marquis of Wyndleton, she was an Osbourne. Just not the one Sir Jonah thought.

"Sir Jonah Sharp, your servant, sir," he said, removing his beaver hat and offering his hand. His hair was seal dark and his equally dark brows made his green eyes all the more striking. They weren't the deep mossy hue of a shaded glen. They were the icy green of the Irish Sea, but they warmed her strangely. "You may not recall me. I was a few forms ahead of you."

Drat! Not only did he know her cousin Rowland, he'd gone to school with him. She took the man's hand, gave what she hoped was a hearty shake, and tried not to wince at his grip. Thank goodness she'd thought to have elegantly masculine gloves made to match her outfit.

Heaven help her if Sir Jonah started reminiscing about schoolboy pranks. She took a big gulp of her coffee while her mind churned furiously. She couldn't help grimacing at the hot, dark liquid. Normally, Serena laced her coffee with cream and at least three sugar lumps, but she figured a man would take it black.

It was horrid.

Sir Jonah settled into the wing chair opposite her and motioned to the servant for coffee to be brought. Even though he was obviously a member of the club, he seemed out of place. Too big, too raw, too...blatantly male to blend in with the other dandified patrons. "I wasn't certain it was you at first. You've changed a good bit since Eton."

Serena hoped her cousin had a reputation for being a man of few words. She didn't dare speak too much for fear of giving herself away. "You've changed too."

"Don't believe everything you hear," Sharp said. "Do you see much of Easterly these days?"

Who the devil was Easterly? Probably one of Rowland's friends. "Not as much as I'd like."

"Truly? You must have called Pax with him then, since the two of you didn't get on when we were in school. I always figured if ever you and Easterly buried the hatchet it would be in each other's skulls."

The brutal imagery made Serena more than a little queasy. Was this really how men talked when women weren't around?

"So, I understand the Duke of Kent is considering making your cousin his royal duchess." Sir Jonah tugged off his gloves and laid them aside as he accepted his coffee from the hovering servant. His hands were far too large for fashion, which required a man have small, neat hands to match his small, narrow feet. Nothing the least diminutive about Sir Jonah's polished Hessians either. Serena's palms began to feel clammy inside her kid gloves, but she wasn't about to remove them. "How do you rate Lady Serena's chances in the race for a royal heir?"

Crude as well as violent. Male conversation was definitely not what it was cracked up to be.

Irritation fizzed in Serena's belly. It was bad enough to be an object of speculation over her possible match with the duke. The tabloids first coined the vulgar phrase "Hymen Race Terrific" to describe the sons of King George's dash to the altar in order to provide their mad father with a legitimate grandchild. Seeing it in print was infuriating enough. Hearing it spoken of in public made her quietly livid.

"I think Lady Serena stands a better chance of becoming English royalty than some German-speaking upstart of a princess," she said staunchly.

Rumors that Prince Edward, the Duke of Kent, was sending envoys to the duchy of Saxe-Coburg-Saalfeld infuriated her father to no end. "We're English, demmit!" he'd say over the dinner table when the subject of a possible alliance with the sister of Prince Leopold arose. "The future monarch of England should not be raised speaking Deutsch!"

Perhaps if her mother were still alive, she'd have tempered the marquis's propensity for swearing, but Serena doubted it. One of her earliest memories was of sitting on her father's lap, listening in horrified fascination while he spouted words her governess had assured her would lead to eternal damnation. Eventually, she assumed coarse language was merely a masculine trait. Based on her experience with her father, she'd expected to hear a good deal more profanity at Boodles than she had. Perhaps it was time to cement her male identity with a bit of the vulgar tongue.

"If the Duke of Kent would move his royal arse and

offer for Lady Serena straight out instead of dancing about the issue, the match could be made by this time tomorrow," she said.

"It's seems you know your cousin's mind on this matter." Sir Jonah's lips twitched in a half-smile. "The lady's willing, is she?"

"Not that it's any of your business, Sharp, but yes, she is. What woman wouldn't accept the suit of a royal duke?"

"One who values herself for more than her ability to conceive an heir."

That stung. She was much more than her gender. Hadn't she chafed at the limits placed upon her by virtue of her sex so much she was willing to endure a little real chafing in order to pierce the male sanctuary of Boodles?

"A *royal* heir. That makes all the difference in the world," she corrected, clutching her coffee cup so tightly she was sure her knuckles went white beneath her gloves. "Becoming the wife of a royal duke is not the same thing as becoming the wife of, say…a mere baronet."

Sir Jonah splayed his hand over his chest. "You wound me, Osbourne."

Serena doubted it. He wasn't taking her seriously at all. It was suddenly very important to make him understand why she'd accept the Duke of Kent's proposal without a second thought. "Any woman can bring a child into the world. Only a very few can give birth to a future king. Just imagine the opportunity to mold and shape the child who will one day reign."

"Careful. It almost sounds as if *you'd* be willing to bear the duke's child, Osbourne."

Would her cousin think that an insult to his manhood and demand satisfaction? Masquerading as Rowland was much more complicated than she'd expected. She decided to take Sir Jonah's words as a joke and laughed, careful to keep the pitch of her voice low.

"Very droll, Sir Jonah. I don't remember you being so clever when we were in school." She hoped he hadn't been the school's resident wag, but she couldn't resist delivering a verbal slap.

"Another blow. You must give me a way to get even." He set down his coffee and skewered her with a penetrating gaze. "Will you make a wager?"

A bet could be a dicey proposition. Suppose she lost. Would Sir Jonah search out her cousin and demand he pay? "It depends on what you have in mind."

"A question about which you have definite ideas. You say Lady Serena will wed the Duke of Kent. I say she will not."

She tamped down a sigh of relief. It couldn't even be considered gambling since she had some control in the outcome. She'd make sure the duke chose her. The day an English maiden couldn't best some German lady hadn't dawned. "Very well."

"Good." Sir Jonah leaned forward, balancing his elbows on his knees. "And now for the stakes. Since you're Lady Serena's cousin and have inside information, it seems only fair that the odds reflect that. Say, ten to one?"

Even at those odds, it was actually unfair for her to make this wager with the man, but something about Sir Jonah's smug smile made her want to smack it off his face. He deserved a drubbing.

"Done. Ten to one."

He signaled to a man dressed in light blue livery. "Mr. Filbee, bring the book if you will."

Serena had heard tales of Boodles' infamous wager book. Countless gentlemen had lost homes, lands, and fortunes simply by signing their names in that ledger. No matter the cost, a lost wager was a debt of honor that would be repaid, even if it meant turning one's family out on the street.

Mr. Filbee disappeared into a back room and returned bearing a leather-bound volume, quill, and ink. Once he was prepared to take dictation, he gave Sir Jonah a quizzical look. "The nature of the wager, if you please."

"Let's keep this discreet since a lady is involved," Sir Jonah said to Serena. He gave her a pointed look and for a moment, her belly squirmed, fearing he'd realized she wasn't her cousin after all. Then he turned back to the liveried servant. "Take this down, Filbee. 'On the question of whether or not a certain young lady, known to us both, will wed a certain gentleman who shall remain nameless, Mr. Rowland Osbourne is of the opinion the match will be made. Sir Jonah Sharp disagrees. The stakes shall be one hundred guineas to ten.' There. That should do it."

Serena sputtered. "One hundred guineas?"

"You agreed to ten to one odds," he reminded her. "I thought we'd make it interesting."

She'd have to sell some of her jewelry, while being careful not to sell the larger pieces her father might notice missing, to make good on a wager of that size.

"Thinking of a higher amount?" Sir Jonah rubbed his chin, considering his options. "As your uncle's heir apparent, money is probably no object for you. Having the expectation of becoming the Marquis of Wyndleton someday probably means there are plenty who would advance you any sum you'd care to name. It would be a stretch for me, but I could go a thousand to one hundred if you like."

"No, no, one hundred to ten is fine." Her voice had crept up half an octave in excitement. She bridled herself to pitch it lower. "Perfectly fine."

Mr. Filbee finished recording the wager in his book, then handed it to Sir Jonah for his signature. He signed with a flourish and handed the quill to Serena.

She couldn't sign her cousin's name. Forgery was considered a crime on par with murder, and was dealt with just as harshly. And even if it wasn't a crime, she didn't want to commit a lie to pen and paper. So she simply signed "Osbourne."

It's true, she reassured herself. She wasn't the one who named her as Rowland for Mr. Filbee. If there was a discrepancy with the facts in the Boodles Book of Wagers, she hadn't been the one to introduce it.

She was slicing her conscience with a mighty thin blade, but she *had* managed to sign her name in the exclusively male ledger. A warm glow of accomplishment surged through her. This was much more satisfying than drinking the bitter black coffee.

"Thank you, Mr. Filbee; that'll be all," Sir Jonah said. Then he settled back into his chair and grinned at her. When she didn't return his smile, his gaze wandered over her head toward the open door. Bracing cold rushed over them as someone entered. "I say, Osbourne, have you a brother I don't know about?"

"No." The Osbournes were notorious for small but hearty families. Few children were born to them, but those who were tended to live to maturity and a ripe old age. At eighty-two, Serena's Grand-mère Osbourne could still cut a respectable reel, but even she had been an only child. "I have no brother," Serena said.

"Then you have a doppelganger, my friend. That fellow yonder has a wispy attempt at a mustache, but otherwise, your twin just walked in the door."

Serena twisted to peek around the tall wing of her chair. *Drat!* It was Rowland. He wasn't supposed to be in Town until the Season started. She shrank back into the chair, wishing she could seep into the tufted cushions.

"Looks like the doorkeeper is reluctant about admitting him," Sir Jonah said calmly. "As he should be. One Osbourne at a time is enough for any establishment. Well, my lady, how would you like to play this?"

"My lady? I'm not—"

"Spare me your denials. You haven't time. If you wish to quit this place without being found out, follow me." He rose and began walking toward the door to the kitchen where servants were coming and going, bearing trays heaped with steaming caffeinated bliss and small glass bowls of the club's famous Orange Fool.

If she were apprehended in Boodles and exposed as herself, she could kiss any chance of a royal betrothal good-bye.

Serena scrambled to her feet and broke into a trot after Sir Jonah Sharp.

Two

A person unknown was seen fleeing the premises of Boodles this afternoon after impersonating a member of the club in order to gain admittance. Mr. Rowland Osbourne, whose identity was nefariously assumed, is offering a reward of five pounds for information that leads to the miscreant's apprehension. The management of Boodles also wishes to press civil charges against the culprit over the matter of upturning a vat of cream during a daring escape through the kitchen. Sadly, Boodles' Orange Fool, the club's signature dessert, has been scrubbed from the menu until the impostor is found as an incentive for parties with knowledge of the perpetrator's identity to step forward.

From Le Dernier Mot,
The Final Word on News That Everyone
Who Is Anyone Should Know

"HONESTLY, MY LADY, HOW DID YOU EVER MANAGE TO get so much cream in your hair?" Amelia Braithwaite asked as she emptied yet another pitcher of tepid water over Serena's head.

"Please don't scold, Amelia." Serena ran her palms over her wet hair, satisfied by the squeak of cleanliness. When Amelia held out an oversized towel of soft Turkish cotton, she rose from the hip bath and allowed her governess-turned-companion to wrap the cloth around her. "I've had a trying enough day as it is."

"It'll be far more trying if your father's coach comes to collect us and finds you unable to return home because you are indisposed by virtue of too much Orange Fool."

Serena rolled her eyes. Their plan had been perfect. The little white lie used to cover Serena's clandestine adventure was that she was taking tea with Amelia Braithwaite's ailing aunt. Fortunately, Aunt Cleo was the picture of health, lived within walking distance of Boodles, and was the proud possessor of a deep copper tub. The old lady was also delighted to live vicariously through Serena's exploits.

"The girl's right, Amelia. No harm done," Cleo Braithwaite said. Serena's pale pink column dress and matching pelisse had been laid out on the bed to keep them from wrinkling. Cleo smoothed out the muslin walking gown with her deeply veined hands. "When I think on the scrapes my young charges got into back in my day—trust me, things might have been very much worse. Suppose Lady Serena hadn't been able to escape, for example."

Still draped with the towel, Serena disappeared behind the dressing screen and dried herself. Then she slipped into her chemise, barely restraining a shiver. Her escape had been a near thing. If not for Sir

Jonah, she'd never have managed to dodge and weave through the kitchen and out the back door. Then once they'd made it into the alley, he served as her rear guard, lobbing chunks of gravel at their pursuers with wicked accuracy. It was enough to keep some distance between them and the gang comprised of Boodles' kitchen staff till they reached Sir Jonah's gig, which he'd left at the livery on the corner. He wasted no time on politeness, hefting her onto the narrow seat without so much as a "by your leave." Then he tossed a few coppers to the stable boy as he leapt onto the seat beside her, slapped the reins over the mare's back, and the smart equipage flew over the cobblestones.

Sharp had become testy with her when she wouldn't allow him to return her to her father's elegant town house. She insisted he leave her at the corner of Brewer Street and Brindle Lane. From there, she could walk back to Aunt Cleo's rented rooms without implicating anyone else in her scheme.

He finally bowed to her wishes. As she clambered down from the gig at the appointed crossroads, she thanked him.

"I don't want your thanks," he'd said with a stern look. "You owe me, Serena. I'll collect one day. Remember that."

He chirruped to the horse and was gone before she could castigate him for addressing her so familiarly. Of course, to be fair, he was in the right. One couldn't be jammed onto a gig's narrow seat alongside someone while coated with cream without becoming somewhat familiar.

Upturning the vat of Orange Fool was probably not

part of Sir Jonah's plan when she first tailed him into the kitchen. Everything had happened so fast as they shoved through the knots of servants. Then suddenly, the world went slick and foamy and their pursuers were slipping and sliding in the sweet peaked drifts of white spreading over the brick floor. Enough cream landed on Serena and Sir Jonah to make them blend in with the similarly doused servants for a moment, which was a sticky blessing.

But she wasn't sure accepting Jonah's help would turn out to be a blessing in the end. She *owed* him. It was an uncomfortable sort of debt.

And something she was uneasy sharing even with Amelia.

At twenty, she was old enough not to need a governess any longer, but her relationship with Amelia was a complicated one. When Serena was twelve, her mother had died suddenly. Amelia had stepped into the gap. Then after Serena's studies were complete and Amelia declared there was nothing more she could teach her, Serena insisted she stay on as a companion.

Of course, it was usually dowagers who hired someone to stay with them for the sake of company, but Serena couldn't bear to lose Amelia. She was mentor, friend, teacher, and confidant all rolled into one. When Serena became a royal duchess, she planned to take Amelia to the palace with her.

It would be unthinkable to be plunged into the strange world of the royal family without someone she trusted to lean upon.

But she still didn't feel like sharing Sir Jonah's involvement in what happened at Boodles.

For one thing, she wasn't sure what she'd say about him. *The man made my insides jiggle like jelly.* No, that would never do.

She stepped into her pantalets, grateful for the smooth silk against her abraded thighs. "You're right, of course," she said, peeping around the dressing screen and nodding to Aunt Cleo. "No harm done. And I was able to cross a few things off the list."

"List?" Aunt Cleo said. "What list?"

Amelia shook her head and cast her eyes heavenward. "A list of forbidden pleasures."

"Don't scowl so. It spoils your pretty face," Serena said, parroting the admonition she'd received from Amelia countless times. "Besides, I can't help it if you raised me to be the curious sort."

"Careful, child. You know what curiosity did to the cat."

"I'm no longer a child," Serena said. Even to her own ears, that sounded a good bit more petulantly childish than she wished. "In any case, a cat has nine lives, you know."

Amelia's lips pursed in a small moue of disapproval. "Then you well and truly used up one this day."

"Tell me more about this list of yours." Aunt Cleo wanted to know.

"I have it here." Serena crossed to the bed and retrieved a much folded bit of foolscap and a pencil from the beaded reticule lying next to her gown. She smoothed the paper flat on the side table.

"Item one: Wear men's clothing in public." Serena struck through the words with her pencil. "Item two: Gain admittance to an exclusively male club."

She crossed that off as well. She could have added "Enter into an ill-considered wager and sign one's name in the ledger of gambling records at said male club," but she didn't think she ought to tell Amelia and her aunt about that either. It had been enough for her to regale them with descriptions of the brass and waxed wood décor of Boodles and complain about the bitterness of black coffee. Serena's expurgated version of her escape through the kitchen provided Amelia and her aunt with more than enough vicarious excitement for one day.

Serena handed the piece of foolscap to Aunt Cleo while Amelia laced her stays and cinched them tight. She could recite the rest of the list in her sleep.

Item three: Smoke a cigar.
Item four: Ride astride.
Item five: Drink until one is insensate at least once.
Item six: Have one's fortune told by gypsies.
Item seven: Dance the—

"Dance the waltz?" Aunt Cleo said, aghast. "Don't you know that's positively indecent? I read all about it in the *Times*. Utterly disgraceful, they say. Why, you may as well add 'Allow a gentleman to paw one in public' to the list."

"It's a perfectly legal dance. The Prince Regent approves it," Serena said.

Aunt Cleo raised a wiry gray brow. "It may be legal, but the fact that His Royal Highness has embraced it is proof enough to me that the waltz is not respectable."

"Neither is any other item on the list," Serena said,

casting a quick smile to Amelia over her aunt's head. Amelia's help had come grudgingly, but she'd finally agreed to assist in fulfilling the list. "Come, Auntie Cleo. Don't you remember what it was like to be young? No lasting harm will come if I indulge in a few small adventures. Discreetly, of course, and only once. After all, experience is the best teacher, Amelia always says."

Amelia shot her a pointed look. "And sometimes the most brutal."

So far she'd escaped her experience with nothing more sinister than a coating of cream. Serena shrugged and lifted her arms to let Amelia drape the gown over her head. The muslin fell in soft folds to her ankles. Men's clothes were an adventure, but she was ever so much more comfortable in her own things. Wool chafing one's unprotected thighs was indeed brutal.

"At least no lasting harm will come from fulfilling the list—*if* Serena's more careful than she was on this day," her governess amended.

"I'll be careful." She took the list back, refolded it, and squirreled it away in her reticule. There was another item on the list, but she hadn't committed it to paper.

The Duke of Kent was much older than she, fifty if he was a day. Rumors of his cruelty in Gibraltar had led to his being removed from the governorship there. A life of dissipation did not lend itself to a healthy countenance. He may have demonstrated his potency by siring a gaggle of bastards on a number of mistresses, but he didn't seem the sort who would make old bones. Serena was under no illusions about what kind of husband the Duke of Kent would be to her.

Benign neglect was the best she could hope for once she delivered an heir.

But there it was. In order to get a child, she'd have to submit to the duke, to allow herself to be taken, probably without an ounce of tenderness if Kent's distant wooing was any indication. If not for the possibility of mothering the future King of England, she'd never agree to the match.

But in a world where women weren't allowed to do anything of significance, birthing a monarch and shaping his character seemed the most important thing to which Serena could ever aspire.

However, that didn't mean she was content to live strictly for the phantom child she might one day conceive. She dreamed of a few things for herself before she left this world. She wanted to experience romance. She wanted to feel passion. She wanted to know what it was to give herself to someone she cared for and be given to in return.

She doubted she'd find those things in her marriage, but she still didn't dare write them down. She only listed the last item in her mind, knowing she'd probably not accomplish it before she wed and bore a child.

But later, somehow, there'd be time for her.

"Lady Serena, stop your wool-gathering. You didn't hear a word I said." Amelia's voice pulled her out of her musings. It always took her aback a bit when Amelia called her "lady." In private, she insisted on familiar address. The insertion of her title when she and Amelia were within earshot of others always felt like a barrier erected between them. "Your father's coach is here."

Serena put on her bonnet and tied the ribbons in a jaunty bow under her chin, mentally reciting that last secret pleasure she couldn't write down.

Item eight: Lie with a man for no other reason than because I want to.

❧

Jonah leaned forward over his horse's outstretched neck and crooned urgent encouragements as he careened down Rotten Row. He never laid a crop on Turk's withers. The gelding had a willing heart and Jonah would do nothing to break its spirit.

However, he thought he might enjoy giving Lady Serena Osbourne a good sting on her wool-clad bum for her exploits that afternoon. What could she have been thinking to dress as a man and invade Boodles like that?

It was a good thing he'd been shadowing her and figured a way to spirit her out of there. If she'd been discovered, she'd have been mired in more scandal than anyone could have gotten her out of.

Not even her powerful father, Lord Wyndleton.

He squeezed the gelding with his thighs and Turk poured on more speed. Jonah moved with him, letting the pounding rhythm clear his mind. Just breathing. Just flying. Just letting his heartbeat fall into time with the measured strides. No random thoughts. No troublesome memories stabbing through his brain.

Life was better when he didn't give himself a chance to think.

But Turk couldn't run forever. They were nearing a horse trough, so he eased up and reined in the Thoroughbred. Jonah dismounted and led his gelding to the stone basin. Turk's sides heaved, and his glossy chest was wet with sweat. Heart pounding and with perspiration blooming on his face, Jonah was as blown as his mount. Then a gentleman approached them and Jonah suddenly wished he'd kept riding whether he and his horse needed a rest or not.

"Hullo, Sharp." It was the Honorable Fortescue Alcock. He'd been seated on the park bench near the trough, a newspaper spread before him obscuring his face until a moment ago. Alcock was a Member of Parliament, a maker of unholy alliances, and a burr under Jonah's saddle for the last few months. "This isn't the fashionable time of day to ride, you know."

The sun had dipped below the treetops of Hyde Park. Their still naked limbs sent long snaky shadows across Rotten Row.

"I'm not here to see and be seen. Turk needs the exercise." And Jonah needed the measure of peace those few moments spent flying over the ground afforded him. Sometimes he thought they were all that kept him sane.

"You need to punish yourself as well. I understand."

Jonah's fingers curled into fists, but he bridled himself. Knocking Alcock into next week would be satisfying for a moment, but it would only give the man more power over him.

"Don't look so surprised. I've read your dossier, remember. It's only natural that you'd seek absolution for your deeds. Riding yourself and your horse to exhaustion is a socially acceptable method of self-flagellation," Alcock said with an oily smile. "You have a long history of doing very bad things, Sir Jonah, albeit for very good reasons. The ends may justify the means, but I doubt a past like yours makes for restful sleep."

"How I sleep is my own business."

"And where you sleep is mine," Alcock countered. "How is your current assignment coming along?"

Fortescue Alcock was determined that the line of Hanoverian kings would die out with the Prince Regent. If the younger sons of King George were thwarted in their race to produce an heir, the Crown would devolve to another ruling house. Jonah had been tasked with seducing and ruining Lady Serena Osbourne so she would no longer be considered as a possible wife for the Duke of Kent.

No, *tasked* was the wrong word. *Coerced* was more like it.

"It's proceeding apace." Jonah narrowed his eyes at Alcock. "Don't worry. I agreed to do it. It'll get done."

"It had better. I understand your brother is keeping company with a lady well above himself. It'd be a shame if, say…new information about your dishonor at Maubeuge should put an end to such idyllic love."

Jonah had been implicated, along with his friends Rhys Warrington and Nathaniel Colton, in a disastrous defeat in France just days before the decisive Battle of Waterloo. Facts were fluid things, Alcock had explained. They could be bent to whatever use he chose. He claimed to have evidence that would either exonerate them or, if he so wished, see them all convicted of treason for colluding with the French and leading their men into an ambush. The ensuing scandal would ruin Jonah's family.

"I imagine it would be impossible for your brother to marry the Earl of Enderling's daughter if—"

Fast as thought, Jonah snatched the man up by his lapels and held him aloft, feet kicking as he tried to scrape his toes on the ground.

"I agreed to do your dirty work, Alcock." Jonah gave him a quick shake, like a terrier might a rat. "I didn't agree to listen to you talk about it. Bother me about this again and I'll find a way to permanently close your mouth."

Alcock paled to the color of rancid suet, but his lips remained firmly shut.

Sometimes, Jonah thought as he shot the man a wolf's smile, *it's good to have a dangerous reputation.*

Three

The London Lyric Opera opened their season with a ponderous production of Mozart's Cosi Fan Tutte. *It was not the company's finest effort. However, ham-handed acting and a tenor of dubious talent aside, the premier was judged by all to be thoroughly entertaining. Of course, this is most likely because the real theatre is always being played out among the bon ton that makes up the audience.*

From Le Dernier Mot,
The Final Word on News That Everyone
Who Is Anyone Should Know

THE TENOR MUFFED HIS HIGH NOTE, BUT HIS CLAQUE insisted on applauding loudly and long in any case. The practice of having a paid group of clappers was new to English opera, but the Italian singer had brought this devoted group with him. Serena suspected the long trip from Italy had rendered them all tone deaf, but they made enough noise that the maestro was obliged to give the downbeat for a reprise.

"Maybe he'll have better luck this time," Serena

said to her friend, Lysandra Grey, who was seated beside her in the elegant Wyndleton box.

"And this opera will last long past midnight if they keep repeating arias till the singers get them right." Lysandra sighed. Then she leaned over to stage whisper into Serena's ear, "He's staring at you again."

Serena lowered her opera glasses. "Who?"

"Sir Jonah Sharp, of course," Lysandra said. "Who did you think? He's been ogling you all night. I haven't seen such an intense stare since my terrier treed a squirrel in the garden."

"There's a flattering comparison. Squirrels are merely rats with fluffy tails, you know."

"Shh!" Amelia said from Serena's other side. "You'll miss the cadenza."

"So will the singer, most likely." Serena sent her governess an apologetic grimace. Amelia had always had a weakness for Italian tenors, whether they choked on their high notes or not.

Lysandra made a "hmph-ing" sound and sat back in her seat, arms crossed beneath her exquisitely displayed bosom.

Serena often envied her friend's curves, but she allowed that a buxom figure might have its drawbacks. Binding her less than generous breasts to fit into the men's clothing had been hard enough. It would have been impossible if Serena had been shaped like Lysandra. No one would ever mistake her friend for a man, no matter what she wore.

Of course, Sir Jonah hadn't been fooled by Serena's disguise one bit. She wondered what had given her away.

Serena glanced at the box directly across the theatre from her father's exclusive seats. Sir Jonah Sharp wasn't paying the least attention to the singers and dancers on the stage. He met her gaze without embarrassment at having been caught looking at her.

Throughout the overture, she'd felt eyes on her, heavy and knowing. She lifted her head, like a grazing doe that senses a watcher in the thicket, and met Sir Jonah's green eyes. She looked away immediately, but while the soprano sang an aria about how desperately she missed the tenor who'd been called away to war, Serena was acutely aware of Sir Jonah's steady gaze despite the dimness of the theatre.

Lysandra leaned in again and this time cupped her hand around Serena's ear. "Honestly, what have you done to attract the man's attention like that? Sir Jonah's been dogging your steps for the last fortnight."

"I doubt that. If we've crossed paths, it's likely because London's circle is a tad small before the Season starts." After the near disaster at Boodles, Serena had hoped to avoid Sir Jonah completely. Unfortunately, she'd encountered him at several social venues since then—the piano recital at Lady Harrington's, the Orphans of Veterans of Foreign Wars charity dinner, and she'd even spied him a few rows behind her at an Academy of the Arts lecture.

"The man seems to have forgotten he's only a baronet," Lysandra said waspishly, earning her another shushing from Amelia.

"His father, Viscount Topfield, is well regarded," Serena said, not sure why she felt compelled to defend the man. Even though her friend was an earl's daughter, Lysandra always put much more stock in titles than Serena did.

"I heard a rumor about a possible match between Sir Jonah's brother Harold and the daughter of Lord Enderling, an earl, no less," Lysandra said, careful to confine her whisper to a mere wisp only Serena could hear. "Even if Harold Sharp stands to become a viscount one day, no one can deny his reach is exceeding his grasp with that match."

"A man cannot be held to account for his brother's actions. What has that to do with Sir Jonah?"

Lysandra cocked a brow that suggested Serena was a dull-witted child. "Perhaps Sir Jonah has similarly high aspirations."

Or low ones. His direct gaze suggested nothing remotely resembling honorable intentions. He made her feel hot and irritable and as if her stays had been laced too tightly. He looked at her as if he *knew* her.

Which was ridiculous. Just because he'd aided her in an indiscreet adventure, it did not give him leave to assume a familiarity between them that categorically did not exist.

Serena stewed through the rest of the collections of duets and ensembles. Tepid applause interrupted her musings, and the curtain mercifully fell on the opera's first act. Liveried servants turned up the gas lamps for intermission and Serena blinked at the light.

She resisted the urge to glance in Jonah's direction. She knew without knowing how that he was still watching her. She'd felt partially hidden by the darkness. Now that Sir Jonah could see her by lamplight, she had the same odd sensation she experienced in dreams sometimes—the squirmish one where she appeared in public as bare as an egg.

Amelia stood. "I do so love Mozart, but he does tend to waffle on sometimes. It feels good to move about. Shall we take a turn around the lobby?"

Serena followed Amelia and Lysandra out of the box and down the corridor that curved around the mezzanine. Mr. Tunstall, her ubiquitous footman, followed. In the absence of another male escort, Tunstall always hovered in the shadows when Serena moved in public. He was tall and well-favored, in the manner of such servants, but he was her father's creature. Any misstep Serena made would be summarily reported to the marquis.

Now is when it would be exceedingly handy to have a brother. Of course, Serena didn't intend any activity her father would frown upon this evening, but if she did, she suspected a brother would have been much easier to bribe into silence than the footman.

By the time they reached the broad marble stairs leading to the lobby, it was choked with other theatre-goers and they had to thread their way through the crowd. Punch was being served off to one side of the lavish space and the other women gravitated toward it. Serena headed for the row of doors. The footman fell into step with her.

"No, Mr. Tunstall, you needn't accompany me. I only wish a breath of fresh air. Please see to Lady Lysandra and Miss Braithwaite instead."

His mouth tightened into a thin line, but he couldn't very well countermand her direct order. "Very good, milady." Tunstall turned on his heel and left.

Serena was free to squeeze past the knots of opera-goers, successfully avoiding being dragged into discussions on the relative merits of the mezzo as opposed to the saucy maid character, who was in danger of stealing every scene in which she appeared. Finally, Serena reached her destination, and the doorman opened the brass-studded portal so she could escape the press of people.

It was a fresh March night, not warm enough for the Thames to begin admitting its distinctive seasonal tarry fish smell, but cool enough to make her wish she'd brought her wrap.

"Good evening, Lady Serena."

She realized that she'd been hoping all along to find him suddenly at her elbow. "Sir Jonah."

He held out a cup of punch. "It's not Boodles' coffee, but it's wet."

She thanked him, took a sip, and made a face. It was as weak as she expected. "They must have borrowed the receipt from Almack's."

"Careful—one of the patronesses may hear you," he said with a chuckle. "Those ladies aren't ones to forgive a slight."

"I rather doubt I'll be blacklisted."

"They did refuse to admit the Duke of Wellington once, but I suppose you're right."

He drained his own cup in one long gulp. Serena diverted her gaze. She wasn't used to such raw appetites. Most gentlemen sipped their punch in a genteel, measured manner. Sir Jonah obviously wasn't the type to do anything by halves.

"You'll have people fawning on you right and left once you're royal," he said.

"So you thought you'd beat the rush and begin fawning on me now?"

"I never fawn. However, if it seems that I've been following you, you're right. I have," he admitted, "but only because you interest me, Serena."

She'd been called many things—accomplished, well-connected, even beautiful once or twice by people who wished to curry favor with her powerful father—but never interesting. "Why do you find me interesting?"

"Frankly, because you're different."

She made the sound Amelia scolded her for often. "Ladies never snort, Serena," she'd say. Unfortunately, Serena did so with alarming frequency. "In case you hadn't noticed, being different is not a quality which is highly prized by Society."

"It is by me." He fixed her with his almost hypnotic gaze. "In my experience, too many young ladies are as interchangeable as a matched set of andirons."

Serena blinked, breaking the spell, and buried her nose in her punch cup for a moment. "Oh, you charmer, you. I wasn't aware your experience included many young ladies. Most say you favor lonely widows and wayward wives."

"You mustn't believe everything you hear."

What about the other things whispered about him? Like the mysterious way he came by his knighthood. Usually, the commoner who was honored with the elevation to baronet had performed some service to the Crown and that service was trumpeted about by said commoner until his listeners were tempted to box their own ears.

Sir Jonah had never uttered a word in public about how he'd earned his baronetcy.

But that didn't stop the rumor mill from grinding out possibilities, some of them quite unsavory. By the light of the gas lamp, she noticed a small scar bisecting one of his eyebrows. Instead of spoiling his appearance, it gave him a rather dashing air, as if he were a pirate king or a gypsy lord.

A dangerous man to know.

She burned to ask him how he came by the scar, but if she did it would seem as if she were interested in him as well. And she wasn't. Not a bit. He was too rough, too direct, too…taking off his tailcoat.

There, in front of God and everybody who cared to glance their way, Jonah Sharp was peeling off his jacket. Gentlemen never did such a thing. To be seen in public in only his waistcoat and shirt was more than a little scandalous.

And made her breath catch strangely in the back of her throat.

She glanced around at the other opera-goers who were taking the air. Anyone might see her with this half-dressed fellow.

He draped the tailcoat over her shoulders. "You were shivering."

This surprisingly thoughtful half-dressed fellow. The fine merino was infused with the warmth of his body along with his distinctive scent—musky and rich as a deep forest with an undertone of leather.

"Thank you. The air is a bit brisk this evening." She hoped he didn't think her shiver had anything to do with standing so closely to him. She handed him her empty punch cup and pulled the lapels together in front. It was almost as if he were holding her close.

She'd always had a vivid imagination, but no good could come from that sort of fancy.

"Why did you sneak into Boodles in the first place?" He set the cups down on the brickwork railing leading to the door.

She took a step back and found her spine pressed against the brick facade of the opera house. "I don't have to answer to you for my actions."

He braced a hand on the wall next to her head and leaned toward her. "Since I risked a bit to get you out of there, I think I deserve to know why you were in the club in the first place. Never say it was for the coffee. I could plainly see that you didn't care for it."

"You're right. It was as bad as that punch."

"Then why masquerade as your cousin and invade Boodles? And may I remind you that you owe me?"

His face was only a hand's breath from hers. "If I tell you why I was there, will it cancel the debt?"

He nodded.

"Very well." She straightened so he could see she wasn't intimidated by his nearness. "I did it so I could cross it off the list."

"What list?"

This was trickier ground. "You'll laugh."

"Perhaps, but tell me in any case."

"It's my list of forbidden pleasures. Things I wish to do simply to revel in having done them," Serena said. "Haven't you ever wished to do some secret thing?"

"I don't consider pleasures forbidden." His smile

was wickedness itself. "And if I want something, I make no secret of it."

She blinked hard at that. "Well,"—she swallowed back the strange tightness in her throat—"in the case of my exploits in Boodles, the pleasure was over-rated. Men's clothes are not nearly as comfortable as I'd imagined they would be, and as you said, the coffee is not as high a quality as I can find in my father's dining room."

"Maybe so, but you have to admit the company was pleasurable." The wickedness was gone from his smile, but it was no less engaging.

She couldn't resist smiling back. "I'll allow the company was tolerable."

"Only tolerable? Hmph. I can do better than that. Perhaps you'll concede that a man cannot be at his best when he finds himself awash in Orange Fool."

She laughed, despite her determination not to encourage him in his interest in her. He liked her because she was different, he said. He too was very different from other men of her acquaintance. The viscounts and earls and foreign dignitaries that graced her father's home were polished and poised.

And patently false, she realized.

Whatever else Jonah Sharp was, she sensed he was letting her see a side of him he normally hid from the rest of the world. Known for gruffness and being taciturn to the point of rudeness, this Sir Jonah was… unconventionally charming.

"What else is on that list of yours?" he asked.

She bit her lip, wondering if she should tell him.

"Very well, don't tell me the whole thing. Just

the next one." He leaned in and whispered, "What forbidden pleasure will you try?"

His breath washed over her neck, but even though it was warm, it left a shiver in its wake. She pulled his tailcoat tighter around her. "You'll laugh."

"I didn't laugh before, did I? Besides, your secrets are safe with me. I won't tell a soul."

The man had helped her out of a deucedly awkward scrape. She decided to trust him. "I'd like to smoke a cigar."

This time he did laugh. Then when she didn't join him, he sobered immediately. "You're serious."

"As an apoplectic fit."

"Why?"

"Because after a formal dinner, smoking cigars is something men retreat into their secret enclave to do while the women are relegated to tea and cordials in the parlor. I'd just like to know what's so appealing about it and why it's forbidden to my gender."

"A good cigar is a fine thing, but I suspect you'd find it as overrated as Boodle's coffee."

"But unless I try one for myself, I'll never know for sure," she argued. "It's one thing to be told what it's like to do something. It's quite another to do it."

"Truer words were never spoken." He frowned at the tips of his polished Hessians for a moment. It made Serena wonder what sort of experiences he'd had that hadn't turned out as expected. Then he lifted his head and smiled at her again, but this time the smile didn't reach his eyes. "What if I could help you cross this particular pleasure off your list?"

Her heart tripped along a bit faster. "How?"

"My town house is only a short distance from here. I have recently received a shipment of cigars fresh from Havana, one of which I'd be pleased to share with you."

Serena's breath hissed in over her teeth. "Will you bring it to me secretly?"

"No." He chuckled, a deep rumble that seemed to vibrate in her chest as well. "You wouldn't know what to do with it. And besides, don't you think your father would know if you invaded his smoking room to try to light up?"

That was true enough. Her father would notice if a single grape were out of place in a fruit bowl. "You can't mean to simply tease me with this. What do you propose?"

"Tell your companions you feel ill and need to go home early," he suggested, "but that they should stay to see the end of the opera."

"My footman will insist upon accompanying me."

"Have him put you into a hansom. It will ensure you arrive at your destination and he can stay to squire the other ladies home later. Besides, I have it on good authority that your Mr. Tunstall considers himself quite the Mozart aficionado. He'll stay readily enough."

Serena sighed. "Probably even for this less than stellar production. Wait. How do you know about Mr. Tunstall's musical tastes?"

"When I'm interested in someone, I make it my business to know as much as I can about them, including the people with whom they surround themselves."

"That sounds vaguely military. Have you been reconnoitering me?"

His mouth twitched in a half-smile. "I've learned

the hard way that it doesn't pay not to." Then his smile faded as he returned to business. "Once you've gone a block or two in the hansom, signal for a stop and I'll be right behind you with my gig. We'll go to my town house. You can smoke your wicked cigar. And when you're ready, I'll drive you home, long before the end of the last ovation here at the opera."

"There are any number of things wrong with that plan. For one, someone might see us together." For another, she'd be unchaperoned with a man. In his home. Alone.

"Doubtful. Everyone who is anyone, or even thinks they are, is here at the opera. You know how lengthy Mozart is. You'll be home in your own bed before the applause ends. No one will see us together."

The plan seemed made to order for knocking another item off the list. And it had the dubious benefit of providing a few more forbidden elements. She hadn't even had the courage to add "Spend time alone with a man who is not a relative" to her list, but she'd considered it. Amelia would be scandalized by the idea, so it was yet another secret pleasure she'd held only in her mind.

"What do you say, Serena?"

"Did I give you leave to use my Christian name?"

"You did." When she looked askance at him, he added, "When you followed me through that Orange Fool."

If his aim was to see her embarrassed, he'd have left her in Boodles. And she didn't see how she'd ever fulfill her wish to try a cigar in any other way.

"Well?" he asked.

She removed his tailcoat and handed it back to him. "Go collect your gig."

Four

Lady S. was seen leaving the opera early last night. One wonders if it was truly from a sick headache, as this reporter heard, or if the woefully inadequate tenor attempting to sing the role of Ferrando did in her ladyship. Either way we wish the lady well, especially since she is one of the young, chaste, and hopefully fecund potentials sprinting in the Hymen Race Terrific. Godspeed, Lady S. And may the best virgin win!

From Le Dernier Mot,
The Final Word on News That Everyone
Who Is Anyone Should Know

JONAH KEPT HIS GIG TO A SEDATE WALK IN ORDER TO allow enough distance between it and Serena's hansom. If he was going to win her trust, it wouldn't do to occasion idle talk should anyone notice that they were leaving the opera at around the same time. The irony wasn't lost on him that by so doing he was actually protecting her reputation when his commission from Alcock was specifically to ruin it.

But if he was going to upend the girl's life by

destroying her chances with the royal duke, the least he could do was make sure she had a little fun before he did it. And Lady Serena's ideas of fun were certainly out of the ordinary.

He'd expected her to be a typical pudding-headed debutante, totally silly and easily swiveable. Instead, she was the sort who donned men's clothes and set out in search of a good cup of coffee. The world might call her mad, but Jonah thought he understood her.

She wanted to experience life before she was shut up in a royal cage.

He knew something about feeling enclosed. Jonah's cage wasn't royal, but it had bars, nonetheless. Each night, they lowered on his mind and he relived the hard paths he'd been obliged to tread. Everything he'd done had needed doing for the common good, for king and country. And he'd been willing to do them at the time.

But he hadn't reckoned on the weight of those deeds afterward.

The hansom stopped ahead of him and he halted half a block away. Lady Serena climbed down from the hired conveyance and waved the driver on.

A woman who's willing to hazard herself merely for the sake of having an adventure.

She was truly unique.

Easy, Sharp, he told himself. *Remember what you're about.*

It was all right for him to be intrigued by her, but it wouldn't do to start admiring her too much. As with his other assignments, a certain professional distance must be maintained. So long as Serena Osbourne gave herself to him freely, his conscience would be clear.

As soon as the hansom clattered away, she lifted her skirts and broke into a trot in his direction. He wished the lamplight were a little brighter. At that pace, she ought to be showing a good bit of ankle. Jonah climbed down from the gig so he could help her up onto the seat.

When he joined her there, she grinned up at him.

"This feels positively wicked," she said. Her eyes sparked with enjoyment. The subterfuge only added to her sense of adventure, he realized. That could be useful later.

He smiled as he drove the gig down an alley and stopped before a small stable. A groom appeared to take the mare's head and tend to the gig.

Jonah helped Serena down, offered her his arm, and led her to the back door of his town house. He supposed it might have seemed a bit more imposing if he'd arranged for her to come in from the front. His decorating tastes were simple, but not inelegant. The Gainsborough in the foyer had cost him far more than he should have spent on something as nonessential as a painting, but the small landscape had a soothing quality that he couldn't ignore. Once he'd seen it, he had to have it. Every room in his home was sparsely furnished, but each piece spoke to him of comfort and tranquility—something he'd had precious little of in his life.

But whether they entered from the alley or the marginally fashionable street, his home was probably not grand enough to impress the daughter of a marquis.

The kitchen wasn't large, but a banked fire lit the small space with a rosy glow. Jonah knew it was spotless. Mrs. Hampstead, who came in and worked days, was a stickler for keeping the floors clean enough to eat from. Garlands of onions and garlic were strung from the rafters, and the herbs growing in the windowsill gave the room a pleasing, savory aroma.

"This way," he said, taking Serena's hand and leading her in the dark.

When they reached the front parlor, they met his manservant Paulson, who was holding a candle. Blinking and fumbling with his jacket buttons one-handed when he realized Jonah had a female guest, Paulson made polite inquiries about the opera and offered to bring them refreshments.

"No need, Paulson," Jonah said as he took the candle and led Serena up the main stairs. "We'll be in the study. Tell the groom not to unhitch the mare. I'll be taking the lady home shortly."

Ordinarily when a lady visited Jonah's town house this late in the evening, she'd be there for the next sennight. If Paulson was surprised that this one would not be staying, he gave no sign. But then, Jonah had hired him specifically for his deadpan expression.

A closemouthed servant was a good thing. One with a closed face was priceless.

Jonah squired Serena to his study, stirred up the fire, and lit the lamp.

"May I?" He helped the lady off with her cloak and laid it across the back of one of the matched Sheraton chairs before his hearth. Lady Serena strolled around the room, taking in the burled oak desk and ornately carved chair. She lingered by the bookshelves, running a fingertip over the spines as she checked the titles.

"Scott, Voltaire, Shakespeare—this is a good collection," she said.

"You sound surprised."

"Your reputation is that of a man of action. Your library suggests a more contemplative soul."

"Perhaps you'll allow it's possible to be both." Even so, he tried to contemplate as little as he could to avoid being sucked back into his less-than-wholesome past. A book was a diversion, an escape from unsettled ghosts. "The humidor is to the right of the desk."

It was a freestanding piece made of rich Brazilian rosewood, as refined a bit of joinery as he possessed. The interior was lined with cedar and held several trays to house his collection of fine smokes.

"It's quite lovely." She stroked the pyramidal top. It occurred to him that the lady was the tactile sort. She'd smoothed her fingertips along the fine merino lapels of his topcoat when he'd draped it over her shoulders outside the opera house. Now she was touching his books, his humidor. If she was as sensual a creature as she seemed, it would make the job of seducing her that much easier.

And far more pleasurable.

"In fact, your entire home is very pleasant," she said as she opened the humidor. The aromatic scent of fine tobacco wafted from the box and filled the small room.

"Again, you sound surprised. Did you think I lived in a cave?"

"No, it's just not…well, to be honest, you have the reputation of being something of a libertine. But this home doesn't speak of excess."

"Too Spartan for you?"

"No, too calm for you, I would have thought." Her lips twitched in amusement. "Any man who can cover an escape with Orange Fool doesn't seem the sort to be at home with such serenity."

"I'm gratified to have provided you with a mystery."

"Oh, I hate mysteries. They torment me until I can winkle them out."

"Good," he said with a grin. "You shall have to spend more time with me then. I look forward to having you uncover my secrets and unravel me completely."

Her eyes flared a bit at that. He'd meant it to sound vaguely naughty. The fact that she realized it meant her thoughts were traveling down the same road as his.

"Remove your gloves, Serena."

"I beg your pardon!"

"If you handle a cigar with those white gloves, you'll find them hopelessly stained when you're through," he said. "Allow me."

He took one of her hands and turned her wrist up. Her elbow-length gloves were cinched tight at her wrists with a couple of seed pearl buttons. He undid them now, making sure to allow the pad of his thumb to stroke her exposed skin. Then he brought her wrist to his lips and pressed a lover's kiss on her pulse point. Her heart was fluttering like a butterfly's wings. One finger at a time, he tugged at the glove, finally pulling the silk slowly over her skin.

Judging from the hitching rise and fall of her breasts, he was making her nervous. Or aroused. He'd settle for either.

"I can do the other one now." She stepped back a pace to put some distance between them, fiddled with the buttons, and removed her second glove.

"Speaking of time," she said, though they hadn't been, "how long will this take?" She picked up one of the Havanas and brought it to her nose for a whiff, refusing to look at him.

He crossed over to the small liquor cabinet and poured two snifters of brandy. "To truly enjoy a cigar takes about an hour."

"So long?"

"It's a complicated process." He handed her a brandy and took the cigar from her. "First the cigar needs to be cut properly. Then lit and then—"

"Yes, yes, I'm sure it's all quite fascinating. Since I only intend to do this once, I don't need to know all the details. Would you light it for me please?"

He shrugged. "You're missing out on the full experience."

"That's all right. You see, what I really want to know is...what *do* gentlemen talk about while they're smoking their cigars?"

"This and that. It depends on the company."

"Politics?"

"Not as often as you might think. Even Members of Parliament prefer to confine their political wrangling to the well of the House when there's a good Havana to be had."

"How about religion?"

He chuckled until he realized she was serious. "It hardly ever comes up."

"Then what do gentlemen discuss?"

"Racing outcomes. Gaming news. Business ventures they are considering or seeking a partner for. Whether a new shipment of cigars has come in."

"Oh." Her shoulders sagged.

"Disappointed?"

"Yes. When ladies gather together, sooner or later the conversation always seems to turn to gentlemen. Don't men ever talk about women?"

"Quite often." Jonah bent to light a cedar spill on the fire. He used the long taper of wood to preheat the foot of the cigar, careful not to touch it with the flame. Then he tucked the cigar between his teeth, drawing in slightly as he continued to hold the flame near the tip.

"What do gentlemen say?"

"About what?"

"About women?"

"In a moment. This is a critical juncture." If he didn't light the cigar evenly, it would taste bitter. Since he wanted this to be a pleasant experience for her, it was important to get this right. He rolled and drew air through the Havana till the tip glowed. Then he blew a neat smoke ring into the center of the room. "There you are."

"Is that one mine?"

"If you like. Now have a seat and hold it like so." He showed her how to balance it between her thumb and forefinger. Fortunately, the distraction spared him from answering her question about what men had to say about the ladies in their lives. Most gentlemen of his acquaintance were circumspect about their *amours*, but a few felt the need to boast, often with details that would have curled the hair of the lady involved. "If you wish, you can dip the end in your brandy before taking a draw. Most smokers appreciate the combination of spirits and tobacco."

She held the cigar out and gave it a squint-eyed gaze. Then she touched the end to the surface of her brandy and brought it to her mouth. At the last moment, she stopped.

"You were going to tell me what gentlemen say about ladies while they're smoking their cigars?" Then she slipped the end of the cigar into her pink bow of a mouth.

Jonah was unprepared for the sudden rush of blood to his groin. There was something decidedly erotic about a beautiful woman with a thick Havana between her lips. But before he could answer her question or, more importantly, explain how to draw the smoke in and hold it in her mouth without inhaling, a knock came at the door.

She quickly handed the cigar back to him.

She might be unconventional, but she wasn't ready to be seen as such by anyone but him. The knowledge was oddly endearing. He enjoyed sharing her secrets.

"Come," Jonah said.

The door opened slightly and Paulson stood at the threshold. "Beggin' your pardon, sir, but there's a runner here for you."

"Take the message."

"The fellow is under orders not to give it to anyone but you. He claims he'll wait until you've time to see him, even if it means he sleeps on the front steps all night." Paulson dropped his voice to a whisper. "He says it has to do with a certain French incident. He seemed to think you'd know from that what it is about and who has sent him."

Maubeuge. Try as he might, Jonah couldn't seem to leave that disastrous defeat behind. And neither could his friends, Warrington and Colton. Both were implicated in the scandal with him. They had also been similarly ensnared by the less than Honorable Fortescue Alcock to despoil other virgins who were being courted by the other royal dukes.

"Very well. Thank you, Paulson. I'll only be a moment," he said to Serena. Then he gave her a wink and handed the cigar back to her without letting Paulson see it. "Try not to let it go out."

◈

Drat! Just when he was about to tell her what gentlemen really talked about. Did they wax rhapsodic about a lady's hair or the shape of her figure? Did they admire her fine manners or value her piano playing on a cold winter's night? Had Jonah ever heard a man talk about a woman's insights into his favorite author's work?

Just what did gentlemen think about the ladies in their lives?

She'd long ago come to terms with the way of the world. Society decreed that she was unable to support herself. A wellborn lady could dabble in water colors, but not make a business of selling them. She might volunteer for charity work but could not toil for hire. A lady needed the protection of a good man or her life would shortly become untenable. But didn't the dependency run both ways?

Don't they somehow need us as much as we do them?

And not just for playing hostess or producing an heir.

She eyed the glowing tip of the cigar, which was growing paler by the minute.

"Try not to let it go out," Jonah had said.

As if she couldn't do such a simple thing. Remembering the way Jonah had drawn on the cigar and then produced a perfect smoke ring, she brought the cigar to her lips and inhaled.

A coughing fit exploded from her lungs. Her body's reaction was so violent, she nearly dropped both the cigar and the brandy.

"How utterly vile!" This was worse than black coffee by several thousand degrees of magnitude.

Drat. Jonah would think her a weak female, unable to rise to the occasion of a masculine pleasure.

She put the cigar down, balancing it on the silver tray on his mantel. Its tip glowed at her, malevolent as a single red eye. How could she pretend to enjoy this miserable thing, and for a whole hour, no less?

The burning tip began to fade again. If she let the dratted thing go out, Jonah would know she hadn't had the courage to see this adventure through. He'd think her weak. Her father had always drilled into her that the world could tolerate many flaws, but weakness was not one of them.

There was nothing else for it. As if it were a spoon filled with castor oil, she picked up the cigar, and, with shoulders squared, she brought it again to her mouth.

❧

The messenger was hunkered before the fire in the parlor, warming his hands before the cheery blaze.

"State your business and be quick about it, man," Jonah said. "I have a guest I cannot keep waiting."

"This shouldn't take long, sir." The fellow straightened and turned around. There was something familiar about the man's hooked nose and receding hairline.

"I know you. Mr. Clyde, I believe. You're in Lord Rhys Warrington's employ, are you not?" Jonah was pleasantly surprised. He'd expected the runner to have come from Mr. Alcock with yet another ultimatum. He'd never believed in punishing the bearer of bad tidings, but he'd have been sorely tempted in that case.

"Yes, I've been with his lordship for many years," the man said, twisting his cap in his hands. "I'm gratified that you remember me, sir."

"Ordinarily I would ask how my friend fares, but I do have a pressing matter I'm attending to at the moment," Jonah said. "What message have you for me?"

Mr. Clyde's eyes slid up and to the right as if the message might be found hovering there above his head. "Lord Rhys asks will you join him and Nathaniel Colton at the Blind Pony in Whitechapel two days hence at ten o'clock in the evening?"

"Why?" Jonah wasn't afraid to walk any street in the city, but some environs led to violence more quickly than others. Just because he was more than capable of defending himself didn't mean he relished doing it.

"Lord Rhys has information concerning a person who has agreed to testify as to your innocence in the matter of Maubeuge."

"That's excellent news."

"Yes, it is, but not all is well." Mr. Clyde's woeful expression reminded Jonah of a basset hound. "The man is no longer in London and the three of you must agree on a plan to find him."

Jonah paced the length of the small space in a few quick strides. If they could secure this witness and clear their names once and for all, perhaps he wouldn't have to ruin Serena Osbourne. He hoped he wouldn't.

Not that he didn't want to bed her. That wasn't in the least dispute. But if he spoiled her reputation, he'd destroy her spirit and that was becoming a thoroughly repugnant prospect. He found her a delightful oddity among young ladies. She deserved to be celebrated, not shamed. Jonah turned back to his friend's servant.

"Tell your master I'll be there."

Five

A little bird whispered to this reporter that Princess Victoria Mary Louisa of Saxe-Coburg-Saalfeld, sister of Prince Leopold, may have stolen the march on one of the British misses competing in the Hymen Race Terrific. According to rumor, correspondence has been flying across the Channel at a breakneck pace. If a certain Lady S. wishes to catch a certain royal duke's eye, she had better do it speedily or we may be forced to endure yet another monarch for whom English is not his mother tongue.

From Le Dernier Mot,
The Final Word on News That Everyone
Who Is Anyone Should Know

"Serena. Wake up, dearest."

The gentle voice was a blessedly familiar one and Serena followed it, albeit unwillingly, up through several layers of oblivion. She opened one eye, then promptly squeezed it shut again when a narrow shaft of brittle sunlight struck it.

Humming softly under her breath, Amelia threw back the thick damask draperies at both of Serena's windows with a rustle of fabric. The sound of the wooden casement being pushed up and the subsequent wash of brisk air made Serena burrow further beneath her coverlet.

"Are you still feeling ill?"

She ran her tongue around the inside of her mouth. The rancid taste of the cigar clung to her hard palate and teeth. She didn't answer, but flipped the blankets back to cast a bleary-eyed gaze at Amelia.

"You poor dear." Amelia hitched a hip on the side of the bed as she leaned forward to smooth Serena's hair back from her forehead. "No fever, so far as I can tell, but you do look a bit green."

Serena sat up and drew a deep breath, which set her coughing. Evidently some of the cigar smoke she'd inhaled had taken up residence in her lungs and her body was still intent on expelling it. A lock of hair fell forward to graze her cheek. The reek of smoke was strong on it. How could Amelia not smell it?

"What a horrid cough. If I'd known how ill you were, I'd never have let you go home by yourself last night. Especially since the tenor never quite lived up to his potential." Amelia crossed over to the small table where a breakfast tray waited. "Do you think you could take some tea and toast?"

"I'll try."

Amelia fixed Serena's tea just as she liked it, adding a dollop of milk and two sugar lumps, and brought the cup and saucer to her. "Do you think you could also try to tell me the truth?"

"What do you mean?" Serena accepted the tea and buried her nose in the cup.

"You smell as if you spent last evening in a smoking room."

"There were several gentlemen smoking outside the theatre when I took some air between acts." That was at least true.

"I know you didn't arrive home by the hansom your footman hailed for you. Sir Jonah Sharp brought you. Mr. Brownsmith said the gentleman carried you into the house because you were too overcome to walk and his gig was the only conveyance on the street. There was no hired vehicle."

She had hazy recollections of Mr. Brownsmith's concern when Jonah swept in with her in his arms. The steward directed him up the grand staircase and into Serena's bedchamber so her chambermaid could help her into bed. She'd counted on discretion from the help, but she should have realized there were no secrets in a great house with so many servants. "I wasn't aware our steward is in the habit of discussing me with others."

"Mr. Brownsmith is hardly carrying tales, if that's what's worrying you. He spoke to me, and me only, in strictest confidence. Now what happened after you left the opera house?"

"I…became so ill in the hansom that the driver was concerned enough to stop. Luckily, Sir Jonah happened along and…" Looking into Amelia's concerned face, Serena realized she couldn't lie to her. "No, that's not what happened."

Amelia sat on the edge of the bed again. "Tell me, dear."

"I crossed item number three off the list."

Amelia's eyes grew wide. "You smoked a cigar?"

"Yes, but apparently I didn't do it right." Serena told her about Sir Jonah's offer to help her experience that forbidden pleasure. She explained how they'd managed for her to sneak away from the opera, then out of the hansom and into his gig within a few blocks. To Amelia's credit, she didn't interrupt or chide, though her lips were drawn in a tight line.

"Everything would have gone swimmingly if Sir Jonah hadn't been called away from his study by a messenger at the wrong time. He hadn't instructed me how to merely hold the smoke in my mouth without inhaling, and while he was gone, I... well, how could I know there is a special knack to smoking a cigar?"

"And that's how you came to be ill?"

She nodded miserably. By the time Jonah had returned to the study, she was retching into the rubbish bin beside his desk. Embarrassment heated her cheeks as she recalled how the man had held her hair back and pressed a clean handkerchief to her forehead while she emptied her stomach.

"That was most unwise, Serena. You were unchaperoned in a man's home," Amelia said. "If it were discovered, you'd be ruined."

"Yes, I know, but I was so violently ill, there was no question of anything untoward happening." And nothing untoward ever would happen between her and Sir Jonah. She doubted he'd ever be able to look at her again without remembering how sick she'd been.

"At least the experience was wretched enough, you needn't worry that I'll make a habit of cigars," she said in an attempt to lighten the mood.

Amelia refused to be mollified. Her brows drew together in a frown. "We shall have to put out the tale about you becoming ill in the hansom and Sir Jonah happening along to offer assistance. I assume the gentleman can be trusted to be discreet enough to go along if he hears that version of events."

The ride home in his gig was a blur in her mind, but what Serena remembered most clearly was the way he drove one-handed. His other arm was around her, supporting and warming her as her head lolled on his shoulder. She couldn't recall what he said to her exactly, but she remembered his voice, low and soothing as they rattled over the cobbles. Despite being more than a little mortified, she'd been strangely comforted by this man she'd known for so little time.

"He'll be discreet," she assured Amelia.

A quick rap sounded on the door to Serena's bedchamber. Then without waiting for permission to enter, her maid Eleanor breezed in bearing a dozen yellow roses arranged with a bit of baby's breath in a crystal vase. "Oh, good. You're awake, milady. These flowers arrived for you just now. There's a card."

The maid set the vase down on the small table with a lyre base near one of the windows. "That'll do, I reckon." Then she plucked out the card and brought it to Serena. "Your father wishes to see you as soon as you're able, milady. He knows you've been indisposed, so there's no need for haste. Shall I lay out your day dress?"

"Give me half an hour to finish my tea and eat a bite, Eleanor. Come back then and I'll be ready to rise."

"Lady Serena will need a bath before she dresses to

see his lordship. Please see to it." Amelia waited for the maid to leave before adding, "We must wash the smoke from your hair. Your father is no fool, you know."

Then she crossed over to bury her nose in the fragrant bouquet. "Hothouse roses in March. These must have cost the earth. They're from the Duke of Kent, I presume?"

Her royal suitor must have been having her watched very closely if he was already apprised of her leaving the opera early on account of illness. Serena tore open the gilded note. The message was written with an aggressive hand, the strokes thick and angular. More than one blotch of ink marred the foolscap.

But the words were gentleness itself.

I trust these blossoms find you feeling better. Forgive me for ruining your adventure.

It was signed simply with a "J."

"The flowers are from Sir Jonah," she said, carefully refolding the note. Perhaps he wasn't as repulsed by her as she feared. A little thrill shot from her wrist up her arm, the same wrist he'd kissed as if he were a pilgrim worshipping before a shrine. "How thoughtful."

Amelia's expression grew even more concerned. "Have a care, Serena."

"Why? Doesn't this signify that Sir Jonah will protect my good name? He didn't even sign the note properly. How much more discreet could he be?"

Amelia sat once more on the bed and took both Serena's hands. "Trust me, dearest, you don't want to become involved with the wrong man."

"We are not 'involved.' I simply had a bit of an adventure with him that didn't go as I hoped."

"Two adventures," Amelia corrected.

"I suppose if you want to be a stickler about it, yes, but the incident at Boodles was not planned."

"I wouldn't be too sure about that." Amelia rose and walked to the open window. She shut it down with such a vigorous shove, Serena feared for the panes. "Men sometimes spend a great deal of time arranging for things to happen in a seemingly natural way."

"You're too wary, Amelia."

"And you're not wary enough. I would not see you harmed."

"The man whisked me away from a potentially scandalous situation at Boodles. Last night, I'm embarrassed to admit he tended me when I was quite ill, and after that, he brought me home safely and without exciting anyone's notice." Serena tucked the note from Jonah under her pillow. "Now he sends flowers. I fail to see the intended harm in his actions, and I don't understand your misgivings."

"I hope you never do." Amelia crossed her arms over her chest and stared out the window.

Serena considered her friend for a moment. Amelia had never mentioned having a man in her life. She'd been born the daughter of a baron, but since she had no brothers, the estate went to her cousin when her father died. The new baron allowed Amelia's mother to use the small dowager's cottage on the estate, but it was in such disrepair and so damp, Amelia's mother succumbed to the ague during her second winter there. Her cousin refused to provide a dowry for Amelia. But he did find a way to place her as a governess to Serena—though more likely to gain influence with the Marquis of Wyndleton than to secure a future for Amelia.

Serena considered that a very lucky day for her. Now she wondered how Amelia felt about exchanging her expectations of marriage and a family of her own for taking care of an admittedly difficult girl who'd just lost her mother. Had her friend enjoyed a *tendresse* for some swain that was upturned when a dowry wasn't forthcoming?

"You speak as if you've been hurt by a man, Amelia. I know your cousin behaved abominably toward you, but was there someone else as well?"

Amelia turned suddenly, a hand splayed across her chest. Her lips parted as if she were about to say something, but then she closed them firmly.

"It won't do to keep your father waiting," she said as she made for the door. "I'll send Eleanor to you."

⁂

"There you are, daughter." Serena's father rose from behind his massive desk and came around it to plant a dry kiss on her cheek. "I understand you've been unwell."

"I'm fine now, Father." She hoped the thorough scrubbing with tooth powder had expunged the last of the cigar scent. "It was only a passing malady."

"I'm demmed glad to hear it, my dear, demmed glad. Please have a seat." He indicated one of the two leather wing chairs before the blue Delft stove that heated his study. He settled into the other chair and steepled his hands before him, his heavy signet ring glinting in the gaslight.

Unlike Amelia, her father wasn't a fan of letting

sunshine invade his home. "Fades the taxidermy," he always complained. Since the shelves of his study were crowded with stuffed badgers and grouse, and a somewhat mangy black bear reared on its hind feet in one corner of the room, the drapes were habitually drawn in his study and the gas lamps lit. He cocked his head and studied her as if she were one of his many hunting trophies.

"Now, be so good as to explain how you came to be separated from Miss Braithwaite and Lady Lysandra at the opera and found yourself in the company of the hairy-legged honyock who brought you home, ill and disheveled."

"Sir Jonah is not a…" What on earth was a honyock? And how could her father know if his legs were hairy or not? All Serena knew was that Jonah's lips on her wrist ought to be listed among the seven deadly sins. "He was…most helpful."

"I'll be the judge of that. Tell me, daughter."

Her father's voice was soft, but the imperative edge beneath the words was undeniable. She drew a deep breath, laced her fingers together, and recited the lie she'd started to tell Amelia. It was surprisingly easier the second time. Her conscience pained her, but the truth would not give her father comfort and the lie wouldn't hurt him.

"…and so, since the driver of the hansom was so distraught over my illness, Sir Jonah very kindly brought me home in his gig," she finished.

Her father's brows arched as he considered her words and then settled when he finally decided to accept them. "Your color is poor, Serena. I'm sending you to Wyndebourne. You'll leave on the morrow."

"But Father, the Season will start in another month or so and—"

"And by then you'll be back in London. If you're recovering from a malady, however transitory, a little time in the country is just what's wanted to put the roses back into your cheeks." His expression changed from one of censure to one of concern. "It will not do for the Duke of Kent to suspect you are fragile or prone to sickness."

"But I'm not."

"I know that, but his advisors may not be aware of the general good health we Osbournes enjoy." Even though the marquis was on the downhill slope of fifty winters, he was still elegantly trim with only a smattering of gray at the temples. He could easily be mistaken for a man ten or fifteen years younger than his true age.

"But if I skitter off to the country," Serena said, "won't that suggest I'm too ill for London Society?"

"No, because the crème de la crème will hear of the charity ball and house party you'll be planning to be held at Wyndebourne just before the start of the Season. The Duke of Kent needs to see you pulling off a brilliant fete that will both do good and make you look demmed good at the same time." Her father leaned forward, took her hands, and smiled at her. Then his smile faded completely. "The threat of the German princess is quite real."

Serena didn't feel threatened by the distant lady. Surely, Kent would prefer a wellborn English miss to become his duchess, but the rumors concerning the duke's correspondence with Prince Leopold's sister obviously distressed her father. "I understand. I shall do my best to make you proud. What charity would you like me to champion?"

"Confound it all, what was that noble cause Lady Hepplewhite was trumpeting at her dinner a week or so back?" Her father's brow furrowed a bit, then he smacked his thigh. "I have it! Our ball will benefit the Orphans of Veterans of Foreign Wars. Not only is it a popular charity with His Royal Highness—the duke was quite the military man himself, you know—it has the added benefit of reminding everyone that this German princess he's considering is *foreign*."

"You're always so clever, Father."

He preened a bit under her praise. "Must be where you get it then, daughter," he said with an indulgent smile. "I'm sure Miss Braithwaite will aid you as you plan the event. Hire all the additional help you need. Spare no expense. Take your modiste with you to Wyndebourne and have her make something dazzling."

Serena warmed to her father's plan. It would be a good deal of work to organize such an occasion, but after her disastrous adventure of last evening, this more conventional one sounded made to order. And she did love the ancestral country seat of the Osbournes. The sprawling Georgian manor house was situated on a bluff overlooking the Channel and surrounded by verdant countryside that would grow more spring green with each passing day.

"Between extra servants, musicians, and modiste, I suspect I'll need a couple of coaches just to transport my entourage to Wyndebourne."

"Better become accustomed to it, my dear. Once

you are royal, you'll never stir a step without a whole demmed gaggle of retainers and aids."

The marquis had meant it as an enticement, but to Serena, being hedged about with so many hangers-on sounded vaguely like a rolling prison. Still, she wanted to please her father and this was the perfect opportunity to make up for the foolish chances she'd taken of late.

A soft rap sounded on the door to the marquis's study.

"Come," he said.

Mr. Brownsmith, the estate steward, entered, his spine ramrod straight despite his sixty-some years. He'd begun his service with the Osbourne family as a bootblack boy, then worked his way up through the ranks of footmen and butlers to follow his father into the position of steward. He had a role in just about every doing of the family, and his pale gray eyes were still sharp enough not to miss a thing.

"Your pardon, milord," Mr. Brownsmith said with a deferential inclination of his head. "I didn't realize Lady Serena was still here."

"She was just leaving," her father announced. He offered her his hand and she took it as she rose. He gave her fingertips a gentle squeeze before he released them. "I'm sure you've already thought of half a dozen things that want doing before you depart for Wyndebourne."

"You know me well, Father." She gave the steward a smile. "Mr. Brownsmith, if you'd be so good as to attend me later this afternoon. His lordship wishes us to host a ball. We need to discuss caterers and musicians and myriad other things before I leave London."

"Very good, milady."

The marquis watched her leave, her slender back

and sprightly step reminding him fleetingly of her mother. He waited for the old ache to throb, but time and other cares had reduced his grief over losing his marchioness to mere wistfulness and mild regret. Once the door closed behind his precious daughter, he took his seat behind the desk again.

"A gentleman unknown to me brought my daughter home last night when she was unwell. However much I appreciate his timely assistance, I cannot allow that to stand. It is untenable that anyone should form an acquaintance with Serena unless I have approved it," he said. "Well, Brownsmith, what have you discovered about this Sir Jonah Sharp?"

The steward pulled a small journal from his inside waistcoat pocket and thumbed through the dog-eared pages. "Jonah Adrian Sharp—second son of Lord Topfield."

"Hmm. Good man, that." Even though he and Viscount Topfield were on opposite sides of the political spectrum, they'd worked together on the issue of child labor in the House of Lords. Nothing had been done to correct the problem yet, but he and the viscount had made some inroads with key peers. "But Sharp is not his heir. I take it the young gentleman is without prospects."

"That is correct. However, he did earn his baronetcy." Brownsmith consulted his notes once again. "And he owns a tidy property in Wiltshire, which produces a respectable income, as well as a house in Town. I could find no evidence of inordinate gambling debts. By all accounts, he seems to have done well with his investments."

So he's not looking to borrow money from Serena, the

marquis thought. *There's a mercy.* "How did he come by his baronetcy?"

Brownsmith snapped the journal shut and stowed it back in his pocket. "That seems to be something of a mystery. Whatever service Sir Jonah rendered the Crown, it is not something he noises about."

The marquis drummed his fingers on his desk. "Commission our most trusted Bow Street runner to discover this information. Prinny may have elevated the gentleman on a whim. Perhaps Sir Jonah merely removed an inconvenient harlot from the Prince Regent's bedchamber."

"I think not, milord." Mr. Brownsmith took the journal out again and made note of the order to hire a runner. "Sir Jonah's reputation is…more shadowy than that. There are rumors about a military incident shortly before the Battle of Waterloo and—"

"If he's bloody well still accepted in Society, it couldn't have been that bad." The marquis waved a hand, dismissing the matter. "There are plenty of rumors about the Duke of Kent's military service as well, come to that." The royal duke's harsh discipline of the soldiers serving under him when he was governor of Gibraltar led to a scandalous mutiny and finally his recall to England. "I believe it's time I had a conversation with *Sir* Jonah Sharp. Send Oliver and Ulrich to collect him."

"Very good, milord. Where would you like him deposited?"

"Bring him to the usual place."

Six

When a potential crown is at stake, one wonders to what lengths a father will go in order to ensure his daughter's success in securing the most brilliant of matches. Likely all usual constraints are cast aside. And if that's so, this reporter wonders what possible reason the Marquis of W could have for engaging a certain baronet whose reputation for skullduggery and mayhem is well known, if not well documented, in an arguably forced clandestine conversation?

From Le Dernier Mot,
The Final Word on News That Everyone
Who Is Anyone Should Know

JONAH HAD NEVER BEEN TO WHITE'S. IT WAS DEUCEDLY difficult to gain entrance to the hallowed halls unless one's name was listed on the rolls. He wasn't a member of the club, and frankly, the Tory-leaning reputation of the place didn't commend itself to him.

However, with Lord Wyndleton's two beefy lieutenants marching in lockstep on either side of him, Jonah was ushered in without challenge. Easily his match for height and weight, the fellows who walked beside Jonah had the look of a pair of pugilists, one sporting a permanently lazy eyelid and the other a cauliflower ear. They escorted Jonah past the fabled table in the bow window on the ground floor where the fashionable elite held court, and on to an alcove in the back of the main room of White's.

Seated in a splendid Tudor chair, its age-darkened wood a throwback to a more barbaric time, was the Marquis of Wyndleton. The man was certainly wearing his station. His superfine tailcoat was meticulously tailored to mold to his form. His waistcoat was cloth-of-gold, and his white cravat was starched in a series of complicated knots that would have baffled even Brummell.

"Sir Jonah Sharp," Wyndleton said, his blue eyes going steely. "How good of you to join me. We have not been formally introduced. I am—"

"I know who you are, milord," Jonah said. "And—"

"And quite frankly," the marquis cut in, determined to one-up him in interruptions, "I didn't give you much choice in coming, did I?"

Jonah shrugged. "On the contrary, I had two choices. I could accompany these…gentlemen willingly, or I could lay them both out."

Lord Wyndleton smiled unpleasantly. "I'd bloody well pay good money to see that."

If I'm to be thrown out of White's, I may as well give them good reason. Quick as thought, Jonah shot out both arms and brought his fists up in explosive jabs to the two guards' jaws. Then he delivered elbows to their guts, doubling them over, and finally swept their legs out from under them with a whirling kick. While the men groaned on the polished floors, Jonah liberated a chair from a nearby table and sat, crossing his legs unconcernedly. A coterie of staff members from the club came skittering up.

"Sir, we must ask you kindly to leave these premises forthwith," the head waiter said, his face flushed and his eyes wide. "This club tolerates no physical violence."

"Nothing untoward has taken place, Watkins," the marquis said as his guards struggled to rise. "A misunderstanding only. Think nothing of it."

Watkins clamped his lips shut. Without another word, the servants bowed and returned to their duties.

"Well, that's a good trick," Jonah said. "One word from you and people disregard the evidence of their own eyes."

"That's because once I point out their error, my inferiors generally realize that the world is not as they see it."

"How is it then?"

"The world is as I say it is," Wyndleton said grandly.

"How convenient for you."

"For them as well." The marquis examined his fingernails for a moment and then folded his aristocratic hands on his lap. His heavy signet ring glinted brightly. "It removes the burden of decision-making from less able shoulders."

"I hope you haven't made the mistake of numbering me in that group," Jonah said. "I'm perfectly capable of both seeing the world clearly and making my own decisions about it."

The two pugilists were upright now and looking to the marquis for further instructions.

Lord Wyndleton gave his guards a weary glance and waved the men away. They retreated to a nearby table where they could keep an eye on him and Jonah while licking their wounds over cups of hot chocolate and finger sandwiches.

"Those decisions of yours are what interest me, Sir Jonah," the marquis said. "Perhaps you'd care to enlighten me about which one led to your elevation to a baronetcy."

Jonah had never told a soul about it, and he damn well wouldn't start with this man simply for the asking. "I performed a service to the Crown."

The marquis squinted one eye at him in a withering gaze. "Obviously."

"I am not at liberty to share the specifics."

"I assure you, Sir Jonah, I have His Majesty's utmost trust."

"As do I." Jonah met the marquis's glare without a blink. "Which is why I can't discuss the matter."

Lord Wyndelton's color deepened and a muscle worked furiously in his cheek. "Then let us turn to a matter you will discuss or I'll know the reason why. You brought my daughter home from the opera last night. How did that extraordinary circumstance come about?"

"I'm sure Lady Serena has already explained the situation to you. I have nothing to add to her account," he said, hoping she'd neglected to mention her unhappy experience with his Cuban cigar. "I was glad to be of service and trust the lady is recovered from her illness."

The marquis frowned. "She ought not to have left the opera alone. My daughter is a remarkable young lady in many respects, but she's far too casual about her personal safety."

Jonah cut a glance at the two men he'd recently introduced to the floor. "I'm frankly surprised you didn't send those two with her to the opera."

"They wouldn't have been able to stay awake," Wyndleton said with a curl of his lip. "I made the mistake of settling for sending her footman who was easily distracted. And my daughter absolutely rebels at the idea of having guards dogging her steps when she moves in Society."

Jonah suppressed a smile. The will of the indomitable Marquis of Wyndleton was thwarted by his slip of a daughter. Obviously, he wasn't the only one for whom the world was as he proclaimed it.

"The lady will have to change her mind on that issue if the match with the Duke of Kent comes to pass," Jonah said. "Royalty is never without company or protection."

"Quite, though convivial company is to be preferred over obvious security providers." Lord Wyndleton's expression turned thoughtful. "I pride myself on being a discerning judge of character, and it occurs to me that you have several useful qualities, Sir Jonah."

"Such as?"

"You know how to hold your tongue, even when not doing so might be personally beneficial for you. You seem to have a care for a lady's safety as well as her reputation. And you are more than able to handle yourself in a tight spot." He shook his head at the two guards who were stuffing their maws with delicacies from White's menu. "Look at them. Totally oblivious to the fact that their time in my employ is fast drawing to a close."

"I wouldn't be too hard on them, your lordship. Any man can be taken by surprise."

"But you weren't, were you? You think before you act, unlike those two, who can hardly take a trip to the privy without a 'by your leave.' Therein lies the difference between a gentleman and the man who by birth and inclination is more than half brute." The marquis leaned forward. "Sir Jonah, I wonder if you would see your way clear to attending a house party and charity ball at my country estate."

"I shall have to consult my schedule. When will this event be held?"

"Actually, I was hoping you would leave with Lady Serena's entourage on the morrow," Lord Wyndleton said. "Since you are a gentleman, I won't insult you by offering you pay, but I would consider it a great personal favor if you were to consent to become my daughter's guard…without her knowledge, of course."

Steady on, lad, Jonah told himself. *Don't jump at the bait too quickly.* "Lady Serena would not thank me for it."

"She wouldn't have to know, but I would and I would be…appreciative." He tugged down his gleaming waistcoat. "I have many friends at court. New peers are created every day, but only if one has the connections required to see letters patent to fruition."

The marquis wanted his help very badly if he was ready to dangle the possibility of a peerage before him.

"That won't be necessary." Not to mention once

Jonah fulfilled his commission to Alcock to seduce Serena, the marquis would no longer have reason to be grateful. "But I am willing to assume responsibility for your daughter's safety."

Just not her purity.

A niggling ache bloomed in his chest. He hadn't felt it in years, but he recognized the sensation with a start.

It was his conscience.

He tamped it down. He had his own family to protect. His brother's happiness shouldn't be destroyed because Alcock threatened Jonah with the scandal of treason. He steeled himself to his task. The end justified the means.

"Very good, Sharp. Present yourself at my town house before eight o'clock on the morrow. You'll travel with my daughter to Wyndebourne."

"Lady Serena is an intelligent young woman. She'll wonder at my inclusion in her party."

The marquis tapped his temple for a moment. "Have you an interest in horseflesh?"

"I keep a fair stable at my country home."

"In that case, you may put out that you intend to inspect the stock at Wyndebourne with an eye to purchasing a new brood mare. After that, you may as well stay on since I'll see to it that you're invited to the house party and ball."

"That'll do." Jonah rose. "Good-bye, milord. If I'm to leave town tomorrow, I have matters to attend today."

The marquis frowned. "Most people ask to be dismissed from my presence, yet you offer not so much as a 'by your leave.'"

"No," Jonah said as he turned to go. "I don't."

Jonah pushed into the Blind Pony with scrapes on his knuckles and a hole in his garrick that was not at the seam. One of the gang of ruffians he'd encountered had brandished a wicked dirk, but with a few deft moves, Jonah had relieved him of it and sent the crew scattering like roaches caught in sudden lamplight. Unfortunately, not before the fellow managed a slash to Jonah's outer coat.

He mentally castigated his friends again for choosing such a sketchy place for their meeting.

Jonah was naturally cat-eyed, but this pub was so dim even he couldn't make out most of the patron's faces. As he scanned the low-ceilinged common room, he saw a hand raised in greeting from the booth in the far corner. As he drew closer, he recognized his friends, Rhys Warrington and Nathaniel Colton, nursing pints of dark, yeasty-smelling ale. A third pint waited on the rough plank table before an empty place.

Jonah slid into it and took a long swig of the drink. It was execrable. "Who ordered this horse piss?"

"It's not so bad once you start on the second one," Nate said. "You're late, Sharp."

"And if that frown of yours is any measure, you're obviously out of charity with the whole world," Rhys observed. "What's wrong?"

"My new coat is ruined thanks to this meeting." And several of the local ne'er-do-wells were missing several teeth. "Why did you insist on such a spotty location?"

"Desperate times call for desperate measures and

we didn't want Alcock to be aware that we are joining forces. You should have dressed down for the occasion," Rhys said. Both he and Nathaniel were disguised in the rags of a common worker—slop trousers and long shirts topped by shapeless capes. A pair of floppy-brimmed hats obscured their faces from all but the most determined observers.

"I am who I am wherever I go," Jonah said. His friends both rejoiced in a "Lord" before their names. It might be a lark to them to pretend to lesser status. A commoner's lot struck Jonah too close to the bone. "Why should I pretend to a lower station?"

"It might save on your tailor's bill," Rhys said. "But seriously, what's troubling you?"

"For starters, unlike the pair of you, I haven't finished my commission for Alcock." Jonah knew he was endangering not only his own family, but his friends' as well by the delay, but the last thing Jonah wanted to admit was that his conscience was keeping him from accelerating his plan to seduce Lady Serena. "Besides, you both cheated."

That earned him a chuckle. "Alcock didn't specify how we were to keep the ladies from wedding a royal duke," Rhys said, "though I must confess I didn't intend on marrying Olivia myself at first. What about you, Colton?"

"Farthest thing from my mind. But I admit to being happily ensnared in the parson's mousetrap with my Georgette." Nate raised his mug. "To our wives."

Rhys clinked mugs with him while Jonah eyed them both stonily.

"Do not expect me to follow suit."

Nate shrugged. "Very well, but it's something to consider."

No, it wasn't. People whispered about his brother Harold, the future viscount, setting his sights too high by courting the earl's daughter. The ton would have a field day if a mere baronet lifted his eyes to the only daughter of a marquis. Not that Jonah gave a tinker's damn about what was said about him, but it galled him that Serena might become fodder for wagging tongues on account of him.

Then how in hell do you intend to ruin her chances with the royal duke without offering her up to the gossip mill?

Jonah raised his mug and drained it. Nate was right. The wretched stuff improved with increased quantity. The guilty ache in his chest migrated lower to simmer uneasily in his belly.

"On to the purpose of this meeting," Rhys said. "We've learned that Alcock's supposed witness, Sergeant Leatherby, has taken ship to Portsmouth. We have reason to believe he's still there since according to Alcock, the man has a wife in the vicinity, but we need to find and detain him in case he decides to set sail for parts unknown."

"I'll be leaving for the Wyndleton country estate tomorrow," Jonah said. "That's close to Portsmouth, I believe. Within an easy ride, at least."

"Good. You can locate the man and have him bound over to the magistrate. We'll come and collect him as soon as you send word."

"Wait a moment. What happened to the 'we' in 'we need to find and detain him'?"

"A married man's life is not his own," Nathaniel

said. "Georgette has us scheduled for a number of dinners and events to support that charity house of hers in Covent Garden."

Rhys grinned. "And I'm happy to report that my lovely wife is in…an interesting condition and blossoming daily, so she wouldn't appreciate me haring off to Portsmouth on an extended fishing expedition of this sort."

"Would she appreciate you being branded a traitor?" Jonah said sourly. "It could still happen, you know."

"I know." Rhys's smile faded. "We either need to find that witness and compel his testimony on our behalves, or you need to keep your assigned virgin from wedding a royal duke. Which is why we want to help you with your part of Alcock's plan, if we can."

Jonah looked at his two friends. They'd both suffered after the horrific loss at Maubeuge. Rhys had attempted to bury his grief in endless rounds of pointless debauchery. Jonah had heard that Nathaniel had actually spent time in common lodgings living rough among the desperately poor of Whitechapel while he sought oblivion in opiates. His family finally sent a runner to find him and bring him back against his will till he could be made to understand that his family still stood by him.

And what had Jonah done to try to forget? Things that further scarred his soul, things that left him with hands that would never be clean. They were things that needed doing for the good of king and country, and he wouldn't undo them, but "the end justifies the means" was beginning to ring increasingly hollow in his heart.

He didn't hold out much hope for himself. However, if he could help his friends regain some semblance of righteousness, he owed it to them to try.

"All right, I'll see if I can find this Leatherby. But if someone doesn't wish to be found, they can hide fairly easily. Even in plain sight." His friends, for example, looked so out of character in their disreputable garb, none of their set would recognize them. That realization caused a new and frankly outrageous brain brat to hatch in Jonah's head and whisper in his ear.

"Does your family still keep that hunting lodge on the road to Portsmouth?" he asked Rhys.

"Yes, though it's vacant right now. To my knowledge, there's not even a caretaker."

"That's all to the good." It would occasion less suspicion if the place was a bit derelict. "I'll be using it for only a short time, I expect. Now here's what I want you to do…"

Seven

While on the road to Brighton a fortnight past, Lord and Lady Sangerton's coach was set upon by a pair of highwaymen. The brigands relieved the earl of his diamond studs, his gold signet ring, and even the mother of pearl buttons on the fall of his trousers, as well as a strongbox filled with an undisclosed number of valuables. From Lady Sangerton, the robbers stole only a kiss—after informing the lady that she'd already suffered a loss, for the ruby pendant at her throat was assuredly paste.

As it happens, Lord Sangerton had lost the genuine necklace in a game of poque at Boodles some two months previously and had substituted a paste replica without his wife's knowledge.

Lady Sangerton has reportedly left London to visit her family in the Lake District with no plans to return for the foreseeable future.

At least not, one suspects, until Lord Sangerton recovers the real necklace.

From Le Dernier Mot,
The Final Word on News That Everyone
Who Is Anyone Should Know

"Honestly, Serena, I have no idea how you can read with the coach rocking so." Amelia raised a perfumed handkerchief to her nose. Despite the supposed strengthening properties of the lavender scent, her complexion was pale.

"It's no trouble," Serena said as she held the tabloid to the shifting light spilling in through the slit in the window curtain. "Here, let me read it aloud to you. There's a rather amusing piece about highwaymen."

"There's nothing amusing about highwaymen," Amelia complained. "Especially when one is on a journey."

Amelia wasn't a very good traveler in the best of times, but Sir Jonah had insisted that Amelia and Serena take the forward-facing squabs. He shared the other seat with Serena's maid, Eleanor, whose sleepy head was nodding precariously close to his shoulder. Serena had hoped to bring all the servants she'd need for the house party and ball with her to Wyndebourne in a couple of coaches, but Mr. Brownsmith would only let her take Amelia and Eleanor. He promised to send the rest after her in a day or two, assuring her that there were already plenty of willing hands in the estate's employ at Wyndebourne.

She suspected it was the steward's way of maintaining control over the event she was supposed to plan.

One nice thing about marrying a royal duke, she mused, *will be servants who don't still see me as the child they helped raise.*

"Those highwaymen actually did the lady a favor," Serena said after she finished reading the short article aloud to her companions.

"I fail to see how," Amelia said.

"She had no idea her husband was the real thief. They opened her eyes."

"So the serpent did to Eve, but the knowledge of good and evil gave her no joy," Amelia countered. "Do you think Lady Sangerton is happier for knowing of her husband's gambling losses?"

"It's not the losses so much as the fact that he tried to hide them. It is deception which speaks to his lack of character," Serena said. "And happier or not, Lady Sangerton owes those highwaymen. I'd certainly want to know if someone close to me were perpetrating a fraud."

Sir Jonah shifted uncomfortably on his seat. It occurred to her that the big man was not accustomed to traveling by coach and was undoubtedly feeling confined.

"Would you care to signal a halt so you can ride for a while, Sir Jonah?"

She asked more for her sake than his. With every sway of the coach, Serena was strangely aware of how close his knees were to hers. Occasionally, their legs brushed against each other and a desperate tingly sensation shot up her thighs with each contact. It was why she was so intent on *Le Dernier Mot*. Ordinarily, she didn't make much time for tabloids, but by feigning interest in the gossipy rag, she could cover her hitched breaths with pretended outrage at something she'd read.

"No, I'll stay where I am," Jonah said after he lifted the window shade to peer behind them at the horses following the coach. "The outrider in charge of Turk weighs a good bit less than I, so it's a rest for my horse to carry a lighter load on a journey of this length. Looks like he's doing fine with him. Your mare is keeping up as well."

"I suppose she is mine, though I've never ridden her. Father bought her for me and couldn't pass up this opportunity to send her to the country."

The coaching company advertised a nine-hour journey over the fifty-odd miles separating London and Portsmouth. However, Lord Wyndleton had requested a slower pace and more frequent stops to accommodate both his daughter's comfort and the horses being ridden along behind.

"I have to agree with Miss Braithwaite about the highwaymen," Jonah said. "Articles like the one in your tabloid are attempts to make romantic Robin Hoods of them, but they are actually quite ruthless for the most part."

"But no doubt our driver carries a gun," Serena said.

"I didn't see one, and besides, a blunderbuss is a notoriously unreliable weapon," Jonah said. "But don't fret, milady. I would never allow harm to befall you."

Serena wondered if that was what was behind her father's insistence on sending the baronet with them. If his lordship had had any inkling of the misadventures she and Sir Jonah had already shared, he'd never have allowed him to set foot inside the coach, much less become a guest at Wyndebourne.

She shot a quick glance Jonah's way, relieved to find him peering out the window again.

Despite the fact that he'd played nursemaid to her after the cigar, he was still willing to head off for weeks of rusticating in the country with her. The memory of that failed foray into forbidden pleasures made her cheeks heat with embarrassment. It was a painful reminder that not all intimate moments were romantic ones.

Not that I want any romantic moments with Jonah Sharp.

"Suppose a highwayman realized who you were," Amelia broke in. "He might rightly assume you'd be worth a good deal more than any jewels we're carrying."

"You're borrowing trouble," Serena said.

Amelia leaned across the small space and put a hand on Jonah's forearm. "If we should be stopped, don't worry about our things. They can be replaced. Take the extra horses and ride away with Serena as fast as you can."

"Amelia, please."

"It would go against my conscience to abandon you and Lady Serena's maid," Jonah said.

"But it goes against sense not to," Amelia said with forcefulness Serena rarely heard from her. "You must promise me, Sir Jonah."

"Oh, for heaven's sake, there's not a brigand in sight!" Serena stuffed the folded tabloid back into her reticule. She certainly wasn't going to read the article about footpads in Chelsea aloud now lest Amelia see one behind every tree.

"I suppose you're right," Jonah said to Amelia as if he hadn't even heard Serena's objections. "In such an instance, that would be the most prudent action."

"But—" Serena began.

"But it's highly unlikely we'll be set upon by high-waymen," he said. "Didn't you read that the pair of brigands was seen on the Brighton road?"

"That's right," Serena said. "Chances are good they

wouldn't risk a different area, would they? After all, miscreants of that sort need a bolt hole someplace close, I'd imagine, and—why are you smiling like that?"

Sir Jonah gave up and let out the chuckle he'd evidently been suppressing. "The turn of your mind never fails to amaze me."

"How so?"

"You seem to know a great deal about the practical needs of a pair of felons."

"It's pure logic, nothing more. I'm only using the mind God gave me."

"Remind me to thank Him. You have a very nimble mind."

His odd compliment made heat bloom up her neck and spread across her cheeks. Some women were praised for their eyes, their swan-like necks, and white hands. Sonnets had been composed to the dimples on a lady's knees in some of the more salacious love poetry she'd read. She'd never heard of a man praising the way a woman's mind worked.

It was the nicest thing anyone had ever said to her.

"You know, on second thought, I believe I will ride for a bit." Sir Jonah rapped on the coach's ceiling and the team of four dray horses came to a lumbering halt. He lifted the curtain and peered out. "It's cold but clear. Would you care to ride as well, Lady Serena?"

She wouldn't be able to use her muff, but she had a pair of good gloves in her pocket. Her pelisse was fur-lined. If she wrapped her muffler around her neck twice, she'd be warm enough.

"You can't, dear," Amelia said. "The mare isn't equipped with a side saddle."

That settled it. "I'd greatly admire the chance to ride, Sir Jonah."

❧

The March sun promised warmth, but the brisk wind gave it the lie as it whipped away any hope of heat. The shivering outriders were quick to disappear into the coach with Amelia and Eleanor. Despite the cold, Serena fairly danced with excitement as she tried to figure out how to mount the horse without totally sacrificing her modesty.

"Turn around," she ordered Jonah before she put her left foot in the stirrup and hauled herself onto the back of the mare.

Her column dress was a bit narrow to ride astride without hitching it up almost to her knees, but when she undid the row of buttons on her pelisse from the hem to her waist, she was able to spread the warm coat over her legs and drape the excess over the horse's rump behind her.

"Very well, you may turn back around now."

He walked over and pulled aside her pelisse, baring her ankle.

"What are you doing?"

"Checking to make sure you can reach the stirrups on both sides. These are too long." He bent and made quick work of adjusting the straps on the stirrups.

If he was distracted by her nearly naked legs—her pantalets were thin enough to be almost transparent, after all—he gave no sign. The situation made Serena's skin tingle with something more than cold. After he finished the left side, he went around to the right to shorten that one. Finally, he took her booted foot in hand and pushed it further into the stirrup.

"Heels down," he advised before mounting his gelding in a fluid movement.

"This is item number four, you know," she said.

He gave her a quizzical look.

"On my list of forbidden pleasures." It was likely to remind him of her last failed adventure, but she was so excited about this one, she couldn't resist sharing. "I've always wanted to ride astride."

"Then I'm gratified to help you cross another small escapade off your list."

Jonah's eyes sparked with amusement, but she didn't care. It might seem a small thing to him, but it was yet another experience she'd been denied until now. She settled into the saddle, a surge of accomplishment washing over her.

Of course, it would be better if she could figure out how to make the horse move forward. When she rode aside, she merely chirruped to her mount or perhaps drummed its side with one heel to encourage it to walk on.

As if she'd asked him, Jonah said, "When you wish to proceed, squeeze the horse between your thighs."

"*Thi*—" She couldn't bring herself to repeat the word. Granted, she was a bit unconventional and they had shared some unique situations with each other, but the man had the temerity to say "thighs" to her, bold as brass, as if it weren't a serious breach of etiquette. "A gentleman would have said 'limbs,' you know."

"Perhaps if he were speaking of a tree," Jonah said with a wicked smile. "I believe in direct discourse."

Indirect discourse might have been vague, but it also wouldn't have made her cheeks heat.

Sir Jonah signaled the coach driver, and when the equipage began rolling, his mount trotted after it.

Serena's mare stood stock-still.

Squeeze the horse between your thighs.

That was something new. She gave the mare an experimental squeeze.

The horse ambled forward.

Serena clicked her tongue on the roof of her mouth and the mare broke into a trot. She moved with the horse, lifting herself in time with the mare's gait. Between posting and squeezing the mare again and again to keep her moving forward, Serena decided that riding astride might not be as freeing an experience as she'd hoped. At least the constant squeezing and rocking kept her from feeling the cold. She caught up with Jonah in short order.

"So, don't you think it's about time you told me what else is on that list of yours?" he said.

"Why? So you can make fun of me?"

"Would I do that?"

"In a heartbeat."

One of his dark brows arched. "Nonsense. I helped you with the cigar, didn't I?"

"For which I'm not sure I should thank you." Sometimes she still thought she could taste that horrid smoke. "Besides, whether or not you *helped* me with the cigar is highly debatable."

"I saw you home safe when things went awry at least." He shook his head. "That's the problem with adventures. They don't always turn out as we expect."

She shot him a sidelong glance. "What adventure have you had that didn't turn out as expected?"

He laughed. "Where would I start? My brother and I got into countless scrapes as lads. None of which was our fault, you understand."

"Of course not," she said with a laugh. "I am always bitterly disappointed when I'm blamed for the things I do. Now, upon what sort of boyish misdeeds did you and your brother embark?"

"I remember one time when Harold and I decided we'd had enough of our tutor and determined to make our own way in the world with the little education we had. So we packed a satchel apiece and lit out, leaving Topfield Manor and a long row of undone sums behind us."

Serena tried to compose a mental picture of Jonah as a boy. It was hard to add enough softness to his chiseled features to imagine him a snub-nosed, dirty-cheeked child. "How old were you?"

"Oh, I was a sage of seven and Harold must have been all of eight. We obviously knew far more than the adults in our lives," he said with a grin. "All the best stories we'd ever heard took place in a woods, so we headed for the timber on our father's property, determined to kill our own meat and live off the land."

She chuckled. "Armed, were you?"

"Don't laugh. I'm still quite deadly with a slingshot."

"Does need for that skill come up often?"

"Not as often as I'd like. In fact, I did manage to get a squirrel for our stewpot that night, but unfortunately neither Harold nor I was much good at starting a fire since we'd neglected to pack tinder and flint. Then it started raining. So there we were—hungry, damp, and totally out of sorts with each other."

Trees pressed in on either side of the road and if she half-closed her eyes, Serena would imagine the young Jonah and his brother tramping along, soggy and dispirited, through the woods. "Since you were such wise lads, I'm surprised you didn't think to pack emergency food supplies."

"We didn't, having been in a bit of a hurry to escape the arithmetic on our schoolroom board," he said. "We didn't think to bring water, either. At least the rain let us ease our thirst a bit, but being soaked to the skin does put a damper on an adventure. After the drenching, we decided to give up and go home, but—"

"Let me guess. You didn't know the way."

He tapped a finger alongside his nose to indicate that she was spot-on. "We'd wandered far deeper into the forest than either of us had ever gone before, and it was growing darker by the minute. So I suggested we climb a tree to the top. From that height, I reasoned we ought to be able to see the roofline of the manor house and at least know which way to go."

"That sounds like a good plan. Seems you were a sage at seven after all."

"Lots of plans sound good when you're just talking about them, but the actual doing of them, aye, there's the rub." Jonah sent her a searching look and for a moment his expression turned so serious, she wondered if he was thinking about something other than his boyhood misadventure. Then he seemed to shake off the introspection and launched back into his tale. "Harold wasn't such a good tree climber. Before we reached the topmost boughs, he lost his hold and took a bad tumble. Broke his arm."

"Oh, no. What did you do then?"

"The only thing I could do. I made my brother as comfortable as possible at the foot of the tree and tried to keep him warm. Our father's foxhounds found us the next morning. Harold had the indignity of having his bone reset by the local surgeon. Must have hurt like billy-o because he yelped like a little girl."

"I'll have you know I've never yelped in my life even when I was a little girl."

"I ask your pardon. It is dangerous to generalize. Present company excepted, then. After the cast was on, Harold suffered through the misery of being unable to swim in the pond all summer." Jonah shook his head at the memory. "Poor lad."

"And you escaped the adventure scot-free."

"Hardly," he said with a lift of one brow. "My bum was birched good and proper. I couldn't sit without a pillow for a week."

"Well, if Harold hadn't broken his arm surely he'd have joined you in your punishment."

Jonah shook his head. "He's the heir, you see. Our father always delegated corporal punishment to one of the servants, and it's deucedly hard for a fellow to blister the backside of someone he'll have to call milord one day. So I was my brother's whipping boy. Of course, Harold was always made to watch. Since he frequently had as many tears rolling down his cheeks as I by the time the birching was done, I like to think he suffered with me."

He fell silent then. The creak of the coach ahead of

them and the rhythmic cadence of the trotting horse's hooves filled the yawning quiet.

"Are you and your brother still close?"

"Not really. We've gone our separate ways as men."

"Still, it must be good to have a brother," Serena said. "I've often wished for a sister."

"It sounds as if you've been lonely."

"No," she said too quickly. "Well, perhaps a bit. I have friends, of course, but that's not the same thing. And then there's Amelia—I have no idea what I'd do without her." The small muscles in Serena's groin ached from all the squeezing she was doing, but she was too embarrassed to ask Jonah if she was riding astride correctly. Honestly, sidesaddles were ever so much easier. She forced her attention back to their conversation to take her mind off her throbbing legs. "But to have a sister, someone who shares a part of you, who's more like you than anyone else, and who will be in your life forever—well, that must be quite wonderful."

"Nothing lasts forever."

"I know. I don't intend to sound so daft, but you know what I mean. Even if one loses a sibling, they are still there in one's heart. It's the love that lasts, even when all else is gone." Serena sighed. She'd never experience the love of a sister.

"Cheer up, milady," Jonah said. "The Duke of Kent has a large and semi-gregarious family. Once you wed the royal duke, you'll have plenty of sisters-in-law in your life. Though I doubt you'll enjoy that adventure quite as much as you think."

She wasn't enjoying riding astride as much as she'd hoped either. All that confounded having to squeeze the horse to make it go. The insides of her thighs were on fire, and trudging up a hill that was steep enough to slow down the coach wasn't improving the situation. She wondered if the mare would stop dead if she stopped squeezing…

But before Serena could try it, a gunshot rent the air and she heard a man's voice bellow from somewhere ahead of the coach.

"Stand and deliver!"

Eight

Lady S. has been conspicuous by her absence about Town of late. Rumors of a grand fete at the Wyndleton country estate to benefit the Orphans of Veterans of Foreign Wars tease our ears, but we've yet to hear definitive proof of such a coming attraction for the upper crust. One wonders if the fact that another emissary from the royal duke was seen taking ship at Wapping Dock bound for the Continent might have something to do with the lady's swift exit from Society's eyes.

From Le Dernier Mot,
The Final Word on News That Everyone
Who Is Anyone Should Know

JONAH LOOSED A FULL-THROATED "YAH!" AND GAVE Serena's mare a swat across the rump with his hat. Serena was only just able to keep her seat when the horse leaped into a headlong canter. They shot past the coach and past the pair of disreputable-looking fellows with long curling mustaches and spiky pointed beards on their equally disreputable horses. The brigands were ordering the occupants of the conveyance out and the driver to lay down his smoking blunderbuss.

Evidently the weapon was as unreliable as Jonah had said, for the two highwaymen seemed to have taken no hurt. They shouted for her and Jonah to stop.

"Keep going," he ordered and gave the mare another swat when she showed signs of flagging.

Leaning desperately over her horse's neck, Serena flattened herself across the mare's back and stretched out into the gallop with her. She'd cantered along Rotten Row in her sidesaddle, a jaunty gait that earned her a reputation for being a fine equestrienne.

But she'd never engaged in a careening, hell-for-leather gallop over uneven and unknown terrain before and certainly not astride in an unfamiliar saddle on an unfamiliar horse.

"That's it, sweetheart," Jonah crooned. Serena wasn't sure if the endearment was meant for her or the mare. Either way, they flew faster, the mare's hooves lobbing dirt clods behind them with each stride.

Serena buried her fingers in the thick mane and fell into a rhythm with the beast. They moved as one, her breathing measured in time with each rise and fall.

It was primal. Exhilarating.

Selfish!

Amelia and Eleanor were being accosted by those ruffians, and here she was enjoying her reckless flight. Her chest ached. She was the most wretched, the most horrible...

She raised herself up and pulled back on the reins. "We have to go back."

Jonah snatched her reins away and led her, still at a brisk canter. "No, we don't."

"But what if they harm or abduct Amelia and Eleanor—"

"They won't. Your friend and servant may lose a bauble or two, but that's all. Highwaymen want easily portable wealth. A screaming, kicking woman is not portable," he said as he led her along at a somewhat slower pace. "Your friends are in no physical danger so long as they are willing to part with a few small things."

"You sound very certain."

He was. The two highwaymen were his friends, Rhys and Nathaniel, in such clever disguise he almost didn't recognize them himself. They'd agreed to pose as miscreants so Jonah could spirit Serena away from the watchful eyes of Amelia Braithwaite for a while. And whatever miniscule amount of booty they collected in this sham robbery, his friends had promised to send back by anonymous post.

"Why don't you simply woo the girl, Sharp?" Nate had asked when Jonah first suggested the idea to them at The Blind Pony.

"Serena isn't like most women," he tried to explain. "She wants excitement. She's lured by the unknown. She needs adventure…a hint of danger."

"God help you," his friends had said in unison.

God help me, indeed.

Jonah wondered if that counted as a prayer as he led Serena's horse off the road and down the overgrown lane that wound around to the Warrington hunting property.

"Where are we going?"

"A friend's family has a lodge hereabouts. If memory serves, this looks like the way to it."

"But ought we not make for the nearest town to report the robbery?"

"Of course we should," he said as he handed back her reins. "If you wish to see *your* name in that tabloid next week."

Her lips tightened in a thin line, but he knew he'd won that point. However much Serena might enjoy indulging in gossip, she didn't relish being the topic of it.

A gabled roof, the thatch dark with age, peeped through the barren trees. Wind rattled through the naked branches, playing a tuneless ditty. Jonah and Serena broke through the dense woods and the cottage came into full view. After the depressing forest, it was a welcoming sight even if there was no smoke rising from the chimney.

"It doesn't seem as if anyone is here," she said, the timidity in her tone surprising him a bit.

"It would be unusual if there were. This is a hunting lodge, remember, and it's customarily only occupied during the fall." When they stopped before the humble dwelling, he dismounted. "We'll wait here for a bit until the highwaymen have left."

"But what about Amelia and Eleanor?"

"I'll warrant they are more concerned about you than fearful for themselves." Rhys and Nate had promised to be charming brigands rather than terrifying ones.

"That's probably true…of Amelia, at least. She'd keep her head if the Apocalypse was upon her. However, Eleanor is apt to go to pieces."

"It should be over fairly quickly," he said as he tied both horses' reins to the porch rail. "Highwaymen don't like to dawdle. As soon as I feel you'll be safe, we'll rejoin your party. Let me help you."

She looked down at him from the mare's back. "But will I be safe alone here with you?"

"I don't understand. You were alone with me in my home and didn't seem at all concerned."

"We were not alone. Your servant Paulson was there."

As if Paulson would ever interfere with anything Jonah intended to do. "You'll be safe, Serena. I have no cigars with me so I can't imagine you'll get into any sort of misadventure." He raised his arms to steady her. "Lift yourself in the stirrups and throw your right leg—"

"Limb," she corrected. "Right limb."

"All right. Throw your right *limb* over the mare's rump, and I'll help lower you down."

She raised herself to comply, but stifled a small groan and settled back into the saddle.

"Is something wrong?"

"Yes. No." Her face crumpled in misery. "I think I'm not meant for riding astride."

"Nonsense. You kept your seat brilliantly."

"And now I can barely get out of it." She raised herself again and this time gingerly swung her leg as he'd instructed. Jonah wrapped his hands around her waist and eased her to the ground. She took a hobbling step.

On a forced march in the military, Jonah had ridden himself raw once, but that had been after two days and nights in the saddle with few breaks. Serena had barely been on horseback for an hour. "Wait a moment. You shouldn't be this sore."

"If I'd had my sidesaddle I wouldn't be. And I'd have kept pace with you in it too," she said, a bit of her usual vinegar returning. "But honestly, how do you bear squeezing your horse the whole time?"

"The whole time?" He snorted. "You mean you've been tensing your muscles constantly since we began riding?"

"You said I had to if I wanted my horse to walk on."

"Only to get started." He tried mightily not to laugh but failed. "Once the horse has started moving, you relax and ride normally."

"You didn't say that," she said with a sniff, and then walked stiff-legged toward the door. "How was I supposed to know? This lack of explicit instruction is exactly what went wrong with the cigar. You failed to—oof!"

Jonah scooped her up.

"Put me down."

"A lady who's been squeezing the stuffing out of a horse for an hour deserves not to have to walk." He bent to turn the knob and then gave the front door a nudge with his foot. It swung open and he carried her into the main room of the lodge.

All the furnishings had been covered with white sheets against the dust. He bore Serena to the nearest sofa-shaped object and lowered her to her feet. Then he pulled off the sheet, wadded it up, and tossed it into a corner.

"Sit," he ordered.

"I'm not a child. I don't require being ordered about."

Jonah gave a derisive snort. "I thought you wanted explicit instruction." Then he softened his tone. "Please sit, Serena. How am I to tend your injury otherwise?"

Her knees seemed to collapse at that, and she plopped onto the softly bristled velvet. "My injury?"

"You have pulled a muscle, several probably, through overwork."

"I see," she said, shifting uneasily.

She must be in real pain.

"And how do you propose to tend it?"

He knelt beside her. "A massage is often the best course of action."

This time it was Serena who snorted. "Do not imagine I will allow you to massage me...there."

"Would you rather explain to Miss Braithwaite how you came to be crippling about when next we see her?"

Serena bit her lower lip and he knew he'd struck a chord. She might enjoy adventures, but she didn't relish appearing foolish because of them. He decided to press his advantage.

"All you have to do is lie still and let me work your sore muscles until they relax. You'll thank me this evening when you are able to sleep without pain."

"It's terribly indelicate."

She was weakening. "Serena, I'll be as delicate about this as I possibly can."

"You wouldn't have to...to look at the area while you...do whatever you must do, would you?"

Hell, yes, he wanted to say. Of course he had to look at her. He burned to look at her. But if a promise not to look meant she'd let him touch her inner thighs, he'd count that a small price to pay.

"I will keep my gaze on your lovely face at all times," he promised.

"All right. But I'm leaving on every stitch of my clothing except for my coat," she said. "You'll have to do your massaging through the fabric."

She undid the silver frogs on her pelisse and shrugged it off her shoulders. Then she lifted her legs onto the sofa, carefully arranging her skirts so even her ankles were discreetly covered, and lay down. She closed her eyes, as if that would put a bit more distance between them. Then they shot open again suddenly, her expression like a wary wild young thing caught in a trap.

"You're sure this is necessary."

"If you wish some relief, yes. You can close your eyes if you like, Serena. It might help you relax." He covered her eyes with his hand and felt her lashes flutter against his palm. "You don't need to watch me to make sure of where my gaze is directed. I promised not to look at any bit of you but your face, and I always keep my word."

"It's not only that." She pushed his hand away from her eyes. "Jonah, you won't tell anyone? I mean, this is…so embarrassing and—"

"Don't worry." Jonah lifted one of her hands to his lips and pressed a kiss on her knuckles. He wished he could have tugged off her gloves and planted his lips on her bare skin, but she had demanded to remain clothed. "Your secrets are safe with me, milady."

She gave him a small nod and let her eyelids drift closed.

No looking. No removing her clothing. Those were pretty stringent rules of engagement. Well, he'd faced greater obstacles than muslin and lace before and overcame them for a much less worthy prize.

He laid a hand on her ankle and went to work.

∽

"Oh!" She jerked when his palm settled on her. Even though she was expecting it, the shock of his touch sent urgent messages flying up her legs and settling to simmer in her belly.

"Easy. I'm only going to remove your boots." He lifted one of her feet. "You're still clothed, but you don't want to mar the velvet with your heels, do you?"

"No," she agreed. It would be exceedingly bad form of her to repay her absent hosts by damaging their furniture. "That's fine, then."

Serena relaxed a bit as he undid her laces and slipped off her cunning little half-boots. Once the boots were gone, she heard him shift so he was closer to her head. When she peeped at him from under her lashes, he was keeping his promise to only look at her face, though his left hand had slid under her hem and was traveling up her leg with languorous slowness.

Her limb! she amended. She mustn't allow him to coarsen her sensibilities.

It was curious how lovely, how naughty a touch could feel, even though its purpose was merely thera-peutic. If he'd moved faster, she might have missed the soft brush of silk against her skin, the whisper of her petticoats as his arm pushed them up. When he reached her upper thigh, he stopped, splaying his big hand over her. Heat radiated through the thin silk of her pantalets, and only about an inch higher, where the pantalets ended in its open crotch design, her skin tingled.

"Serena." His voice sounded a little rough around the edges. "I want you to lift your right leg and bend your knee."

She opened one eye and peered up at him. "You mean lift my right lower *limb* and bend the *appendage*?"

"Whatever will get you to move," he said. "I need to be able to reach the injured area without impediment."

She complied, propping up one leg against the back of the sofa. Then she draped an arm across her eyes. Otherwise she'd be tempted to peek at him again and there was something in his face—a hunger, a craving—that made her unable to meet his gaze. He might not be looking at the inner thigh he intended to massage, but the intensity in his eyes while he gazed at her face made her feel as if he were seeing her soul naked, all her weaknesses totally exposed.

Then his fingers began to move. Gentle, as only a big man can be. Strong, but with a tight bridle on his strength. Her skin rioted in pleasure, and the sore muscles protested for only a moment before surrendering to his soothing touch.

It was most curious. Even though he was touching only her inner thigh, another part of her tingled. She felt all warm and heavy *down there*. A low throb, like an ancient heartbeat, began to pulse between her legs. His hand shifted up, closer to the sensitive folds.

Her breath hissed in over her teeth.

"Does that hurt?"

"No. Not exactly." There was a definite ache, but it was far from unpleasant. His hand moved up, past the top of her pantalets close to the open crotch. A fingertip slid under the silk and touched bare skin.

She was on fire.

He kneaded and circled, close to the private place between her legs, but never quite touching it.

Serena swallowed back a growl of impatience.

When he brushed his palm across her short, curling hairs as he transferred his attention to her other leg, the effect was as startling as if she'd been struck by lightning. Her whole body was alive with sensation, with anticipation, with—

"Serena, have you ever been kissed?"

Her eyes flew open at that. "Well, of course I have. I'm twenty years old, you know."

He continued the gentle massage, easing her sore muscles, but frustrating the living lights out of her by not touching the part of her that most clamored for it. If anyone had told her she'd want a man to touch her *there*…well, it was beyond her understanding. But drat it all, it simply *was*.

"Tell me about your first kiss," he said softly.

"My second cousin Homer Quinsy stole a kiss from me under the mistletoe. I was twelve," she admitted. "He tasted of gooseberry tart. I thought my lips would never unpucker. It was awful."

What his hand was doing to her was anything but awful. She felt hot and cold and feverish and shivery all at the same time. She had the definite sense that his pleasant strokes were leading up to something, but she was afraid to think what, afraid of the outlandish ideas that kept careening around in the nimble mind of which he thought so highly.

"Kissing your second cousin doesn't count."

"There have been others." She'd learned to dance the minuet, and stylized kisses at specified times were as much a part of the steps as the stately promenade.

"How did they make you feel?" he asked.

She frowned at him. "They weren't awful, if that's what you're wondering."

"It's as I thought," he said with a grin. "You haven't been properly kissed."

"Of course I have."

Her father had never allowed her to be courted, even when several extremely eligible men approached him about her during her come-out Season. The marquis had always been angling for the grandest of matches for his daughter. "And that sort of thing takes planning. Negotiation," he was fond of saying. "It's not to be found in a confounded glorified tearoom like Almack's or by keeping company with beardless boys."

Some of the men hadn't been beardless, but there was no arguing with the marquis. None of the potential suitors were fine enough, wealthy enough, or well-placed enough for his only daughter.

"Besides whether you think I've been kissed or not," she said, beginning to have a few doubts, but not willing to admit it, "I think I'm a better judge of whether I've been *properly* kissed than you."

"Seems to me you don't have enough experience to reach a valid conclusion." He leaned close enough for her to feel his breath feather warmly across her lips. "Are you game for another forbidden pleasure?"

She swallowed hard. If she said no, he'd think her a coward. Besides, she wanted to feel his mouth on hers. She wanted it most desperately.

But her voice wouldn't work. Fortunately, he was satisfied with a nod.

Jonah covered her lips with his in a sweet joining. He slanted his mouth over hers and traced the seam of her lips with his tongue. It tickled a bit, but she didn't feel like laughing.

It felt...wonderful.

Soft. Liquid. Pliable.

His hand moved closer to *down there*. It struck her as absurd that she didn't even know what to properly call that part of herself that had suddenly become the center of the universe.

Why on earth don't I have a name for it?

The ache was becoming unbearable.

Oh, God. He's going to touch...But what if he doesn't?... don't make me ask...don't make me beg...oh, there.

A fingertip grazed her curls and she gasped a bit at the shock of delight that shot through her again.

But she didn't break off their kiss. Her lips parted and his tongue slid into her mouth.

Heaven.

His fingers had retreated back to her sore muscles, but there was so much going on what with his tongue tracing her teeth, she forgot about that low ache for a moment. She let him explore. She suckled him a bit and when he withdrew, she followed his tongue back into his mouth. The whole world was wet and warm and giving and demanding.

Then just as she'd decided there was nothing on earth so fine as this man's mouth on hers, his hand moved up to cup her sex.

Nine

We are saddened to report that yet another couple has gone haring off to Gretna Green. Miss Phoebe Lovelace and the honorable (or should we say "not-so-honorable"?) Mr. Bartholomew Bird, fifth son of Lord Sirey, have fled north in their haste to wed. While Miss Lovelace's uncle, Lord Hastings, has reputedly settled a tidy sum on her, Mr. Bird is utterly without prospects, unless one counts the living his father is trying to arrange for him as a country vicar in an unnamed village. Once Mr. B's creditors catch up to them, the couple will undoubtedly be poor as church mice in the parish Mr. B will nominally serve. However, given Mr. B's predilection for spirits, gaming, and, if the rumors are true, wenching as well, one must question his fitness for the pulpit.

One wonders what the lady was thinking. Then again, perhaps the question should be "with what was she thinking?"

From Le Dernier Mot,
The Final Word on News That Everyone
Who Is Anyone Should Know

SERENA PULLED AWAY AND LOOKED UP AT HIM, HER lips kiss-swollen and her eyes wide. Her breasts rose and fell with short breaths. Jonah still held her hot little self in his hand. He longed to explore her tender little valleys, to drive her to shattering pleasure, but he forced himself to stay immobile while she accustomed herself to this new intimacy.

"Well," he said. "Had you been properly kissed before?"

"No," she whispered. "I'd never been properly kissed before. But I suspect there's nothing proper about what you're doing to me now."

"I'm only holding you, Serena."

She squeezed her eyes closed and a single tear slipped from the right one. She was trembling.

"You're doing more than that," she said.

"What does it feel like I'm doing?"

"It feels like you're...you're...I don't know. I'm so confused."

"Am I hurting you?"

She swiped away the tear and opened her eyes. "No. Nothing hurts. Even my sore muscles feel fine now, and I want you to...hold me...but...well, yes, I do hurt. In a way. I ache something awful."

"I can fix that."

"How?"

He moved his hand a bit, settling one finger into her soft crevice.

She drew a shuddering breath.

"I never dreamt I could feel like...I mean...no one told me..." Then her eyes flared with alarm. "Jonah, I can't...we mustn't—"

"I agree. We mustn't," he said. "That's why I'm only going to touch you, and when we are finished here you will still be in the same state of purity you now enjoy, Serena."

"I'm not certain *enjoy* is the right word. Is all this... this throbbing normal?"

"Perfectly."

Her lips went slack for a moment. "You're sure?"

"Trust me," he said. "This is one forbidden pleasure that will turn out better than you expect. I only want to give you delight. Will you let me?"

In answer, she reached up and pulled his head down for another kiss.

Jonah was free to touch her now however he chose. He started slow. He traced the delicate edges of her folds, teased the short curling hairs, and circled her mound till she was arching herself into his hand. Then he dipped into the soft wetness of her.

He found her most sensitive spot and tormented it, first with the pad of his thumb, then with his dexterous middle finger. When he pulled back from their kiss, her expression contorted into that look of anguished ecstasy one sees in paintings on the faces of saints in rapture.

She stretched up to kiss him again and groaned into his mouth. She demanded he give her his tongue. She broke off their kiss, threaded her fingers through his hair, and brought his head to rest between her breasts. Her heart hammered under his ear so hard, he began to wonder if it would burst out of her chest.

He felt her body stiffen. She was close.

"Come to me, Serena," he whispered.

His words seemed to release her, and her whole body spasmed with the force of her shattering release. It started in her lower body and shuddered in both directions. He kept stroking and drew the moment out in exquisite torment. She gasped, small needy sounds that tore at his control and made him wish he could plunge into her soft wetness and join her in the madness of lust. Then the sounds subsided as she rode the waves of bliss to their gentle conclusion. Finally, she quieted but for an occasional hitching breath.

Listening to her heartbeat slowly return to normal, he didn't move his head from her chest. The soft mounds rose and fell beneath his cheek and he breathed in her delicate fragrance, a light hint of orange blossoms mixed with the musky sweetness of her arousal.

She must dab a bit of scent between her breasts. He longed to discover where else she might apply a drop or two of fragrant oil.

He still held her sex, but was careful to keep his fingers motionless. Her delicate secrets would be too sensitive, too swollen and charged, to bear more for a while.

"My word," she breathed.

Jonah raised up to look down at her. Her face was flushed a becoming shade of peach. Her lips were parted in a kissably slack state.

A warm glow surged through him. His body might be growling that they weren't finished yet, not by a damned long shot, but there was definitely satisfaction to be had in seeing a woman brought to such glorious completion. Serena had been utterly fulfilled and he'd kept his promise not to deflower her.

He'd just plucked a few petals.

But her eyes concerned him. She was looking up at him with such doe-eyed languor, his conscience pricked him like a cattle goad.

Had the daft girl decided she was in love with him? That would never do. He was there to do a job, to claim her maidenhead solely to save his family from being tainted by the scandal Alcock threatened to rain down on them. The last thing he wanted was for Serena to develop a *tendresse* for him.

Jonah figured if he introduced her to her own sensuality, she'd probably add lovemaking to that confounded list of hers. And if that happened, Serena was curious enough and adventurous enough that she'd be begging him to take her sooner rather than later, simply because she wanted to cross off the experience.

Making her fall in love with him was not part of the plan.

Then her eyes lost that hazy "don't-give-a-tinker's-damn-about-anything-because-I'm-still-floating" quality, and her brows drew together into a frown. A wary, narrow-lidded expression stamped itself on her features.

"What's wrong?" he asked. "Are you disappointed?"

"In a way."

"What?"

"No, I don't mean that. Not exactly," she said quickly. "It was wonderful. Life-altering, in fact, and I will never forget it. Thank you, Jonah."

Thank you? Somehow that grated on him. She made it sound as if he'd just shined her boots.

She sat up, pushed his arm out from under her skirt, and spread the fabric demurely over her legs.

Limbs, he silently amended. *Even now, she'd want me to think "limbs."*

"Why are you disappointed?" He'd never had a complaint from any of his other lovers.

"It's not your fault. I suppose I'm just upset that I've been kept so ignorant of how my body works," she said as she tucked a stray lock of hair behind her ear.

"I doubt young ladies are routinely instructed in such things."

"Indeed, we are not." Serena pulled on her pelisse and began catching the long row of silver frogs that marched down the front of the long coat. She studiously avoided looking at him. "Otherwise, I could have done this myself."

"Yourself?" *Oh, that mind of hers.* He ought to have counted on her haring off in an unexpected direction.

"Well, couldn't I?"

He couldn't very well say no. His own history of occasional self-gratification didn't comprise his proudest moments, but he'd managed to keep his body's needs in check with it more often than he cared to admit. "Yes, I suppose you could."

"I thought so. Why on earth isn't this information given to young women?"

"Perhaps you should write an instructional pamphlet," he said, sarcasm graveling his voice.

"An excellent idea." She threw her legs over the side of the sofa and reached down to tug on her boots. "Of course, I'd have to use a *nom de plume,* but I rather suspect the pamphlet would sell like hot buns once the word got out."

"You have no need to make money by writing a pamphlet about that."

"Of course not. Money is not the object." She rose and replaced the sheet on the sofa, smoothing the edges neatly. Then she walked over to peer out the window at the horses outside. It occurred to Jonah that she was avoiding meeting his gaze. "The pamphlet could be offered at only marginally more than the cost of the paper and ink. Do you have any idea how many women might be spared from making rash decisions about questionable gentlemen if they knew they could sate their...marital urges themselves?"

"There are lots of reasons women make rash decisions. What about those who choose questionable gentlemen based solely on the fellow's title?" His tone came out more bitter than he intended.

She glanced his way then. "That's another question entirely."

"And one for which you have no grounds to write a pamphlet." He had no idea why, but anger flared suddenly in his chest in a hard, hot knot. "After all, you're set to accept a man you've never met simply because he's the son of a king. When it comes to wedding a title, it appears as if you're no different from any other ninny who ever wore a skirt."

She flinched as though he'd slapped her. Then she turned and stalked out the door without so much as the hint of a limp.

At least he'd managed to massage the soreness out of her groin muscles. The way she held her shoulders, so squarely rigid, he was sure she was sore about something else though.

For the life of him, he couldn't figure out why she should resent it when he'd spoken the truth. And he'd just given the girl a self-admitted "life-altering" experience. Yet all she could do was natter on about writing instructional pamphlets on how to "sate a marital urge" solo. She had no idea how much it cost him to merely touch her when he wanted desperately to bury himself in her. When he wanted to be closer to her than anyone he'd ever known. When he—

Stop it, Sharp, he ordered himself as he followed her outside. *You can't care about her. You can't want her. You're going to muck up everything.*

Without a word and without waiting for his help, Serena hauled herself up onto the back of the mare. Then she turned her mount's head and started off at a brisk trot.

And I'll bet she's not squeezing constantly this time.

He mounted Turk and hurried after her down the lane. She paused at the road.

"Do you think the coach has passed by already?"

It wasn't the most intimate of conversations, but at least she was speaking to him.

He stared at the winter-rutted road in both directions. "No. I see only our tracks. This way."

They rode in silence back toward the spot at the top of a hill where the highwaymen had appeared. Jonah wasn't sure how much time had passed. It had seemed to expand and contract around them while he lost a bit of himself in Serena. But he hoped his friends had finished their little charade and made good their escape.

As they drew near, voices seemed to echo disjointedly off the woods around them.

"Hold a moment," Jonah said.

Serena reined in and cocked an ear. "It's Amelia." A brief smile flashed over her lips. "That's her major general voice if ever I heard it. Whatever's going on, she's definitely in charge. Let's go."

"Wait." He grasped her reins to keep her from riding away without him. She eyed the leather strips in his hands as if she could ignite them with her glare. "I'll give them back if you promise not to keep running away. I only want to make sure you'll stay long enough for me to say something to you before we join the others."

"I don't want to talk about the duke." The wariness was back in her eyes. "Haven't you scolded me enough over something that is beyond my control?"

He handed her back the reins. "I rather doubt that anything in your life is beyond your control. More than any woman I've ever known, you do what you want and say what you want."

"And I am censured for it regularly, I assure you. What is it you want to say?"

"Just this. I gave you an experience today."

She bit her lower lip. "And I thanked you. It was… quite beyond my imaginings."

He held up his hand. "There's no need for you to thank me, because you gave me something too."

She blushed, that same peachy glow that had lit her from within back in the hunting lodge.

"You gave me your trust, Serena, and I want you to know that I do not take it lightly. So it is I who should thank you."

Her mouth twitched. "I rather doubt those words pass your lips very often."

"They don't."

"Then it must have meant something to you too," she said softly. Then she drummed her heels on the mare's flanks and sped away.

Yes, damn it. Jonah urged Turk into a canter after her. *It meant something to me too.*

He just wasn't quite sure what.

Ten

In advance of the Season, a number of the finest families are arranging house parties at their country estates in order to allow their precious debutantes a chance to hone their social skills with close friends of the family before they are subjected to the harsh light of public scrutiny at their come-outs. Society is on pins, hoping for invitations to the most sought-after parties.

By far the most coveted invitation is one to Wyndebourne, a four-story Georgian manor on our fair land's southern coast that serves as the country seat for the Marquis of Wyndleton. Not only is the sea view said to be divine, but it will be the perfect venue from which to watch the last lap of the Hymen Race Terrific unfold for the daughter of the house. Tally ho, Lady S!

> *From* Le Dernier Mot,
> The Final Word on News That Everyone
> Who Is Anyone Should Know

"OH, MILADY!" ELEANOR BLEATED. "YOU SHOULD have seen 'em—a regular pair of gentlemen they were despite their shabby turnout. Honestly, Miss Braithwaite, did you ever see such fine manners?"

"I'd have been more impressed with their fair words if we hadn't been looking down the barrels of a brace of pistols at the same time," Amelia said as she supervised the reloading of the coach's boot. The highwaymen had required all the trunks to be pulled off of the luggage rack and the strongbox brought down from the roof of the coach as well.

"But they didn't take very much," Eleanor said. "Your jewels are all still safe."

"That is unusual, I daresay," Serena said. Along with a number of smaller pieces, she'd packed her ruby necklace and earbobs, an emerald choker that weighed her down each time she wore it, and a length of beautifully matched pearls that reached to her knees unless she looped them multiple times over her head. "What *did* they take?"

Amelia cast Jonah a sheepish glance. "They rifled through your trunk most thoroughly, sir. And I very greatly fear you are missing a set of wrist studs, a horse pistol, and a leather-bound case which I suspect contained your shaving accoutrements."

Jonah swore and muttered something under his breath, but Serena couldn't catch the words.

While Serena was thankful for the apparent chivalry of the robbers, their targeted theft of Jonah's things seemed suspect. Perhaps he'd had a run-in with the pair in the past. "That's all the highwaymen took?"

"Oh, no. They insisted on kissing my hand, milady," Eleanor said with a giggle. "They wanted to kiss Miss Braithwaite's as well."

"No need to encourage such riffraff. I refused them." Amelia cast a dagger glare at the maid.

"Well, it seems you're not so much worse off for your adventure, then," Serena said. She wished her belly would quit jittering every time she glanced at Jonah. Just because they'd had their own unexpected adventure together, it didn't signify a change in their association.

It couldn't.

He was helping the driver and the outriders load up the boot again. As a passenger, he wouldn't have had to do that, but he seemed to be staying busy in order to avoid looking her way, which was probably the wisest course.

She watched while he hefted the trunks and imagined his muscles bunching and flexing beneath his clothing. Which was probably *not* the wisest course.

"Are you unwell, milady?" Amelia laid the back of her hand to Serena's forehead. "You don't seem to have a fever, but your face is flushed."

"I'm fine. It's only on account of the wind," she lied.

Why wouldn't he look at her? She sauntered over to the rear of the coach where he was arranging their considerable amount of luggage in the most efficient configuration. "When we reach Wyndebourne, we'll be within an easy ride of Portsmouth, Sir Jonah. Perhaps we can visit town and replace your losses."

"That'll do. I intended to visit the port in any case," Jonah said as he pulled down the boot's canvas cover and fastened the straps tight. "A…former friend of mine is staying there, and I hope to renew our acquaintance."

Friend. Did he mean a former lover?

Serena, stop being such a goose. Just because they'd

shared a moment, a glorious, heart-stopping moment, it gave her no claim on him. Or him on her. But she could have no more stopped the words that came out of her mouth next than she could have stopped herself from bleeding if she'd been cut. "Who is this friend?"

"Someone from my time in the military. You wouldn't know him. He doesn't move in your exalted circles."

Serena was annoyed at the relief that washed over her when he said "him," but the relief was no less real.

Once the coach was reloaded, the travelers climbed inside out of the wind. Serena wasn't sure how she felt about being back in the confined space with Jonah on the opposite squab. She couldn't very well insist he ride, so she made herself as small as she could, keeping her knees together and making sure they didn't brush his.

It irritated her that he didn't seem the least affected by her proximity. Jonah folded his arms over his chest and closed his eyes, almost immediately feigning sleep.

No one could drop off that quickly.

Of course, the soft snore that rose from him did sound pretty authentic.

She decided to pull back the curtain and watch the Hampshire countryside roll by. There were forests and heaths, winding rivers and hills. In a few more weeks, they'd be spring green and bursting with new life, but now they were weighed down with the last drabness of retreating winter.

Then the coach crested a rise and she was treated to her first glimpse of Wyndebourne in the distance. Slanting sunlight caught the multiple rows of windows, and the manor sparkled like a jewel on its bluff overlooking the sea. Wyndebourne was a study in form and function, balance and beauty. Her chest ached at the loveliness of it.

Far more than the town house in London could ever be, this was her home. It was the place where she'd taken her first toddling steps, where she'd helped her mother plan and lay out the garden that rioted each spring and summer in waves of blooms, where she'd wept her first heartbroken tears…

"What are you looking at?" Jonah's voice was unusually soft, so as not to disturb the other occupants of the coach. Both Amelia and Eleanor, obviously exhausted by their brush with felons, had succumbed to the rocking motion of the coach and were asleep with their heads nodding in time.

Serena met Jonah's green-eyed gaze and wondered how long he'd been watching her. "It's Wyndebourne. We're almost there."

He lifted the curtain and peered out. "A commanding location."

"Trust a man not to appreciate the graceful aesthetics of an elegant house. It's also a warm family home. However, if a defensible position is all that interests you, there are ruins of a castle not far from the manor," she said. "My family has claimed this land since the time of the Conqueror."

"Or the Bastard, depending on which side of history you hail from," he said.

"There are always two sides to every question, aren't there," Serena said. "However, the passage of time generally shakes matters out."

She didn't have much time left before her most pressing question was settled. If her father managed to finalize an agreement with the Duke of Kent, she might be wed inside a month.

She'd been resigned to it and even found the bright spot of parenting a future monarch in the situation, but now there was a dull lump of something new in her chest. A simmering resentment perhaps over being treated as if she were nothing more than an available, suitably noble womb? Or was it fear of being trapped in a loveless marriage with a man she didn't know?

Until Jonah showed her what glory there was to be had between a man and a woman, she'd thought she could grit her teeth and muddle through a royal marriage and mating well enough.

Now she wasn't so sure.

As the coach rumbled up the tree-lined drive, the servants came spilling out of the massive double doors. From a distance, the flurry of activity reminded Serena of a disturbed anthill, all the small figures scurrying about in seeming confusion that slowly attained a measure of order. The faithful Wyndebourne retainers delighted in arraying themselves in a tidy line of welcome whenever any member of the family came home.

It was a constant source of anguish to her father that his immediate family was so small. And that his only offspring was of the wrong gender.

If Serena had been a son, someday Wyndebourne in all its splendor would belong to her instead of her cousin Rowland. Not that there was anything wrong with him. Rowland was a fine fellow and she had no doubt he'd do right by her, unlike some heirs apparent who all but ignored the needs of their predecessor's family. But it did seem unfair that she should be penalized for something over which she had no control.

"You're frowning," Jonah observed. "What's wrong?"

"No, it's nothing," she said. "It's silly really. But sometimes I wish I'd been born a man."

"I'm very glad you weren't."

His words warmed her cheeks. *Drat.* Would she never stop this infernal blushing? Of course, she'd never had better reason to blush. After all, Jonah was acquainted with her womanliness in a way no other man on earth could claim.

The coach lumbered to a halt and the occupants disembarked. Serena was careful to traverse the entire line of servants, calling each by name and inquiring after their families, until she finally came to Mr. Honeywood, the head butler. He was as efficient as the steward Mr. Brownsmith ever thought about being, but his apple cheeks and ubiquitous smile made him seem so jolly, Serena almost thought of him as a favorite uncle instead of a servant.

"A thousand welcomes, milady," he said, his high tenor carrying in the bright cold air. "We trust you'll find everything in order here at Wyndebourne."

"I always do, Mr. Honeywood," she said as she accepted his bow. The butler made certain that the estate was ready to receive and entertain any number of guests at all times. She was sure there would be little to do to prepare for the upcoming ball except choose the menu, engage a decorator, and hire the musicians and dancing master.

Serena swept in through the tall double doors with the rest of the party in her wake. The circular marble-floored foyer rose to a domed ceiling, but the grandeur of the place didn't speak to Serena. She was too busy remembering how she used to take a running jump and slide across the polished floor in her stockinged feet as often as she could get away with it.

"Miss Braithwaite," Mr. Honeywood said to Amelia, "his lordship sent word that your effects were to be moved to a different chamber from the one you occupied the last time you were in residence. If you'll follow me, please."

Eleanor would take her customary room on the topmost floor. As Serena's lady's maid, she was entitled to a chamber that was a bit larger than most of the other servants. Eleanor had cooed over the small window that looked out over the garden and managed to snag some fabric from Serena's old curtains to dress up her space. A series of cords linked Eleanor's chamber to the bell pull in Serena's so she could ring for her maid whenever she needed her.

Amelia and Eleanor began to follow the butler up the grand curving staircase, but Jonah held back.

"Mr. Honeywood will see you to your chamber," she said, gesturing for him to follow the butler. "There are some interesting ones in the east wing. Ask for the Africa Room."

It was furnished with all manner of outlandish pieces, including an ottoman made from the foot of an elephant. Serena had often sneaked into the chamber as a child for the guilty pleasure of running her chubby fingers over the rough hairy hide.

"Where are you going?" he asked.

"To say hello to the garden." She turned away and started through the labyrinth of rooms she'd have to negotiate before she reached the French doors that led out to the back of the great house.

Jonah fell into step beside her. "A little early in the season for a garden, isn't it?"

"Yes. Nothing will be in bloom yet except maybe a jonquil or two." She lengthened her stride, but he kept pace with her easily. "You don't have to come."

"You've piqued my curiosity. 'Hello to the garden,' you say. I've never seen one that required a greeting."

"Why do you insist on making my words sound ridiculous?"

"Did I say it was ridiculous to say hello to a garden?"

"No, but you make me feel…" She waved a hand in the air, as if the right word was hovering there and she could somehow pluck it down. *Nervous. Uncomfortable. Indecisive.* All true, but not things she cared to share with him and no more appropriate sentiment was forthcoming. "Oh, never mind."

She led Jonah through the stuffy parlor with its matching yellow chintz-covered chairs and settee, and past the music room where the Broadwood grand was kept in perfect tune though no one had played it in months. Then she skirted the perimeter of the blue-striped breakfast room that gave onto a stone terrace.

She paused long enough to allow him to open the door for her.

May as well let the man be useful instead of merely ornamental since he's set on accompanying me, she reasoned. Then she resolved to pretend he wasn't there.

The vines that covered the trellis forming an arch

over the entrance to the garden proper had been cut back last fall. By mid-summer, the heliotrope would be so thick and fragrant, it would leave Serena slightly lightheaded when she passed through the portal and into her mother's horticultural dream.

"A garden should never be squared off, dear," her mother used to say. "No hard edges. Green growing things need freedom to follow their own course."

So, it happened, did small girls.

All one spring and summer, they'd spent nearly every day together, side by side, planting, watering, and weeding. With trowel and shovel, they'd dug out a hint of a wandering pathway and placed flagstones at intervals in the pea gravel. There was no design to the place in the truest sense. Higgledy-piggledy was the watchword.

"Where does this rosebush want to live?" her mother had asked. Serena cocked her head to the side for a moment as if she were listening for the rose's quiet, slightly prickly voice. Then she announced that the red rose wanted to live by the statue of Hera because it was feuding with the yellow rose that had already taken the spot near the stone bench and wanted to be as far away from its mortal enemy as possible.

Her mother had accepted this as perfectly reasonable and planted accordingly.

The garden was a horror by French standards. But to Serena's mother, who preferred to let a garden be itself, it was a disorderly triumph.

And even as the garden lay now, in the stillness of waiting for its first tender sprouts to push through the cold sod, it was the place where Serena felt the presence of her mother most strongly. The family crypt in the nearby village church may have held Miranda Osbourne's earthly remains, but her essence, her spirit lived in the garden at Wyndebourne. Sometimes, Serena talked to her there.

"Hello." Jonah's voice interrupted her musings.

"To whom are you speaking?" Serena asked.

He did a slow turn, arms extended. "To the garden faeries or whoever it is you feel the need to greet here."

"There actually is a faery by the fountain." She walked toward the now quiet stone basin that would be pattering with life once the threat of the last frost was past. In several places, the shrubbery on either side of the path was so overgrown, it threatened to choke off the narrow trail. She'd have to cut them back later. "There she is."

Serena pointed to the statuette, nearly hidden in the shadow the fountain. Some sort of lichen was creeping up the faery's dainty stone legs and she stooped to scratch at it with a fingernail. The rough greenish-gray growth refused to relinquish its hold. She'd have to come back with a stiff bristled brush and some bleach.

"My mother loved that little thing," she said softly.

"That's who you're really greeting here, isn't it? Your mother."

She nodded. No point in shutting the man out since he seemed able to read her more easily than a posted placard. "She and I planted this garden together. It may not seem like much to you, but—"

"It seems very fine," he assured her. "I like it."

She couldn't help but smile. When she gave this tour

to most people, they launched into lengthy exhortations about how a formal house like Wyndebourne required an equally formal garden. Still, she couldn't allow Jonah to think she needed his approbation.

"Even if you didn't approve," she said, "I wouldn't change a thing."

"Why does that not surprise me?" Jonah snorted and shook his head. Then his amused grin faded. "What sort of things do you talk to your mother about here?"

Drat the man. He seemed privy to her every thought. "How do you know I—"

"Because if I had a place like this where I felt I could connect with my mother, I would."

"That's quite an admission from a man with a reputation for cold toughness like yours."

He shrugged. "Such a reputation usually works in my favor."

"No doubt. Men fear you and women want to… to fix you."

"That implies I'm broken." His eyes darkened, but the shaded glen of those green orbs promised no calm retreat. "Is that what you want, Serena? To fix me?"

He stepped closer and she almost backed away reflexively. Then she remembered this was her garden. She straightened her spine and stood her ground.

"We can all do with a bit of improvement," she said, taking comfort in one of Amelia's well-worn homilies. "Not that I think you're broken," she hastened to add.

"Sometimes I do." He cupped her cheek in one of his large hands. His touch was so warm, she couldn't resist leaning into it slightly. "Say I were, what would you do to improve me?"

How would her mother answer such a man? There were certainly times when she heartily wished she could hear Miranda Osbourne's calm measured tones. Serena remembered her as being full of wisdom and good humor. And any woman who dealt regularly with Serena's father had to have a few feminine tricks up her sleeve as well.

"I think," she said slowly, "that would depend on the nature of your brokenness."

He traced the curve of her cheekbone with the pad of his thumb. "Suppose my heart were broken."

"I can't imagine you'd ever allow anyone close enough to do that." She swallowed hard. His lips were so near. If she simply tilted her chin up a bit, he'd be on her before—

He didn't wait for her to tip her chin.

Eleven

According to Miss Odelia Longbotham of the Ladies'
Temperance Union, we must note with growing sadness
that gin is the new scourge of the masses. In every narrow
alleyway of our fair city, one may find an inebriate laid low
by this potent, readily available liquor. However, lest the
upper crust feel themselves immune, let us warn them to take
heed. One may just as easily lose one's way by embracing
Madeira or fortified wine.

More evidence will be presented on this topic at the Ladies'
Temperance Union's weekly meeting. Not surprisingly, no
liquid refreshments will be served.

From Le Dernier Mot,
The Final Word on News That Everyone
Who Is Anyone Should Know

JONAH'S MOUTH CLAIMED HERS.

How dare he not wait for her invitation? Indignation
made her stiffen, but it was a futile gesture. She melted
almost immediately. His kiss was more potent than the
strongest fortified wine.

Serena had never been tipsy in her life, but she imagined this might be how too much sherry would affect her. She was hot all over, despite the brisk breeze. All her joints seemed loose. Her knees trembled. In a few heartbeats, she was leaning into Jonah's hard body, accepting his demands and making a few of her own.

She knew this man's mouth. Knew when he'd slant his lips over hers and moved with him. She anticipated his tongue and welcomed it.

How could she know him so well after only one stolen interlude in his friend's hunting lodge?

She might have been surprised by the kiss initially, but now she realized it was an inevitable claiming. A quest. An adventure distilled down to the press of his lips on hers, his heart pounding against her chest, his hands smoothing down her spine and drawing her closer.

Rational thought fled, and that low drumbeat began between her legs again. She was becoming such a shameless wanton. And here of all places, in the garden where she'd spent countless happy hours planting perennials and playing silly word games with her young mother.

Oh, Maman, what you must think of me now.

She wedged her arms between herself and Jonah and pushed, fingers splayed against the broad expanse of his chest. When their mouths separated, she was marginally comforted by the fact that his breathing was as ragged as hers.

"If you intend to fix me, Serena, that's a start." He rested his forehead against hers as his arms circled, drawing her back into his embrace. "That's definitely a start."

It would be so easy to lose herself in his arms again. So easy to press kisses on his neck and taste his salty maleness. So easy to forget that her father was counting her to be even more important to the Osbourne family than if she had been born his male heir. Serena had a once in a lifetime chance to become part of the royal family, grafting the Osbourne name into the House of Hanover for all time.

It was bad enough that Serena feared she was disappointing her mother by dallying with Jonah in their special garden. She couldn't disappoint her father too.

"I don't have time to fix you, Jonah." With a growing heaviness in her chest, she extricated herself from his arms and fled away, up the winding path and back to the relative safety of the house.

I need too much fixing myself.

❧

As Serena had promised, the Africa Room was an interesting space. At least one of her ancestors had been a serious hunter and the tall walls were studded with trophy heads—wildebeest and antelope, giraffe and Cape buffalo. Their baleful gazes were trained down on Jonah's bed with faintly accusatory stares. From the zebra skin stretched on the floor to the fresco of an African savannah on the ceiling, the guest chamber was a feast for curious eyes.

But it was not conducive to sleep.

The rest of the house had settled into a somnolent rhythm, the slow tick of the long case clock in the corridor outside his chamber as steady as a heartbeat. But in the Africa Room, there were too many eyes, too many spirits of departed beasts. Jonah found he couldn't remain in the large tester bed.

The logical thing to do would be to use the bell pull and order a glass of whisky or warm milk to be brought, but he didn't see why his restlessness should interrupt some poor servant's sleep. He'd seen a liquor cabinet in the first floor parlor. If he couldn't pick the lock and help himself, then he'd consider ringing for a footman.

He toed on his house slippers, knotted the belt of his silk banyan at his waist, and headed into the hallway, counting on the moonlight shafting in through the large window at the end of the hall to light his way.

If he were honest, it wasn't just the exotic chamber that kept him awake. He'd dallied with a beautiful woman twice that day without taking a bit of ease for himself. His body rebelled against the scruples his conscience placed upon it, but he was determined that the loss of Serena's maidenhead would be her choice. He didn't want to take her in a moment of weakness. He wanted her to come to him freely, clear-eyed and without illusions.

Of course, he was still going to bed Serena Osbourne. That wasn't in doubt, even if she had made a point of ignoring him at supper.

But he took that as a positive sign. She wouldn't pull away so vehemently if she weren't actually drawn to him. Seduction was a game and this sort of give and take was to be expected. There was time. So long as he accomplished his goal before that ball she was so keen on, everything would be fine.

When he reached the parlor, a thin strip of light showed at the bottom of the door. Someone else was roaming Wyndebourne in the wee hours too. He pushed open the door slowly.

Serena was there. She'd abandoned the comfortable furnishings to lounge on scattered pillows on the Turkish carpet before the fire. A half-filled goblet was in one hand and a half-empty bottle of claret stood on the nearby table.

"What are you doing here?" she asked.

"I could ask you the same thing."

"This is my home, Jonah." Her words were slightly slurred. "I can be anyplace I please."

"And drink anything you please, I see." He recognized the label on the bottle. The vintage was like a top-tier courtesan—French, full-bodied, and devilishly expensive. "Claret is not normally a woman's drink."

"Shh!" She put her fingers to her lips. "Don't tell a soul."

"Let me guess. Getting totally foxed is another item on that infernal list of yours."

She rose to her feet and wobbled to the liquor cabinet to retrieve another goblet. Then she poured some of the pale claret into the second glass and offered it to him. "1790. It's supposed to have been a very good year."

Jonah swirled the wine in the glass to release its perfume, then took a sip. "A very good year," he agreed. He had a good head for liquor, but he realized immediately that this sweet, fruity claret was more potent than most. "Is that your first bottle?"

She grinned, shook her head, and held up two fingers.

"So is the point of this exercise to drink until you're ready to do something foolish?" he asked as he settled into one of the chairs by the fire. "Because if so, I think you're already there."

"Why would I wish to do something foolish? If it's likely I won't remember it tomorrow, what fun would that be?" she said with a slow blink. For a drunk, she made uncommon sense. "The goal is to drink until I'm insensate."

"That can be dangerous."

"All the really good adventures are." Her pupils had dilated so much her eyes were dark wells, ringed with a thin blue line. "The one we had today certainly was."

She walked toward him and came to rest between his knees. Then she tipped her goblet up and drained it.

Her breasts were level with his face and her night rail and wrapper did nothing to disguise her ripe figure. If he reached up and fondled those breasts, she was deep enough in her cups not to protest. With very little persuasion, he might take her right there on the floor before the fire and be done with Alcock's demands.

But a foxed woman couldn't make a free choice to surrender to him. It would be like playing with a marked deck, so he gripped the arms of the chair hard enough to leave indentations from his fingernails and resolved not to touch her.

She leaned over to put the glass on the table next to the bottle, misjudged the distance, and dropped the dear Frankish crystal to the floor. Fortunately, the carpet was thick enough that it didn't shatter, but the stem broke off from the globe.

"Oopsie." She lost her balance and landed with a

plop on his knee. "Mr. Brownsmith will be upset about that. He counts all the crystal and the silver every time he comes and measures out the cumin and dill."

"I'll say I broke it then," Jonah said.

She palmed his cheeks. "Oh, that's so sweet, Jonah. How should I repay you?"

Serena leaned in and kissed him. Even sloppy drunk, her kiss was tentative and sweet. The tender innocence of it made his gut clench. Then she pulled back and frowned down at him. "You're not kissing me back."

"Yes, I am. It appears you've reached your goal. You can no longer feel your own lips, and if that's not insensate, I don't know what is."

His cock tried to remind him that she wouldn't take much convincing and he could have her hem up around her waist. His body cheered this line of thinking, but his conscience still wouldn't let him shag a woman who might not even remember he'd done it tomorrow.

In the past, Jonah had always been the sort who could do what was necessary, devil take the hindermost.

You picked a hell of a time to develop a conscience.

"So you think I met my goal?" Her eyelids were drooping. If he could keep her still, she'd probably drop off to sleep without imbibing more. She'd been so ill over the cigar, he didn't want a repeat performance.

"Yes. I think you can accomplish anything you set your mind to, Serena," he said. "But are you sure this sort of thing is worthy of you?"

She straightened. "Men drink to excess all the time."

"That doesn't mean it's smart."

She shook her head slowly, narrowing her gaze at him even while draping her arms around his shoulders and getting more comfortable on his lap. He gritted his teeth to ignore the way his cock stood at attention, thick and ready, against his belly.

"I would never have thought it of you," she said. "Are you going to be a scold?"

"No, I just care what happens to you, and if you're set on finishing that damned list, I think you'd better tell me why."

She made a little tsking noise. "Language, Jonah. At least swearing is one forbidden pleasure I neglected to add to the list." She walked her fingers down his chest and teased the bit of hair that showed in the V of his banyan. "Why do you care about my list in any case?"

"So I can help you cross the items off," he said. "So I can keep you safe while you act a little foolish."

"It's not foolish."

Drinking herself to oblivion certainly could be. He'd seen men die after a night of drunkenness, choked on their own vomit or falling into a deep stupor and never waking up. It was imbecilic. Pointless—

"It's because of my mother," she said softly.

"I doubt your mother would have wanted you to endanger yourself."

"Perhaps not, but she would have understood. You have no idea what she was like, Jonah." She sighed and laid her head on his shoulder. "She wanted to have adventures. We used to talk about them. She wanted to climb Snowdon."

"Why didn't she?"

"She always said there'd be time someday. When

I was older, perhaps we'd do it together, she'd say. She wanted to visit Rome and splash through every fountain. She wanted to dabble her toes in the Mediterranean. She wanted to write a novel. She had dozens of stories spinning in her head. While we were planting the garden, she'd tell me some of them—not the whole thing of course, but just the ideas for the stories as they tumbled around in her mind."

"Maybe you could write them down for her," he suggested. It would certainly be a safer activity than most of Serena's wild hares.

She rolled her eyes. "I write a decent letter, but I don't have her gift for words. She could spin them off her tongue and make them dance and sing."

"If she never wrote the stories down, they must not have meant that much to her."

"No, it wasn't that," Serena said. "Other things occupied her time. She was too busy running my father's household. Too busy with me, I suppose."

"I doubt she minded that. Doesn't every woman want a home and children of her own to tend?"

"Yes, of course," she said testily, "but don't you see? My mother never had time for herself. She had such hopes. She wanted to do things. Adventurous things. And maybe she would have eventually, but she…" Tears gathered and trembled on her lower lids. "She died when I was twelve."

He drew her closer and pressed her head back onto his shoulder. She breathed deeply and, to his surprise, left her head there. He stroked her hair, hoping she'd nod off, but instead he felt the tension of suppressed grief building in her body. Silence stretched between them, more oppressive with every heartbeat.

"Do you…want to tell me about it?" he asked.

Please say no.

He was no good with this sort of thing. If she needed him to knock someone on their backside, he was her man. Listening and talking and comforting—that was for an entirely different sort of fellow than he. Unfortunately, Serena didn't seem to know that.

"It was a stupid accident," she said with barely bridled anger in her tone. "Someone had spilled lamp oil on the back stoop and hadn't gotten around to cleaning it up yet. Mother was hurrying out to join me in the garden with a tray full of seedlings when she slipped and fell."

Jonah didn't know what to say, so he just kept stroking her hair.

"She hit her head on the iron balustrade," Serena whispered. Then she fell silent and as her breathing relaxed into a slow rhythm, Jonah suspected she'd dropped off between one sentence and the next. Then she suddenly straightened and continued speaking. "She never woke up. I sat with her every day. I read to her. Pleaded with her to come back to me."

A small sob escaped her lips and he tightened his embrace. Pain and grief roiled off her in scalding waves. It was as if she were reliving her mother's loss afresh and Jonah was powerless to do anything to help her.

Except grieve with the heartbroken girl she'd been.

Serena laced her fingers together on her lap, her knuckles whitening. "I prayed the most excellent prayers I could pray, but she just slipped away a little bit more with every shallow breath. She died the day my father came home. I think she was waiting for him…so I wouldn't be alone when she…"

Serena buried her face in his shoulder and wept.

People cried easily when they were foxed, but this was more than the claret talking. In her inmost part, Serena had never gotten over the loss of her mother. Her tears stained the black silk of his banyan. Finally, her nose red from weeping, she subsided into moist hiccups.

Jonah fished in his banyan pocket and pulled out a clean handkerchief for her. He might not have the right words for this unexpected situation, but at least he had the right tools.

She blew her nose like a trumpet.

"So I put together my list of pleasures because my mother never got a chance to do all the things she wanted while she was here," Serena explained, her words tumbling over each other in her hurry to get them out. "She never climbed Snowdon. Never went to Rome. She spent her last days with me planting that ridiculous garden."

"You know," he said slowly, "I'm no expert on this sort of thing, but I suspect that your mother thought spending time with you was the best adventure she could have."

Her chin quivered and he feared he'd said the wrong thing.

"I only told you these things so you'll understand about my list," she said, her voice growing softer but at the same time more urgent. "Don't you see? I can't wait. None of us are promised tomorrow. And when

I come to the end of my life, whenever that may be, I don't want to look back with regret. I don't want to leave this world with anything undone."

Jonah had seen his share of people leaving this world. He'd wager any amount of money that they all felt they had left things undone, but he didn't think she'd appreciate him saying so. And he certainly didn't want her to ask why he'd been present when so many souls "shuffled off this mortal coil."

She sniffed loudly. "But my adventures have gone all wrong. I managed to see you covered in Orange Fool. I was embarrassingly sick in your study over the cigar, and now you find me all mushy and maudlin just because I've had too much to drink." She balled up the handkerchief and shook her head. "What you must think of me."

"I think," Jonah said, rising with her still in his arms, "it's time you found your bed, milady."

Twelve

We note with little pleasure that Miss Jemima Blackstock and Lord Randall Finchley will be posting the banns in preparation for a rather rushed pre-Season wedding. Rumor has it the couple was caught alone together in the Blackstock family library after a well-attended piano concert at the home. While not absolutely in flagrante delicto, the couple's encounter could be most charitably described as "compromising."

A reputation, once lost, is tediously difficult to regain. One hopes this cautionary tale warns other young ladies from even the appearance of impropriety.

From Le Dernier Mot,
The Final Word on News That Everyone
Who Is Anyone Should Know

SINCE SERENA DIDN'T OBJECT, JONAH CARRIED HER OUT of the parlor and up the flight of stairs to the family wing of the great house. She was so still in his arms, he thought she'd dropped off to sleep again until he heard her whisper, "Third door on the left."

He tried to walk quietly, even with Serena's weight

in his arms. Jonah could have moved stealthily through a forest without a sound, but several of the floor boards in the long corridor creaked when he stepped on them. If there were any light sleepers on this hall, they'd hear his approach.

He was relieved once he managed to open Serena's door and close it softly behind them. No one else needed to know she was properly foxed. He laid her down on the big bed and drew the coverlet over her.

"Thank you." Her words were so soft, he had to lean down to hear them. She snuggled deeper into the bedclothes, tucking them under her chin. "You're a good man, Jonah Sharp. If I had an ounce of sense, I'd love you forever."

The next thing he heard was a small, very lady-like snore.

He straightened immediately. Love? There wasn't supposed to be any of that. *Must be the claret talking.*

Besides, he knew better than anyone that he wasn't a good man.

But perhaps it wasn't unusual that she should be entertaining warm feelings for him. They'd spent a good deal of time together over the last few days. The proximity had affected him too. He couldn't deny that he felt *something* when he looked down at her.

It wasn't lust. He had no desire to bed her if she wasn't going to be a willing participant. Drunk sex was never as intense as when both parties were in full possession of themselves.

It wasn't guilt. Not this time. He hadn't gotten her into this sorry state, but he felt more than a little satisfaction over getting her out of it. He'd stay with her now and watch her sleep, just to make sure she was all right. Her head would feel like a cannon shot had gone off next to it in the morning, but if that was the worst she suffered for her overindulgence, perhaps it was worth it for her to be able to cross another item off that pernicious list of hers.

After all, she was doing it on account of her mother.

He shook his head and went to sit in one of the chairs before her fireplace. He didn't know which was more ridiculous—a lady who insisted on breaking all the rules or him being cast in the role of guardian angel.

But that still didn't settle the question of what was behind the strange glowing lump in his chest. It plagued him every time he was in the same room with Serena Osbourne.

His ears pricked to a soft tread and the occasional creak of the hall floorboards. When Serena's door swung open, he went still as a stone, satisfied that he was probably hidden in shadow. The fire in the grate cast enough wavering light into the room to show him Miss Braithwaite stealing close to Serena's bed.

She leaned over and sniffed. There was no mistaking the alcoholic fug hanging about the slumbering form.

"Oh, child," the governess whispered as she settled a hip on Serena's bed, obviously intending to stay a while. "What on earth did you get into?"

"It's more a question of what got into her," Jonah said softly, deciding he'd fare better if he announced his presence now rather than let her discover him there later. "Which as nearly as I can figure was a bottle and a half of the '90 claret."

At first, Miss Braithwaite startled at the sound of his voice. Then she rose from the bed and advanced on him, her stiff-legged gait reminding him of a guard dog with its ruff up.

"How dare you, sir," she whispered furiously. "What are you doing here?" She held up a hand to forestall his reply. "Never mind. It doesn't signify. Get out."

Jonah rose. "Someone needs to stay with her till she wakes."

"Well, it's not going to be you. Have you any idea what the marquis will do to you when he hears that you got his daughter thoroughly intoxicated?" She marched up and poked a finger at his chest. "It doesn't bear thinking of, young man. You will kindly quit this house first thing in the morning or I shall be forced to inform Lady Serena's father of this…this thoughtless abuse of his hospitality."

Damn. That'll put a kink in Alcock's plans.

"What are you waiting for? Someone else to find you here as well?" She was trembling with rage. "If you have the slightest care for Lady Serena, you will go away. And I mean now."

Jonah cast one last glance at Serena, who was so deeply in the arms of Morpheus she likely wouldn't have wakened if Miss Braithwaite had been shouting at him instead of hissing like a rabid cat. Then he skewered the governess with a steely gaze.

"Don't leave her till she's sensible again." He started for the door. "Which in her case may be several years."

❧

"All in all," Serena muttered as she pulled on her stockings, "overindulging in a manly drink was a worse experience than smoking a cigar."

She wiggled her toes experimentally. Even her feet hurt.

At least after the smoking episode, she'd felt marginally better once she'd been sick. She hadn't become ill over the claret, just incredibly fuzzy about things and afraid her head was likely to detach itself from her shoulders and roll across the floor.

Perhaps it would be a mercy if it did.

When the long case clock had chimed four o'clock in the morning, Amelia had become worried because Serena hadn't stirred so much as an eyelash. She'd rung for a stout pot of coffee, a rack of toast, and proceeded to try to rouse Serena from her claret-induced oblivion.

After being shaken awake and plied with several cups of sugar- and cream-laced coffee, Serena was conscious enough to understand that Amelia was quietly livid with her because Jonah had been in her chamber.

"No, of course I didn't invite him," Serena protested. At least, she didn't think she had. She vaguely remembered seeing him in the parlor, and she'd discovered one of his monogrammed handkerchiefs in the pocket of her wrapper. Someone had used it and she doubted it was Jonah since she still had the foul thing.

"A gentleman does not generally enter a lady's bedchamber unless he's sure of his welcome," Amelia said, entirely too loudly.

Every sound was like a bass drum in Serena's ears.

"I was in no condition to welcome anyone. The point is," she said, trying to keep her voice quiet and even so as not to disturb the uneasy equilibrium her shoulders had reached with her neck, "you say you found him simply sitting in one of the chairs. That doesn't sound as if he were trying to take advantage of my diminished capacity."

In truth, she'd been in more danger of succumbing to Jonah without an ounce of liquor in her system back in that hunting lodge, but Amelia didn't need to know that.

"Still, it could have been ruinous if anyone but I had found him here," Amelia said.

She tried to push another piece of toast into Serena's hand. For the last five hours, she'd been cajoling and begging Serena to eat in order to sop up some of the claret in her stomach. Serena choked down a single bite and put the toast back down.

"If I let something happen to you," Amelia said, wringing her hands, "your father would never forgive me."

"But isn't that what life is about?" Serena gave up and nibbled at the toast once more. "Things happening to me. You can't stop it. Why would you want to?"

"Serena, you're being purposely obtuse. You know perfectly well what I mean."

Amelia crossed the room and threw back the curtains—out of spite, Serena figured—to let the morning sun stream in.

She covered her eyes with both hands.

"Where are my tinted spectacles?" she whimpered.

Serena hoped the blue lenses would take the edge off the bright light.

"In the second drawer of the highboy," Amelia said unhelpfully.

"Will you please get them for me?"

"No," Amelia said waspishly. "If you insist on having things happen to you, who am I to stop you from enjoying the full experience?"

Serena shaded her eyes with her hand and walked, stoop-shouldered as an octogenarian, across the room to the tall chest. Eyes closed, she felt her way up the piece of furniture to the second drawer and located her tinted glasses. They didn't change her vision, but viewing the world through the cool blue was a relief. Once she propped them on her nose, she held out marginal hope that she'd live till lunchtime.

Amelia straightened the bedclothes so Serena wouldn't be tempted to crawl back into the bed. "At least we don't have to worry about Sir Jonah Sharp any longer."

"Why, pray tell, is that?"

"Because I ordered him to leave the house this morning. I expect he's gone by now."

"You what? Why would you do such a thing?"

"Because someone needs to protect you from a rake like that."

"He may have the reputation of a rake, but he has acquitted himself like a gentleman with me." She worried the lace on the hem of her night rail and managed to start it raveling. Starting with his brother, Jonah had a long history of accepting the blame and consequences for other people's bad deeds. "I won't make Jonah my scapegoat. He had nothing to do with the claret. I decided to drink it on my own."

"On the list, was it?"

Serena nodded.

"Oh, that stupid list. I never should have encouraged you about it. Honestly, Serena, why are you jeopardizing your entire future for a few moments of foolishness today?"

"Which is more foolish—to dare to try new things or to sit on the sidelines and watch life pass one by without living it as you do?"

Amelia flinched and Serena felt a momentary pang for having wounded her. It wasn't her friend's fault that circumstances had given her so few choices. Even if Serena's exploits were uncovered, she knew she was somewhat insulated from her unconventional experiments by virtue of her wealth and station. She might be passed over by the Duke of Kent. She might lose a few invitations to a few balls, but she'd still be a marquis's daughter, with all the wealth and privileges attending that rank.

Society would censure someone of Amelia's standing heavily for the same missteps. If a governess were discovered dead drunk with a man in her room, she'd likely be given the sack and turned onto the street without character.

"You still had no right to order Jonah to leave," Serena said in a softer tone, in an effort to both be more conciliatory and keep her head from imploding.

"I've seen the way he looks at you, dear," Amelia said. "And the way you look at him. No good can come of it. Someone has to protect you from yourself."

"No, someone needs to protect me from *you*." Even though her head still banged like a smith's hammer, Serena stomped across the room to confront her old friend. "You had no right to send Sir Jonah away. He's my father's guest, not yours. And in the marquis's absence, this is *my* house. I decide when someone has outstayed their welcome. Not you."

Amelia lowered her gaze and looked so remorseful Serena felt a stab of guilt for scolding her. Usually when they wrangled about something, the rebukes went the other way around.

She wondered if Amelia had ever felt guilty for dressing her down. She wouldn't have thought so, but theirs was a complicated relationship. Less than a parent and child, but far more than a governess and her charge. The love Serena and her old friend felt for each other always clouded the issue whenever they butted heads, which thankfully wasn't often.

"I apologize, my lady," Amelia said, using Serena's title as both weapon and shield, a subtle reminder that they could never have a truly fair fight.

"And I'll accept it," Serena said as she headed for the door, "as soon as I find Sir Jonah and convince him to return to Wyndebourne."

Thirteen

Excitement is building for the upcoming Season and its ubiquitous marriage mart. However, by rights, civilized people ought to decry this rampant, mercenary practice of pairing similarly situated couples and uniting them in holy matrimony, whether any true love match exists or not.

But marriage-minded mamas argue, by what criterion shall we base such an important decision if not suitability of rank and wealth? Such commonality suggests common interests and indeed common affection would surely follow.

Since the Flood, like pairs with like and folk have been going through this world two by two. Who are we to argue with such precedent?

From Le Dernier Mot,
The Final Word on News That Everyone
Who Is Anyone Should Know

AT THE TOP OF THE RISE, JONAH REINED IN TURK so he could look down at Portsmouth. Morning fog still swathed most of the docks in a thick gray blanket, with only the tallest crow's nests peeping from the mists. But the rest of town showed signs of waking. The night soil wagon rumbled through narrow streets accepting pungent offerings, followed by the milk and egg man dropping off the household orders. Fishmongers and grocers wheeled handcarts to their corners and set up shop for the day. A faint bit of the singsong patter they used to entice customers echoed up to Jonah in disjointed words and phrases.

When reconnoitering a new place or trying to run someone to ground, Jonah often made use of two equally informative yet vastly different sources of intelligence—the local pub and the parish church. The pubs wouldn't be serving customers for some time since most folk were just now sitting down to breakfast, but the church doors were always open.

Luckily for Jonah, the vicar was the gregarious sort who loved to talk about his parishioners. The gentle reverend was also willing to share a frugal breakfast of bread and milk with a curious traveler in the manse's kitchen.

"You say the man's name is Leatherby, eh?" The man of God tapped his temple. "Seems vaguely familiar, but to be honest, my memory is not what it used to be. But if I baptized a babe, married a couple, or buried someone, it'll be recorded in our church rolls."

He disappeared to his private study and returned to the kitchen with a doorstop-sized ledger in tow. "There you have it, my good man," he said. "The life of the parish since 1800 all in one place. If we need to go back further than that, I'll have to find my predecessor's book."

"I expect this will do," Jonah said as he leafed

through the stiff pages. He'd told the vicar that he was trying to find Leatherby because his military service had earned him a commendation which had yet to be awarded. "Sergeant Leatherby is likely older than I so he won't be listed in the births section. If he's in here, I suspect it'll be in the marriage listings."

The vicar reached across the table and thumbed over to the correct section of the massive book. There, in a neat round script, were the names and dates of all the couples who'd vowed to forsake all others and cleave only to each other till death did them part.

The listings went on and on, page after page.

It never ceased to amaze Jonah that so many people were willing to take on responsibility for another soul for their entire life. The record length for his relationships with the fair sex was barely a fortnight.

"There it is." The reverend, who appeared to be gifted with the ability to read upside down, pointed a finger at a pair of names halfway down the column. "Hammond Barnabas Leatherby and Helen Smallshaw, wed 21 August, 1803."

"Is there any way to know where they live?"

"Not from these records. And if they attend church here regularly, I confess I am not aware of it." The vicar steepled his fingers before him. "And I so wanted to help you find the fellow so you can deliver that commendation. Our gallant military men deserve every honor."

Jonah felt a twinge of guilt over lying to a vicar, but since it was far and away not the worst thing he'd ever done, he figured his newly awakened conscience would give up needling him soon. "Since Leatherby was in the king's service, I believe the couple may have lived separately for a good bit of their married life. Perhaps the missus receives parish assistance…"

"She may. A good many wives of soldiers and sailors are little more than widows without the name. And just as poor, more's the pity," the vicar said, pausing to make a tsking sound with his teeth and tongue. "But that would be in another ledger. If Helen Leatherby is listed there, we should also have a place of residence recorded for her."

The vicar scurried away again.

Jonah continued to glance through the pages of the parish records. "For better or worse, for richer, for poorer," he mused. "I wonder how many of you got the short end of those sticks."

But for the first time in his life, he wondered if his name would ever appear in a parish record linked with a lady's in holy matrimony like this. He doubted it. The marriage vows promised a love without conditions. One that didn't buckle when health or fortune fled away. One that could last through anything.

He doubted "anything" included the likes of him.

Jonah was carrying so much deadweight, he could never expect a woman to shoulder half the load his soul carried.

As he turned the page, a couple of names he recognized caught his eye.

No, it couldn't be.

He stared at the indelible ink, thinking he'd misread the entry, but the names remained the same. *Married, 5 June, 1815.*

"Well, that explains a lot," he muttered.

"Oh, I'm so glad you're finding my ledger helpful," the vicar said as he bustled back in and plopped down the parish benevolence rolls in front of Jonah. "Hopefully, this one will be too."

❧

The sun was starting to set when Jonah caught his first glimpse of Wyndebourne again. His day in Portsmouth had been a disappointment. Helen Smallshaw Leatherby had moved from the ramshackle tenement the parish rolls had listed as her place of residence and none of her former neighbors knew where she'd gone. Jonah had soup in one pub and ale in another, but hadn't been able to ferret out anyone who admitted to knowing Sergeant Leatherby.

In midafternoon, he made a few purchases, replacing his stolen wrist studs and shaving kit. Warrington and Colton had better be taking good care of his horse pistol or he'd throttle the pair of them when he saw them next. He made a quick stop at a booksellers' and then turned Turk's head toward Wyndebourne once more.

Somehow, he had to finagle an invitation back into the household. If he couldn't find Leatherby on his own, it was more imperative than ever that he satisfy Mr. Alcock's demands.

As Jonah crested another rise, he discovered two other riders heading his direction, a man and a woman. The fellow was dressed in the powdered wig and livery of a footman and the woman was wearing a jaunty green riding habit. Even from this distance,

Jonah could see her hat sported a ridiculously long collection of feathers draping out the back.

It had to be Serena.

He dug his heels into Turk's flanks and the gelding leaped into a ground-eating gallop. She began cantering to close the distance between them and they both drew to a halt with about a dozen feet separating them. The footman looked the worse for his bone-jarring canter to keep up with her, but Serena was smiling.

"Back in the sidesaddle, I see," he said with a grin.

"I've found I prefer it. Everything fits so neatly, you see." She peered at him over the tops of her blue tinted spectacles.

"Do those help?" By rights, she'd ought to have a splitting headache after all that claret.

"I wear them from time to time for relief from megrims," she said with a grimace. "It seems they are useful for other maladies as well."

Even self-inflicted ones. Still, he couldn't help but admire her pluck. She might be in discomfort, but she didn't allow herself to wallow in it.

"Kindly give us twenty yards please, Mr. Halpenny," she said to the footman. The servant turned his mount around and trudged away. Serena nudged her mare into a sedate walk onto the narrow trail leading into the woods. Jonah kneed Turk and came even with her.

"I didn't expect you to come looking for me," he said.

She snorted, a singularly unladylike sound, but one he was coming to associate with her. He admired her ability to flout what was expected of her, even in how she expressed herself.

"You flatter yourself, Sir Jonah. I'm only riding for pleasure. Our meeting is but a happy accident."

"So you admit it, then. You are happy to see me."

She cast him a sidelong glance but didn't contradict him. "I was surprised that you left Wyndebourne without a good-bye."

"I was cordially invited not to tarry."

"Yes, well, Amelia regretted those hasty words once I convinced her you were not responsible for my...unfortunate state last evening." Serena nudged her mare into a quick trot as the path ascended up an incline. The long pheasant feathers on her hat undulated with each stride. "She wishes to rescind her request that you leave," she called over her shoulder.

"And what do you wish?" He hurried to catch up with her as the trail widened.

"You're my father's guest, Jonah, visiting Wyndebourne solely for the purpose of buying a brood mare, I believe," she said. "What I wish doesn't signify."

"It does to me."

As soon as the words were out of his mouth, he realized with a sinking feeling in his gut that they were *true*. That strange glowing lump in his chest was caring, confound it! He'd gone from being the seducer to being seduced.

When did that happen?

She didn't say anything. She just looked at him as if she were seeing him clearly for the first time. As if she *knew* things about him no one should know.

Which, of course, she didn't or she'd likely be fleeing from him as fast as her mare and her not-quite-megrim headache would allow.

Jonah nudged his mount on up the path where gray stone glinted through the barren branches. He pulled up before the tumbled-down ruins of a tower and part of a curtain wall. Dressed gray stones littered the shallow indentation of what had once been a moat.

"This must be the castle you spoke of," he said, grateful for anything that might change the subject.

"High marks to your powers of observation, Jonah." Behind her tinted spectacles, her remarkable eyes rolled in playful derision. "Apparently, my fore-bears held this part of the coast against all comers for hundreds of years by sheer brute force. Now my father does the same thing with Acts of Parliament and a judicious word in a well-placed ear. Much more tidy, don't you think?"

"It may appear that things are more civilized now," Jonah said as he dismounted, "but let me assure you, politics is still a blood sport."

She has no idea.

He went over to help her down and to his surprise, she allowed it. She unhooked her knee from the pommel and slid gracefully to the ground, her long skirts billowing.

"You do sit a horse well, milady," he said, not moving to release his hold on her waist. "Either aside or astride."

"Yet isn't it odd that I prefer my sidesaddle after all?" She looked up at him and leaned closer. "In truth, most of my forbidden pleasures have turned out to be not nearly as pleasurable as I expected."

"But not all?"

"No, not all." Her pink tongue flicked her bottom lip. "Of course, some of the pleasures that have come my way lately were things I'd never dreamt of. Our adventure in the hunting lodge was not on the list in the first place, so that probably doesn't count."

"It counted for me, and I don't even have a list," he said with a grin.

Her lips turned up. "I guess I'll count it too then. But on balance, the scales still haven't tipped in my list's favor."

"Does that mean you're giving up on your list?" He hoped she would. Who knew what the next dubious "pleasure" might be and what sort of trouble she'd make for herself?

"No, but I will be more circumspect about accomplishing my goals. I don't want anyone else to pay for my mistakes," she said. "It's bad enough that you were your brother's whipping boy. I won't allow Amelia to make you mine."

"I don't blame her. Finding me in your room was a nasty surprise for her and she does care for you a great deal," Jonah said. "That's a rare enough gift that it's not something to take lightly."

"Surely you have people who care for you."

His parents, while always conscious of their responsibilities toward him and his brother, had never been the demonstrative sort. If his mother had kissed his brow or his father said an approving word to him, he had no recollection of it. Family was duty. Honor.

Not something as ephemeral as a feeling, something that could be altered by a whim or a bout of improper digestion.

"It's not something I concern myself over," he said. Life was simpler if one didn't give a damn.

"Amelia always says we must give to get. Perhaps you haven't let someone care for you because you haven't cared for them first." She leaned in to whisper, "But never fear, Jonah. I care about you and there's nothing you can do about it."

Then after this astonishing admission, she pulled away from him and addressed the footman who'd finally ambled into the clearing.

"Stay with the horses, Mr. Halpenny. Sir Jonah and I are going to explore the ruins."

Then she slipped her hand into the crook of Jonah's elbow and led him toward the barbaric remains of Wyndleton's greatness.

Fourteen

It has come to this journalist's attention that the Duke of Kent is planning to travel this spring, but no one can name his intended destination. Will he hie himself to Hampshire to woo Lady S. or embark on a ship to cross the Channel for a visit to Prince Leopold's court? Our usual sources are dismally silent. The crown jewels aren't as closely guarded as the royal duke's itinerary.

From Le Dernier Mot,
The Final Word on News That Everyone
Who Is Anyone Should Know.

JONAH NODDED, CASTING A MILITARY MAN'S APPROVING eye at the landscape spread out before them. "The first Wyndleton certainly knew how to pick the right spot."

Serena leaned on the balustrade and drew a lungful of sea air. They were too far from the surf to hear the breakers, but the wind carried the briny freshness up to them.

After she and Jonah had explored the grassy-floored and open-to-the-sky chambers that made up the ruined castle, they'd climbed to the top of the remaining curtain wall, well away from the part that had already crumbled. The forest fell away below them, and from this vantage point it was clear that the undergrowth was beginning to shoot out green tendrils. Tiny buds dotted every tree limb. Over the treetops, Serena could see the broad expanse of the Channel spreading away from them in a grayish blue that blurred to a rim of cobalt at the distant horizon.

"When I was younger, I'd come here and pretend we were under siege. Fortunately, my imaginary standing Wyndleton force beat back the invaders every time," she said with a grin as she peeped over the parapet. "Visigoths can be so very inconvenient if you allow them a toehold, you know."

Jonah laughed. "I thought little girls hosted tea parties with their stuffed bears and pretended to mother baby dolls."

"I'm sure some do, but obviously I read the wrong sorts of books as a child." She leaned her chin on the knuckles of both hands. "Or maybe I was trying to be the son my father always wanted."

"You really shouldn't trouble yourself over that, Serena." A deep cleft formed between his brows. "We all disappoint our parents one way or another. Most often because of what we do rather than what we are."

She wished she could smooth away that frown line. "I'm sure you've been a source of great pride to your family. After all, not many men perform a service to the Crown that results in an elevation of station."

He flashed a half-smile at her. "As you delight in pointing out at every opportunity, I'm only a baronet."

"That was horrid of me." She knew her grin didn't match her words, but she couldn't seem to stop smiling. Everything felt right when she was with him. "No doubt you were provoking me sorely when I did it."

"No doubt. Every single time."

"Still, most nobly born second sons are resigned to being merely 'Mister' all their lives. The fact that you did not remain so makes you special." She turned and leaned against the parapet. "What did you do to merit the Sir before your name?"

A wall seemed to rise up behind his green eyes, more formidable than the Wyndleton castle ramparts had ever been. "I can't discuss it."

"Can't or won't?"

"Does it matter?"

"It does to me. If you can't tell me because you took an oath not to, that's one thing." She stopped leaning and paced along the parapet, as fidgety and unable to settle as a sparrow on a narrow ledge. "If you won't tell me because you don't trust me with your secret, that's something else entirely."

He caught one of her hands and held it fast. "Serena, there are some things best left unsaid."

"And those are the things that generally wear a body down till they can't put one foot in front of the other." She sank onto the gray stone with one of the taller crenelations at her back, letting the heat the granite had absorbed during the day seep into her. In times past, the curtain wall sheltered the real Wyndleton defenders from flaming arrows and trebuchet volleys. She wished she could shelter the man beside her as completely. He'd never admit to needing it, but part of her was sure he did. "I've watched you, Jonah. Even when you smile, it rarely reaches your eyes. It's as if you won't let yourself be happy."

"I'm happy enough, Serena. Who said I'm not?"

"Happy enough is a poor substitute for being truly content."

Jonah said nothing. When he didn't join her in the growing shadow of ancient stone, she rose to stand beside him. The sun slipped under the westering clouds and shot long golden rays back at them before it sank into the distant sea. It ought to have been a lovely moment of shared pleasure over the beauty of the scene, but the silence growing between them was beginning to be oppressive.

"Did you find your friend in Portsmouth?" she asked to fill the yawning space.

"No."

"I'm sorry. Perhaps we can send some of the servants to inquire—"

"That won't be necessary."

She was only trying to help him. Why did he thwart her at every turn? "But you want to locate him, don't you?"

"Let's just say it would be better if he doesn't know I'm coming. I'd like to surprise him."

"That doesn't seem very friendly," she said with an odd flutter in her belly. "In fact, it sounds a bit nefarious."

"You've no idea." Jonah rested his palms on the balustrade.

She placed a hand on his. "I'd like to have an idea,

Jonah. I want to understand you. And I've a feeling I won't until you tell me how you won your baronetcy."

"Don't ask me, Serena. Because I might tell you and you wouldn't like what you hear."

"Try me." She gave his hand a squeeze. "How many times have you asked me to trust you?"

"That's not the sort of thing I generally keep count of."

"You don't have to give me a number," she said with a sigh. Honestly, the man was so obtuse sometimes. "Just think back. I trusted you enough to follow you into Boodles' kitchen after only a few minutes of conversation. I trusted you enough to protect my reputation over stealing away from the opera to try that cigar."

She didn't mention the way she'd trusted him enough to accompany him to the hunting lodge when they'd been set upon by those highwaymen. Or the way she'd given herself over to his talented hands. But she was thinking about it so hard, she was sure he must hear her lascivious thoughts. She hurried on to fill the void lest he bring it up.

"Granted, neither of those exploits went according to plan. But the point is, I gave you my confidence," Serena said. "Don't you think it's time you returned the favor?"

❧

Jonah settled down on a fallen stone in the growing dusk. Perhaps it was a good thing the light dwindled by the moment. Once she knew the truth about him, she'd think him a monster. Darkness seemed fitting.

If she fled from him screaming, she'd save herself from his intention to ruin her. He owed her that chance.

"All right," Jonah said slowly, "but I want you to know I have never told anyone this. Not my family. Not my friends."

She dropped to sit beside him. Her willingness to listen didn't seem motivated by morbid curiosity. The look of earnest concern on her sweet face humbled him.

"Whatever you say will stay with me," she promised.

"I'm counting on it." He stared down at his hands. They'd never be clean. Even under kid gloves or doused in fragrance, the blood was still there. The problem now was how to tell her. Where to begin? "You may know that in 1800, an attempt was made on the life of our king."

"I was only three years old when it happened, but I remember it well. It's one of my earliest memories because all the adults in my life were beside themselves over the news." She rested one of her hands on his forearm and leaned against him, letting her head drift companionably to his shoulder. "I'd never seen so many people crying and shouting at the same time."

Everyone in England had been abuzz with the details. According to the *Times*, His Majesty had just entered the royal box at the theatre. While the national anthem was playing, a lunatic named James Hadfield fired a pistol at him. The shot missed King George III by a mere fourteen inches, but after the miscreant was dragged away, His Majesty insisted that the evening's entertainment go on as planned. He even managed to fall asleep during the play as was his custom.

"The assassination attempt didn't change His Majesty's habits, but it affected a number of his inner circle," Jonah said. "They reasoned that if someone could dare to strike at the nation's king, why couldn't they take pre-emptive blows at his enemies?"

Serena said nothing, but the hand she'd laid on his forearm tightened its grip. If she'd given him a worse reaction, he'd have stopped talking then. But now that he'd begun, he felt the need to continue. He might never get the chance to unburden himself again.

"So a group of three influential courtiers formed a secret association they call the Triad for the purpose of identifying those who pose a threat to the House of Hanover. The identities of the three members of this group are secret." Jonah covered her hand with his while he could. She was likely to yank it away soon. "As I understand it, a unanimous vote is required before action is taken."

"What are you saying? That our king is having his enemies killed?"

"No, of course not." Jonah shook his head. "The king is far too mad to know anything of this, and the royal family doesn't want to know. Those who form the Triad make the decisions and shelter them from the truth. And from those who would harm them."

She lifted her head from his shoulder and looked up at him, her eyes enormous in the growing twilight. "What do you have to do with this…this Triad?"

"I'm sure your father would tell you it's one thing to set public policy, and quite another to bring it to fruition. The Triad needs operatives who carry out their not-so-public wishes in a discreet fashion. Every country on earth has a few men who are willing to do what must be done for the common good, even if the doing of it puts them beyond the pale." He breathed deeply and plowed ahead. "Shortly after I graduated from Eton I came to the Triad's attention. You see, I have…certain skills."

Her mouth formed a perfect "O." "You're telling me you were an assassin for the Crown and that's how you earned your baronetcy?"

"And how I kept it." Honors given can be taken away just as easily, but he hadn't accepted an assignment from the Triad in several months. Only the one from Alcock, which was in direct opposition to the Triad's purpose since Alcock wanted to ensure the House of Hanover's royal line would *not* continue. It was an ironic paradox Jonah couldn't help but enjoy.

At first, seducing a noble virgin had seemed a much easier task for his conscience to absorb than the state-sanctioned removal of an enemy of the Crown. But being with Serena had made several emotions he'd stopped having to deal with bubble back to the surface.

She swallowed hard. "How many…"

He dragged a hand over his face. How many nights had he lain awake, seeing the faces, hearing the pleas? "More than I care to recount."

"Who…have you…removed?"

Lord love her, she was trying to avoid calling it what it was. "I won't give you names. It would only endanger you to know them, but suffice it to say I made it look accidental as often as I could."

"Oh," she said. He could almost see her churning through unexplained deaths and disappearances of well-placed persons over the past few years and trying to reconcile them with what she'd just learned. "Where have you…worked?"

"On the Continent," he said. "And here. I pledged to protect our king from enemies both foreign and domestic."

"I see." She tugged her hand away, but at least she wasn't shrieking and fleeing from him. "How long have you done…*this* for the Crown?"

"The first one was right after Eton, before I joined the military."

It had seemed exciting at first. Being singled out by His Majesty's inner circle for a special assignment meant that Jonah was special too.

"I was chosen for my blade skills and tasked with doing away with a suspected Prussian spy by challenging the man to a duel." He served his king well and was rewarded. Unlike his friends Warrington and Colton, who both had a courtesy title affixed to their names merely on account of their births, Jonah had *earned* his honors.

He'd ridden off to war with his head held high. Then after all the death he'd seen on the battlefields in France, he was reluctant to return to the Triad's fold once the war with Bonaparte was over. But once a man was blooded by the Triad, it was difficult to deny their hold on him. Jonah did their bidding. After the disaster at Maubeuge, he was prey to the same self-destructive urge that had driven his friends to debauchery and opiates.

"The first time was easier because my life was at risk too. A duel might go either way, you know. Later I realized even in a duel, there was very little risk to me."

It was no empty boast. Jonah was a swordsman with few equals. And it seemed the less he cared if he survived his encounters with the Crown's enemies, the more likely it was that he escaped without a scratch.

"It doesn't sound as if there was little risk," Serena said. "What of the risk to your soul?"

"Are you going to preach a sermon now?" Jonah looked down at his hands again. They were capable hands. Deadly hands. "You're right, of course. At first, I could complete an assignment and then sleep like the just. Later I came to realize when you take a man's life, for whatever reason, it takes something of you as well."

"A baronetcy was not enough," Serena said softly. "So, this is something you're still doing?"

"Not in the last few months." Jonah had been trained not to question why a target was chosen, but after a couple years, some of the threats he'd been ordered to eliminate seemed to be of a domestic political nature rather than a physical threat to the king. He began declining assignments. His handler had warned him with a thinly veiled ultimatum not to turn down another, but Jonah was almost ready not to care whether his own name came up for elimination by one of the Triad's other operatives.

"Do you intend to continue?"

He rolled the question around in his mind and came back to the reasoning that prompted him to accept the Triad's offer in the first place. "If I perceive a true threat to the king's safety, yes. It is my duty."

She nodded slowly. "I see that. I understand. Someone must protect the king, even if he has no notion they are doing it. I'm sorry it had to be you, Jonah. I can see this has cost you dearly." Then she leaned toward him and, very gently, kissed him on the cheek.

It was a benediction. A cleansing. A minor miracle. Serena saw him for what he was and yet she didn't turn away.

For the first time since he was a boy he felt the hot press of tears against the backs of his eyes, but he wouldn't let them gather.

"I know it was hard for you to tell me," she said softly. "Thank you for trusting me."

When Alcock first tasked him with seducing her, he'd expected Serena Osbourne to be just another silly debutante. Then once he realized she was a risk-taker and a bit of a daredevil, he categorized her as a shallow pleasure-seeker who deserved to be plucked, though he'd make sure she enjoyed the process. Now, she'd taken the side of him he thought no one could bear, the darkest, ugliest part, and she accepted it. After that absolving kiss, he realized she was half-angel.

And she still hadn't flitted away from him.

He palmed her cheek and covered her lips with his.

Fifteen

Lady Breakwater is hosting a gala to benefit the Home for Children of Indigents and Gypsies in Surrey. In keeping with the exotic background of some of these suffering urchins, she has engaged a number of palm readers and crystal ball gazers to entertain her guests.

We predict that a number of fortunes prognosticated by the hired swamis will not prove true, unless they foretell that the attendees of this soiree will be lighter in the pockets by the end of the evening—and not necessarily because they have made a cheerful donation. Look to your wallets, gentlemen.

From Le Dernier Mot,
The Final Word on News That Everyone
Who Is Anyone Should Know

JONAH WASN'T THE MAN SHE THOUGHT HIM. EVEN HIS kiss was different. Now instead of the self-assured kiss of a practiced rake, Jonah's lips were tinged with urgency, with unbelieving desperation. Their mouths molded to each other in a shared breath. Serena could almost feel their souls mingling and flowing back and forth between the two of them, unsure which body to inhabit.

She was still reeling a bit from the revelations of his more than scary past. But when she sneaked a glance at Jonah from under her lashes, she saw only his pain over his deeds. Her own chest ached in sympathy.

She grasped his lapel and tugged him closer, giving him permission to plunder her mouth. He went farther. He slipped a hand under her pelisse to cup a breast.

Warmth surged through her. Her nipples ached at the nearness of his hands but chafed at the layers of fabric that separated her skin from his direct touch.

"My lady," someone called.

Jonah squeezed her nipple through the fabric and longing jolted her. That low ache began again *down there*.

"I say, my lady! It's growing dark. Oughtn't we be returning to Wyndebourne?"

Serena pulled away from Jonah's kiss with reluctance. "I shouldn't let you kiss me so often."

"Maybe I haven't kissed you often enough." Jonah continued to caress her breast. "After all, you started it this time."

"But only because you seemed to…need a kiss."

His fingertips drew circles around her nipple. It was hard as a horn button and throbbed desperately. "And what about you, Serena? What do you need?"

"My lady!"

She shoved aside her body's responses, its clamoring aches and urges. "Mr. Halpenny's right. We must go." She scrambled to her feet. "It's already so dark that we'll have to take the road at a walk, and even if we leave now, we'll be late for supper. Amelia will be worried sick."

Jonah sighed, rose to his feet, and extended a hand to her. "I don't want to be the cause of more anxiety for Miss Braithwaite. But Serena, before we go…" It was growing too dark for her to read his expression, but his voice seemed choked and broken. "I just want to say…"

It was gratitude she heard in his tone, she realized suddenly. He was thankful she'd listened to him. Bless him, it was still so hard for him to speak what was in his heart. "Don't worry, I know. You don't have to tell me."

"I want to." His eyes had gone very dark in the dimness, but the hard glint was gone from them. "I never wanted to tell anyone. I never thought anyone would understand. And I especially never thought anyone would be you. Thank you."

"I can't claim to understand. In fact, I understand very little really except that I can't bear to see you in pain. Please, Jonah. Tell me you'll stop these clandestine doings."

"If I can. I have one more assignment to complete."

It's that supposed friend of his in Portsmouth. The man must be a target.

Jonah took her hand and led her down the stone staircase to the grassy remains of the castle's Great Hall. Serena decided she would do everything she could to discover the man's name.

And, for Jonah's sake, she'd make sure the fellow took the next available berth on any ship leaving Portsmouth.

❧

The next day a veritable army descended upon Wyndebourne—an army composed of modistes, seamstresses, decorators, caterers, and a squabbling troop of musicians. Mr. Brownsmith had handled the invitations from London in order to ensure that no person of importance was overlooked, but he'd sent all the other help Serena had requested to prepare for the house party and ball at Wyndebourne. The new arrivals threw themselves into their appointed tasks with as much fervor as if they were trying to rebuild the glory of Rome in a single day.

It was exhausting just to watch them work.

Serena had to approve every decision. Should they use velvet ribbons or satin to hold back the damask curtains in the ballroom? Which type of petite-fours and what flavor of punch should Cook prepare to be served on the sideboard? She was consulted on the order of dances and whether the constantly drunken pianist should be allowed to remain with the ensemble or if the glory of Wyndebourne would be better served by only a string quartet.

Fittings for her ball gown were about to drive her to tears. Her modiste was using a daring new design, one that required such a snug fit around the bodice that Serena despaired of drawing breath, much less dancing in the thing.

From the deepest dungeon that had been converted into a wine cellar more than one hundred years ago to the topmost garret chamber occupied by the lowliest scullery maid, all of Wyndebourne was being cleaned to within an inch of its life. The brasses and silver were polished, and the hearths of every fireplace scrubbed until the bricks gleamed. Every horizontal surface was dusted and then dusted again. The marble and hardwood floors shined so brightly, Serena could see her reflection in them.

And everywhere she went in her own home, she felt as if she were underfoot.

She managed to escape the dancing master who had insisted upon putting her through her paces the day before. The pompous windbag had tried to wrangle a repeat performance earlier that morning, but Serena slipped into the library when she heard his nasal twang echoing down the corridor toward her.

She needed time to think. She and Jonah hadn't spent a moment of time alone since they visited the castle ruins together and he told her about his unorthodox (and utterly unnerving) service to the Crown. Even though it had felt as natural as breathing to kiss him there beside the crumbling parapet, in the cold light of day she still had to weigh his words. It was hard to reconcile the courtly, if somewhat rakish, Sir Jonah Sharp with the cold-blooded assassin he admitted to being. It made Serena's head hurt to try.

Unfortunately, the library was not empty. Mr. Honeywood was there, supervising a pair of footmen who were grappling with the Doric columns that supported a pair of busts.

"Oh, Lady Serena, there you are. I wonder if I might have a word?" Mr. Honeywood took out a slightly rumpled white handkerchief and wiped his brow. "Mr. Brownsmith sent notice that we'd ought to switch Cicero and Voltaire so that Cicero was nearest the selections of classical literature. What's your opinion?"

"I think everything was fine the way it was." And she didn't just mean the library. Before all this nonsense with the royal duke, her life was just fine. Before she met Jonah Sharp, her life was just fine. Life was ever so much easier when one's insides weren't twisted up in knots all the time.

But she had to admit, it was much less interesting.

"Very good, my lady," Mr. Honeywood said. "I wonder if I might prevail upon you to help me with seating arrangements for the midnight supper after the ball."

"I'm sure you can manage without my opinion. Your knowledge of precedence far exceeds my own. I trust your judgment implicitly."

The butler preened a little under her praise.

"On to other matters then," he said. "It's come to my attention that a troop of gypsies has made camp down by the apple orchard. I know it is the marquis's custom to allow them to stay on Wyndleton land as they pass through each season. But since we are expecting guests and possibly royal ones at that, I thought it might be advisable to send a few of the grooms and stable lads to encourage them to move on with all speed."

"No, don't do that." A frisson of excitement sparked through her. Finally, here was something she could do that didn't involve schedules and menus and tape measures. Her almost forgotten list of forbidden pleasures beckoned. "You are to leave the gypsies be, as it is my father's policy. As far as everything else is concerned, I can see you've matters well in hand. I'm going to ride before tea."

Then Serena made good her escape before Mr. Honeywood could put another decision before her. By some judicious dodging into rooms at the last moment and skittering up staircases as soon as the danger was past, she managed to reach her chamber without encountering the dancing master. Serena secreted a handful of coins in her reticule. Then she rang for Eleanor to help her change into her riding habit and hurried back down to the stables as quickly as she could.

Jonah had been spending his afternoons in the stable, she knew. Each day, he took one of the marquis's brood mares out of her stall to check her conformation, her gait, and to ride the horse around the enclosed paddock. He had not made an offer to buy any of them as far as Serena knew.

And he hadn't gone back to Portsmouth to look for his "friend" either, for which Serena was pathetically grateful. It was one thing to know about his past deeds. It was quite another to know that he was going to be doing it again.

Jonah was riding a high-stepping bay when she reached the paddock. He sat the horse with grace and ease, moving with her as one as she made a few small jumps without hesitation. To Serena's certain knowledge, that particular mare had never been trained to jump.

"You didn't tell me you were part centaur." Serena climbed up on the lowest rail and peered over the paddock fence.

Jonah chuckled. "I'm not. This little bay is a good sort though. Some Arabian blood, I'll be bound, but there's English stock in her too."

"You're right. My father thinks the Arabians are too highly strung and not nearly stout enough for English winters. That mare is one-quarter Thoroughbred."

Serena gave the order for one of the grooms to saddle her mount.

"Why don't you take this one?" Jonah asked as he dismounted and led the mare over to the fence. "I'll saddle Turk and join you. Where are you bound?"

"It's a secret."

"I believe I've proved I can keep your secrets, milady."

And I can keep yours. She'd never tell anyone about Jonah's activities on behalf of the Crown. Not even Amelia. "Suffice it to say, I'm about to cross another item off the list."

"In that case, I'm definitely coming."

Serena smiled. The only time they'd had speech with each other was over the supper table. Then Amelia was there too, so their conversation always had to revolve around the weather or other approved topics. She wanted to ask why he hadn't sought her out, why there'd been no chances for her to ask more questions about his work for the Triad. But she knew the answer to that in any case.

Jonah considered the matter closed.

"Of course, you'll have to ride astride." Jonah walked the mare out of the paddock and handed the reins over to her.

"That should pose no difficulty. I know I only have to squeeze once to get her started now."

"If you forget, I'm always available for a massage," he whispered and then disappeared into the stable to saddle Turk.

Serena's cheeks warmed, but rather than be affronted she was relieved. It meant Jonah was behaving more like himself.

Jonah the Rake she knew and could deal with. Jonah the Shadowy Hand in the Dark, ready to snuff out the life of that poor man in Portsmouth just because he'd gotten crossways of some mysterious Triad…well, that Jonah was someone she wasn't sure she wanted to know.

She adjusted the stirrup height, mounted the mare, and arranged her skirts so that her shins and ankles were modestly covered. Once Jonah and Turk cleared the stable door, she nudged the mare into a trot and set off across the meadow. As soon as they were out of earshot of any of the Wyndebourne help, Serena slowed her mount to a sedate walk.

"Have you begun work on your pamphlet yet?" Jonah asked with a grin.

"My pamphlet?"

"Yes. The one in which you were going to share my…how shall I put this?…massage techniques with the women of the world."

"Oh, that. No, I haven't started work on it yet." Serena refused to let him see he could ruffle her though she was at a loss to control the color of her cheeks. Only last night she'd tried again to reach that pinnacle of sensation on her own. After a frustrated quarter-hour, she decided it was rather like trying to tickle one's self. It wasn't at all the same as when someone else's hand was doing the tickling. "To be honest, my experiments with your…massage techniques have been…less than successful."

If he'd have laughed, she would've reached across the space between their mounts and boxed his ears. But she couldn't really blame the man if he couldn't suppress a smile.

"It's nice to know that men are not as unnecessary as you thought," Jonah said. "Are you going to tell me what item you intend to strike off the list today, or am I to guess?"

"You think you can guess? I should like to see you try."

"Let's see. You have explored the dubious pleasures of tobacco and alcohol. You invaded an exclusively male club while wearing men's clothes. You've mastered riding astride." He gave her a searching look. "I trust you are more comfortable in a conventional saddle now."

"It's tolerable," she said. "But I do still prefer the sidesaddle."

"It's always good to know what you like, but what will the lady try now?" Jonah cocked his head at her, as if that would help him penetrate her thoughts. "I'd guess sea bathing in the nude, but we are headed in the wrong direction. The Channel is back that way."

Serena laughed. "Is that wishful thinking?"

"Yes."

It was only a single word, but he said it with such barely contained fervor, warmth surged over her entire body. For a moment, she imagined how it would be, leaving her discarded clothing on the pebbled beach and dashing into the surf, bare as a peeled twig, with an equally bare Jonah at her heels. The sun kissing every bit of her. The saltwater flowing over her skin, caressing her secret places. Jonah adrift with her in that decadent watery world. Floating together, skin on skin, the kindly sea bearing them up. Would they kiss and sink and lose themselves in the rapture of the deep?

"Penny for your thoughts," Jonah interrupted her highly improper—and probably inaccurate since she'd never actually seen a naked man—musings.

"They are worth far more than that."

"The thoughts of a dedicated sybarite always are."

"A sybarite? I am no such thing."

"Aren't you? You're adventurous, sensual, and willing to go to great lengths to experience new things. If the dictionary were illustrated, by rights your picture should appear beside the word." He tipped his hat to her. "And please know I say these things with the greatest respect for your accomplishments in the field of pleasure seeking."

Serena sat taller in the saddle, hoping a more upright posture would demonstrate an upright character. "Just because I want to experience more of life than most young ladies of my station do, it does not make me some sort of voluptuary."

Serena nudged her mare into a trot beside the silver stream of the river. Clumps of birch and alders clung to the banks, dipping their toes in the shallow water. The air was alive with the fresh breath of newly sprouted green growing things.

"How else would you explain your list of forbidden pleasures?" Jonah's mount kept pace with her. "I've never known anyone who set such concrete goals for new experiences. I commend you for it, Serena. But if life has taught me anything, it is that we must acknowledge who we are."

She reined her mare to a full stop, and Jonah drew

to a halt beside her. "So you think I must admit I am a self-centered sensualist."

"No. But it wouldn't hurt for you to recognize that you are a passionate woman."

The heat of his gaze sizzled over her, and all that was feminine in her responded with moist warmth and a low ache. She gave herself a stern mental shake.

"I'll have you know that not all of the items on my list have to do with sensual things. Some of them are simply new ideas, things in intellectual and spiritual realms that I wish to explore."

"Such as?"

Serena decided she might as well tell him since otherwise she'd be imagining frolicking with Jonah in the surf and he might get her to actually admit it. "I've always wanted to know what lies ahead—haven't you?" And never more than now, when a possible royal match was still in the offing. "If you must know, we are on our way to a gypsy caravan where I intend to find someone who can tell my future."

He cast her a dubious look. "If a gypsy, or anyone else for that matter, could truly foretell the future, they'd be appointed one of the king's privy counselors, not gallivanting around the countryside in a painted wagon."

"This is my list of pleasures, not yours, Jonah," Serena said as she reined her mare into a walk alongside the river. "I didn't ask for your company. Turn back, if you wish."

Instead, he came even with her again. "Even supposing someone could tell you honestly about your future, are you sure you want to know?"

Yes. Was the royal duke going to make an offer for her? If he did, would she still accept? Why did she drift to sleep each night with Jonah's face hovering before her eyes? Why did she feel hollow as a gourd when he was nowhere to be seen and so jittery on the inside when he was? If someone, anyone, could tell her what was coming, what to do, and how to slip this infernal Gordian knot her insides seemed to be tangled up in, she'd be pathetically grateful.

"I don't fear tomorrow," she said. "I want to know."

"Then know this. The future is not fixed. You choose it for yourself, Serena."

The plaintive sound of a single violin wafted over the rise ahead of them.

"There's the encampment," Serena said. "If you're too afraid to have someone read your palm, I'm sure the gypsies have horses they want to sell."

She dug her heels into the mare's flanks and left Jonah in the dust behind her.

Sixteen

Our English lords have been accused of being "games mad."
While it is true that gambling to excess has become the
hallmark of a gentleman of title and property, the wagers
themselves give us insight into upcoming developments in
Polite Society.

For example, currently the odds at White's and Boodles'
are weighted sharply in a certain German princess's favor in
the Hymen Race Terrific. However, we note with interest
that a relative of Lady S. has wagered that the English miss
will triumph over the sister of Prince Leopold. It is also telling
to note that a certain baronet believes she will not.

Who will be proved correct? Only time—and pressure is
mounting on that front, we assure you—will tell.

From Le Dernier Mot,
The Final Word on News That Everyone
Who Is Anyone Should Know

THE GYPSY CAMP WAS CLEANER THAN SERENA EXPECTED
and far more pleasantly aromatic. Pots of stew filled
with some unidentifiable meat, which she suspected

probably wandered there from her father's flocks, bubbled before every caravan wagon. Cardamom and sage and other spices she couldn't identify wafted in the air.

The gypsy men greeted them as they first rode into camp. The young ones were so darkly handsome, if they'd only been outfitted by Brummell they'd have turned every feminine head at Almack's. The older men were hawkishly featured with only a little silver streaking their hair, but all of them were built with wiry strength. As she expected, they had a string of ponies for sale that they were eager for Jonah to see.

The women pretended not to understand her until they heard the jingle of coins in her reticule. Then she was ushered to a wagon decorated with garish orange stripes and introduced to a woman named Nadya.

"A thousand welcomes, my lady." The woman's dark curly hair hung below her multicolored kerchief to her waist. Several strands of golden chains with coins affixed to them looped her neck. Serena had heard that Roma women wore their wealth. If that necklace were truly gold, then Nadya was undoubtedly the queen of this tribe. The woman opened the door to her wagon and bade Serena enter. "Come. We make the tea."

Because the interior of the wagon was well organized and surprisingly bright considering the only source of light was the window built into the door, Serena found it cozy rather than merely small. Rows of drawers had been built into one side, and a fold-down bunk was propped up on the other. A table, sturdily nailed to the floor and topped with a brightly colored cloth, hugged the far end of the wagon. Nadya waved a be-ringed hand toward one of the two chairs. The tea things, complete with a steaming kettle, were already laid out.

"How did you know I was coming?" Serena asked in surprise. There was a spherical object covered with a silk scarf on one of the shelves. Had the woman watched her approach in a crystal ball?

Nadya followed the line of her gaze, laughed, and shook her head, setting her loop earrings glimmering. "Do not be amazed. I did not know it was you. I saw only that someone would come."

The gypsy woman made short work of slicing coarse barley bread and offering pots of jam to go with it. Then she poured two cups of the strong, spicy-smelling tea. While Serena nibbled at the repast, Nadya told her that her family appreciated the way the marquis had allowed the gypsy troop to camp unmolested on his land over the years.

"Your father, he is a good man and holds what is entrusted to him with an open hand. He treats the Roma well and for that, he will be rewarded."

Might as well cut to the heart of the matter. "Will he be rewarded by having a grandchild who will wear a crown?"

"Ah, now we come to it. You are not here simply because that handsome fellow you came with wants to buy a horse. And you have been thinking about what it is you wish to ask. Good." Nadya began to clear off the table. "Finish the tea. I must see your cup. No, no. Hold it with two hands. The more you connect with the cup, the more you concentrate on your questions, the clearer will be my vision."

Serena usually took her tea with milk and two sugar lumps, but Nadya had offered her nothing of the sort. She wrapped her fingers around the cup and drank the bitter dark liquid. Though she tried to suppress it, she couldn't help but grimace at the taste.

"That tea blend, she is special. Is from my grandmother's grandmother and so on, handed down from the beginning," Nadya said. "Is good, no?"

No. But Serena didn't think it would be polite to say so, so she simply nodded.

"There is small bit left, yes? Then give to me." Nadya held out her hand and Serena put the cup into it. The gypsy woman flipped the cup upside down onto a saucer and turned it quickly three times in a clockwise direction. Then she picked up the cup and stared into it intently.

"What do you see?" Serena asked after several minutes had passed.

"Zztt! The spirits, they do not like to be rushed." Nadya turned the cup this way and that, her dark brows drawing together in a frown.

Serena shifted on the hard wooden chair. She wondered suddenly if Nadya had seen something she didn't want to share with her. An accident that would befall her father. A lingering illness in her future. Perhaps Jonah had been right when he warned that it was good not to know too much about what was coming.

"What is it? What do you see?" Serena asked as she bunched her riding skirt in tightly clenched fists.

Nadya set the cup down and closed her eyes. "This

crown which you seek, I have seen it often in the Hall of Dreams. It floats above a child not yet formed. 'Power,' says the rain. 'Wealth,' whispers the wind. 'Honor,' chants the sea." Her enormous dark eyes opened and she stared at Serena as intently as she'd stared at the cup. "So it is for those who hold pride of place in the annals of the Children of Men. After such, all the world follows. But these things are meaningless until you answer one question."

"What?"

"What says your heart?" Nadya asked.

Oh, for pity's sake, the woman was no help at all. "You see nothing in my cup, do you?"

Nadya smiled, but it was not a pleasant one. "In truth, you could not bear all I see."

A cold lump of dread congealed in Serena's belly, but curiosity burned alongside it. She had to know what Nadya could tell her.

Nadya turned and rummaged in the bottom drawer next to her chair. The gypsy woman pulled out a length of cloth and held it up before her. It was a wretched mass of multi-colored threads, hues blurred or fighting each other. Knots snarled in bunches, dotting the surface in no discernible pattern.

"Life, it is like this cloth, my lady. So often it seems choked with problems without reason. We clash with those we hold closest to our hearts. We tear and wound those we should mend and heal."

Serena found herself drawn in by the woman's melodious voice and sensible sounding words.

"The Weaver chooses each thread with care. Each soul will have some sorrow, no matter what choice is made. In each life, there is some joy, however small. But if we were to look ahead and see it all at once, it would wash over us like a pitiless sea."

Nadya crumpled the cloth and let it drop to her lap. Then she reached across the table and took Serena's hand, holding it palm up. She traced the line that curved from below Serena's forefinger around the mound at the base of her thumb. "You have a long lifeline with many years ahead, but not even you would I tell the hour or manner of your death. It is too much for the human heart to bear."

Superstitious shivers passed over her.

"And so I ask you again, my lady, how will you spend the long march of years allotted to you? What says your heart? Will you give it up for a crown?"

"It's not as simple as that." Serena drew her hand back and folded it with the other one on her lap to keep Nadya from feeling her tremble. "There are expectations of me, people who are depending upon me to make the right decision. Sometimes, one is not allowed to please only one's self."

Nadya laughed, a full-throated yet musical sound. "And yet you intend to fulfill all the items on your list, do you not?"

Serena's eyes flared. "How did you see my list? Was it in the cup?"

This time, the gypsy woman's smile was friendlier. "I saw them all, all the little pleasures, all the longed-for adventures you hold in your heart, even the one you fear to write down—to lie with a man simply because you wish it. But your list, it was not in the cup."

"Then where?"

"Some knowledge, it is in the air." Nadya waved a hand toward her low roof. "I do not know from where the knowing comes or why it chooses to come to me. I must not question. I only know I must screw my courage each time to pluck the knowing down with both hands." She leaned toward Serena. "As you must gather your courage to make your own choices."

"Now you sound like Sir Jonah."

"Ah, yes. The handsome one who looks at horses but thinks only of you."

"Really?"

"Listen to your heart. It knows these things already." The woman's expression went suddenly somber. "In your cup I have seen a gate, an opportunity. You must choose whether to go through it. There is also an arch." She picked up the cup and showed it to Serena. With a long fingernail, she traced the curve of tea leaves. "The arch, it is decorated, you see, which foretells of high honor and a coming wedding."

"Then the royal duke *will* offer for me." Her father would be in raptures. She ought to be overjoyed too, but against all expectation, her heart tumbled to her toes.

"That remains to be seen," Nadya said as she pointed to another clump of leaves in the cup. "Here you see a forked line. A decision, it is in your future. And the hourglass so, next to the lip of the cup, says the time, it is drawing near."

Serena squinted at the tea leaves, trying to see what Nadya saw, but it was all just lumps and swirls to her eyes. "Is there…Is there anything in there about Jonah?"

"Do you wish there to be?"

Serena worried her bottom lip. She hadn't known him long and yet the idea of not having him in her life was beginning to be insupportable.

"And now we come to the difficult part," Nadya said. "The Weaver of all life casts down many threads to us. Which strand we take up, which we tossed away, how we decide to knot or befoul or create something beautiful with those we use—it is up to us. We have been given a gift. A terrible and wondrous gift. Over and over again, we must choose." The gypsy woman picked up the discarded cloth from her lap again. "*You* must choose."

This time Nadya presented the other side of the cloth to Serena. Her breath caught in her throat at its shimmering beauty. The horrible knots and mismatched threads on the backside were fitly joined into a glorious pattern, all shot with silver and gold, on the front.

"I warned you before, my lady, that I would not tell you all I see for you. It is too hard to know some things are coming. Life, it must be lived looking forward, but it may be understood by looking back." Nadya spread the cloth on the table between them. "So it is, my lady, when we come to the end of our lives, we look back and see that the difficult things, even the ugly things, work together to create something beautiful. If we *choose* to make it so."

The woman folded the cloth carefully and handed it to Serena. "A gift, to remind you that life is filled with things you cannot yet see." Then she stood.

Apparently, the tasseomancy session was over. Serena emptied the contents of her reticule into the shallow bowl on the table and tucked away the precious cloth. Even though she was leaving with more questions than answers, she wished she'd brought more coins. She thanked Nadya and climbed the fold-down stairs out of the wagon.

Serena stopped at the base of the steps. Jonah was standing with a group of gypsy men, probably talking about horseflesh and the comparative merits of one breed over another. His hair was dark enough to blend in with the others, though he stood half a head taller than the tallest of them.

She waited for that fluttery feeling, the one that started in her belly every time she looked at Jonah, but it didn't come. Instead, there was a warm glow in her chest as if she'd swallowed a live coal.

She started to walk toward him, but Nadya stopped her with a hand to her forearm.

"One thing more, my lady. I think it is in your heart that some things do not require choice. That you may be a greedy child and have both cake and pie as you please."

The gypsy woman looked pointedly at Jonah. "You must remember that others, they too have a choice. And it is in my mind that you may not have both this man and the crown you seek."

Seventeen

We note, with barely concealed tittering, that the Prince of Wales has been to his tailor once again. However broad they try to make his shoulders by piling on epaulettes of enormous size, a haberdasher's accessory cannot conceal so many gustatory sins.

Clothes may make the man, but unfortunately they cannot make a Prince Regent.

According to reports, Lady S.'s new ball gown for the much ballyhooed upcoming fête at Wyndebourne is cut in a daring French style. We wait, with unconcealed anticipation, to see if the modiste's craft can produce a royal duchess.

From Le Dernier Mot,
The Final Word on News That Everyone
Who Is Anyone Should Know

"WELL?" JONAH LACED HIS FINGERS TOGETHER SO Serena could step into them to mount her horse. She nodded her thanks and settled her boots, heels down in the stirrups, but she didn't say a word. "Aren't you going to tell me what Mme. Nadya said?"

"No."

Before he could protest, she reined the mare's head around, kicked her into a canter, and set off along the riverside path.

Jonah mounted Turk in one fluid motion and pounded after her. But between her head start and the way she flattened herself on the mare's back to urge her to more speed, Serena would not allow him to come within a horse's length of her all the way back to the stable.

A fracas was erupting in the paddock around a young stallion that reared and snorted, refusing to let anyone close. All the Wyndebourne groomsmen and stable boys were hanging on the fence, watching and cheering, as one man tried to loop a rope around the animal's head and muscle it into submission. No one was available to tend Serena's and Jonah's horses.

Serena was off her mount and leading her into a stall as Jonah clattered into the stable behind her. He looped Turk's reins around a nearby pole and stomped after her.

"I told you this gypsy business was a bad idea. Now what did that woman say to upset you so?"

He was utterly unprepared for the way she blind-sided him. If Serena had been one of the Triad's assassins, Jonah would have been dead. But instead of attacking him with intent to harm, she threw herself into his arms, palming his cheeks and pressing hungry kisses to his mouth.

Well, whatever Mme. Nadya said deserves a "Hallelujah, amen!"

Jonah had been kissed by some experienced lovers, worldly widows who knew exactly what they wanted and how to get it from a man, and once by a courtesan in Paris who doubled as a Triad spy. He thought he knew all there was to know about the delicate byplay of mouths, teeth, and tongues.

He was wrong.

What Serena lacked in finesse, she made up for in enthusiasm. No other woman in his experience had kissed him with such rapacious need, with such hunger, with such desperation. He was granite hard between one breath and the next.

Jonah walked her backward so her spine was flattened against the stall. Blessed woman, she parted her legs so that when he bent his knees to press against her, his hard length rubbed against the soft crevice between her thighs.

Too much restrictive clothing, too many layers of fabric separated them. Even so, the world dissolved in heat and friction and blinding need. Without conscious volition, he undid the silver frogs at her throat and trailed his lips down her neck and lower as he continued to unfasten her bodice.

She gasped and arched her back, lifting the tips of her breasts above her boned stays. She made little needy sounds as he found the hard button of her nipple and sucked it through the thin linen of her chemise.

Serena knocked his hat from his head and threaded her fingers through his hair, encouraging him to remain at her breast. He bit down on her and she cried out.

"Oh, God. We have to stop," she said, though the way she rocked herself against his pelvis belied her words.

"I could've sworn you liked it."

"I did. I do." When he covered the wet spot on her

chemise with his hand and caressed her breast, thrumming her nipple with his thumb, her eyelids fluttered and she drew a shuddering breath. "But someone may come. Someone may see us."

He claimed her mouth again, swallowing up her protests. She melted into him and even reached around to grasp his buttocks and pull him closer.

Little minx.

It would take very little effort to convince her to lie down with him in the fresh straw there and then. But however much he wanted her, he wanted her first time to be perfect even more.

With Herculean resolve, he straightened to his full height and looked down at her. "You're right, Serena. Not here, not now."

"Oh, you!" She pounded his chest with a closed fist once, and then let her head sink against it. "Why do you have to pick now to be so agreeable?"

He honestly didn't know. If all he was after was finishing his commission for Mr. Alcock, he was going about things all wrong. He'd ought to just lift her skirts, unbutton the flap on his trousers, press her back against the stable wall, and show her what a good hard swive was like. His body applauded this idea with a solid ache and several pulses of his cock.

And if he wasn't here to satisfy Alcock's demands, what the hell was he doing?

His chest constricted. Whatever this thing was he was feeling for Serena, it wasn't going to let him off easy.

"I'll come to you by night." The words poured out of his throat before they passed through his brain.

"No, it's too risky." She looked up at him, her eyes

languid, her lips kiss-swollen. "There are too many people in Wyndebourne, servants and such. You might be seen."

"I can be damn near invisible when I wish to be." Jonah was a large man, but she had no idea how stealthy he could be when the occasion called for it. He'd evaded trained agents and covert operatives. The day he couldn't outmaneuver a gaggle of servants hadn't dawned.

She ran her tongue over her bottom lip. "Tomorrow the guests from London will start to arrive."

He pressed a kiss to her forehead. Very gently, he began to refasten the frogs on her riding habit's bodice. "Then I guess I'll have to come tonight."

❧

Serena walked back toward the great house, trying to convince her heart not to leap out of her chest. Jonah had stayed behind to see to the horses and to give her time to collect herself. As far as she could tell, putting a little distance between them wasn't working. She was sure her cheeks were still flushed. And she was achy and wanting all over.

I'm becoming such a shameless hussy.

It was beyond foolish to agree to allow him to visit her chamber by night. Why had she not told Jonah no?

Of course, she really couldn't blame him. She was the one who'd thrown herself at him.

She couldn't even say why she'd done it. She was just so confused after everything that Mme. Nadya had said to her. The gypsy woman didn't make her future any clearer. If anything, it was more hopelessly muddled than the backside of that intricately woven cloth.

How could she make a rational choice when every time she looked at Jonah all she wanted to do…was give herself to him? Of course, she was excited by the new and strange sensations that coursed through her body whenever he was near. And his kisses were a revelation.

"But it's more than that," she muttered as she crunched along the pea gravel path back to the house. It wasn't just that she wanted Jonah's strong body next to hers. She'd told him once that men feared him and women wanted to fix him. Serena wasn't sure she was equal to the task, but she wanted to try.

After his confession at the castle ruins, she understood more about what needed fixing. Even in defense of the king, taking a life was no small matter. She feared for his soul. In the back of her mind, she remembered her vicar saying once that love covers a multitude of sins.

She stopped dead on the path. *Love*?

Was that what was causing this terrible jumbled up feeling inside her?

If it was, she was in even more trouble than she thought.

Because the day was fine and she needed to move in order to settle her body's unruly urges, she strode all the way around the great house and came in by the front door. Mr. Honeywood greeted her and took her bonnet once she'd untied the bow beneath her chin.

"Your modiste requests another fitting this afternoon," Mr. Honeywood said.

Serena rolled her eyes. Yet another round of pokes and pins. "Very well. Tell her to join me in my chamber in an hour. No, make it two."

If Mme. Boulanger insisted on cinching the bodice of Serena's ball gown another quarter-inch tighter, she was ready to threaten to attend the ball in nothing but her skin.

She blushed as she imagined what Jonah would have to say about that.

"The post has come, my lady." Mr. Honeywood's round, honest face beamed at her. "Acceptance notes for the house party and ball are flying in."

Serena shifted through the stack of envelopes and recognized her friend Lysandra's ornate script. She tucked that one into her pocket, intending to pore over it later when she could fully enjoy her friend's giddy mix of gossip and foolishness.

In the pile of acceptance notes, there was also an envelope addressed to Jonah.

The paper was fine milled, cream-colored, and of good quality. No fragrance wafted from it, so Serena decided it likely wasn't from a former lover. Besides, the envelope was addressed with a masculine hand, the lettering bold and only slightly slanted.

Serena turned the envelope over. A red blob of sealing wax held it closed. She didn't recognize the crest embossed in the wax, but when she slipped a thumbnail under it the entire seal lifted slightly. She wondered if this letter contained a clue to the identity of the man in Portsmouth. With very little effort, she should be able to pry off the seal, read the note, and then reseal it without Jonah being any the wiser.

Serena glanced around. Mr. Honeywood had left her alone in the foyer so that he might attend to other duties. She slipped Jonah's note into her pocket and hurried to her chamber.

Her escritoire was well-stocked. Paper and pens, inks in several colors, and a sharp letter opener that proved equal to the task of removing the red sealing wax in a single intact blob. She pulled out the single sheet of foolscap and read:

> *My dear Sharp,*
>   *We wait anxiously for news. Have you located Sgt. Hammond Leatherby in Portsmouth? Remember that Colton and I stand ready to assist should you need us.*
>   *Unless we hear from you, expect to see us at the Wyndebourne ball. With any luck, all this unpleasantness will be done by then.*
>   *Your servant,*

It was signed "Warrington" with such an elegant flourish Serena was certain this fellow didn't consider himself *anyone's* servant. Whoever Warrington was, he must have some doings with the Triad since he was interested in someone in Portsmouth just as Jonah was.

Some unfortunate named Sgt. Leatherby.

She wondered what sort of assistance this Warrington was offering. Several scenarios sprang to mind, none pleasant.

Serena was determined to help Jonah shake free of this shadowy part of his life. And the only thing that would truly help him was if the man could not be found. That way he wouldn't have to kill him.

Serena refolded the letter with care and slid it back into the envelope. She spent a few minutes melting a drop of red wax onto the back of the original seal and closing the envelope tight again. Jonah would never know she'd intercepted his letter.

Then she rummaged through her jewelry case. She'd exhausted her supply of coin when she went to see the gypsies, and it wouldn't have been enough at any rate. She needed to offer Sgt. Leatherby enough to take him to someplace in the Americas and see him set up in a new life.

"That should put enough distance between him and the king to remove all possibility of his being a threat," she reasoned. *And remove all need for Jonah to stain his hands again.*

She decided on the emerald choker. It was more than generous and she'd never liked it much in any case. Then she went to find Mr. Honeywood.

He was refereeing a dispute between the decorators, who were festooning the ballroom with satin streamers, and the musicians who were trying to practice in the same space, without the pianist who was evidently foxed again.

"I need your help on a matter of some urgency," she said once Mr. Honeywood joined her in the hallway.

"Of course, milady. I hope you know you may always count upon me."

She flashed him what she hoped was a disarming smile. "I need someone who has a detailed knowledge of Portsmouth and the families who live there, someone who is capable of finding a person who may not wish to be found. Have we someone with those qualities in our employ?"

Mr. Honeywood's eyebrows formed sideways question marks. "Yes, milady. One comes to mind."

"Good." Relief washed over her. She hadn't

known what she'd do if he'd said no. "This person must also be the soul of discretion who may be relied upon never to tell anyone what I ask of them. They must also be dependable enough to be trusted with no little amount of wealth, which they will have to hand over to another party. This person must then be capable of compelling this third party to remove himself from England forever."

Mr. Honeywood nodded solemnly. "He is."

He, a man then. Serena was glad because she feared this assignment might be dangerous for a woman since it was likely to involve slinking around some of the poorer quarters of Portsmouth. "And one last qualification. He must not ask why. About anything."

Mr. Honeywood's brows shot up at that, but he recovered quickly, adopting his usual pleasantly vacant demeanor. "Very well. He shall ask who then." He straightened his shoulders and smiled. "I'm your man. Whom shall I find for you?"

"You, Mr. Honeywood?"

"I would trust no one else for an assignment of this obvious delicacy. And our under-butler is more than capable of stepping into the breach here at Wyndebourne in my absence." A shrieking brou-haha erupted behind them in the ballroom. Mr. Honeywood's shoulders sagged and he sighed deeply.

"Very well. Come with me and I'll explain all." The assignment was likely to see him out of Wyndebourne until the house party and ball were over. When the squabbling between the decorators and musicians erupted afresh behind them, Serena suspected Honeywood might be relieved.

Eighteen

On the chance that His Royal Highness, the Duke of Kent, will make an appearance at the Wyndleton ball (though we suspect that this is a rumor spread by those who have wagered in favor of Lady S.'s fortunes), acceptance notes have been flying from London to the lovely Wyndebourne estate. As a matter of record, it must be noted that the odds at White's have swung markedly in Lady S.'s favor. However, as with any game of chance or romance, the slightest misstep by the principals involved can ensure they can swing just as quickly in the other direction.

From Le Dernier Mot,
The Final Word on News That Everyone
Who Is Anyone Should Know

AMELIA BRAITHWAITE PUT DOWN HER SEWING AND pinched the bridge of her nose. Her eyes hurt from overstrain. She missed her usual room at Wyndebourne with its cozy appointments and much smaller bed. The tidy space always made her feel cosseted and safe. This new chamber seemed cavernous by comparison.

When the marquis arrived, she'd ask to be switched back to her old room.

The table runner she was embroidering was a lost cause. Even with all the candles burning, it was too dim for close work. She might have better luck reading the second volume of *Rob Roy* that had arrived by post that day since the print was of generous size, but she wasn't in the mood for Scottish angst.

Over and over in her mind, Amelia kept reliving the argument she'd had with Serena after her latest fitting. The girl was near tears over her ball gown, but she wouldn't allow Amelia to comfort her. It wasn't like her to be so weepy, especially over a question of fashion, something Serena usually considered inconsequential. But she refused to confide her true troubles, which was also out of character. No amount of cajoling would make her budge, and they fell to squabbling about place cards for the upcoming midnight ball, of all silly things. Finally, Serena had fled the room and then refused to come down for supper. She sent back the tray Amelia had sent up to her untouched.

Even when Serena had been mourning her mother's death, she'd never shut Amelia out like this.

She put her hand over her eyes and sighed. She loved Serena as much as if she were her own blood, but sometimes the girl was a sore trial to her soul.

When she heard a faint scraping noise, Amelia peered between her parted fingers. The wall opposite the fireplace seemed to be opening and a cloaked figure stepped from behind a previously hidden door.

She shot to her feet, her hand to her throat.

"Be easy, Amelia," came a familiar masculine voice. "It's only me."

She might be sliding toward her fortieth year, but her heart leaped up as if she were a debutante. "Leonard."

Amelia skittered across the room and melted into the arms of the Marquis of Wyndleton. His cloak was damp and his cheeks cold, but his kiss was warmer than the blaze in the grate.

"We weren't expecting you till the end of the week," she gasped between kisses.

"I couldn't wait." The usually staid marquis cupped her bum and pulled her close to his hardness. "Just got in. Hellacious trip from London. I'd have been here hours earlier, but the bloody coach broke an axel just outside of Liphook. Lord, you smell good."

She parted her lips, surrendering to his questing tongue and letting his urgency wash over her in scalding waves.

"Like your new chamber?" he asked with a rakish grin when he finally let her come up for a breath.

"I do now." She pressed another kiss to his neck and then helped him off with his wet cloak. "I had no idea that secret door was there."

"No one has. That's how it stays a secret," he said as he stripped off his jacket. "This chamber is connected with my own by a clever little passageway."

"Really? This is not the marchioness's room." That grand chamber had been closed off since Serena's mother died. Amelia had never set foot in it, but she'd heard the servants nattering about the room's gilt-edged furnishings fashioned in the French style and the dear Flemish tapestry that covered one wall.

"In times past, this room was set aside for the lord's mistress." He pulled her back into his arms. "It's a good bit larger than your previous chamber and much more convenient for our purposes."

She stiffened in his arms. "But Leonard," she said with a sniff, "I am not your mistress."

"I know, love."

"But the servants—some of them must know of the connection between the chambers. I'll move back to the old room first thing tomorrow." She pulled away from him and crossed her arms over her chest, giving him her back. "I will not be made an object of speculation by the below-stairs gossips."

"I doubt any but Honeywood know of the passageway. Lord knows, there are enough cobwebs to prove no one's been cleaning back there. And our butler is far too tight-lipped to noise about any of Wyndebourne's secrets." Leonard came up behind her and slipped his arms around her waist. Then he ran his lips over her nape in the way he knew she liked. Little tendrils of pleasure bloomed over her skin. "Come, Amelia. I've missed you so. Don't be so fussy."

"Fussy? You think I'm being fussy? How very inconvenient of me." She whirled on him. "What wife doesn't want to be confused with a man's mistress?"

"Most men love their mistresses more than their wives and you have the unique position of being both to me, my dear. Utterly forbidden and entirely church-sanctioned. No wonder I can't get enough of you." He caressed her breasts through the thin fabric of her wrapper and night rail. A wicked smile lit his face.

He bent to tug down the neckline of her night rail, kissing along the edge of the lace there.

With effort, Amelia pushed him away. "It's been nearly three years. How long are we going to keep this a secret?"

"As long as we must. Charles Fox kept his marriage to Elizabeth Armistead a secret for ten years, you know," he said as he untied the bow between her breasts.

"The fact that Elizabeth Armistead had been a courtesan before she married him might have had something to do with it."

"And so did the fact that he knew she'd never be accepted at court even after the marriage was made public," he said.

"I am no courtesan." Amelia pulled her wrapper tight around her and stalked away from him. "You think I would not be accepted?"

She'd been born a gentleman's daughter. It was only bad luck that she'd had no brother to ensure she retained her place in Society when her father died. Even so, everything in her urged her not to play the lady now. She longed to lie down on the bed and spread her legs for this man she loved, but she was so tired of pretending to be merely his daughter's companion.

"Of course, you would be accepted eventually, but right now it would—"

"You're ashamed of me."

"Never." He grasped her shoulders and forced her to face him. "Never," he repeated. "But I'm a pragmatist. If I didn't have a marriageable daughter we need to protect from the foolishness of the ton, we wouldn't even be having this discussion."

She hated to admit it, but he was right. From the beginning, she and the marquis had been drawn to each other. Leonard maintained his distance during his period of mourning, but once he removed his black armband, he pursued his daughter's governess with single-minded intent.

Amelia refused to allow him into her bed. He'd never know the nights of frustration that had cost her, but in the end, Leonard had proposed because he had to have her.

They agreed to marry in secret and keep their fiery passion under control when they found themselves under the scrutiny of others, for Serena's sake. Leonard claimed it didn't matter to him what the world said about his making a commoner his marchioness, and he was chafing to drape her publicly in the jewels and honor of her true station. But they both knew it would not redound to Serena's favor if their union became public knowledge.

Especially not now, when Leonard's daughter was poised to become a member of the royal family.

Still, Amelia chafed at being hidden away, as if she were a lunatic aunt in the attic. As if Leonard were embarrassed by her. She turned in his arms and gave him her back.

He bent his head and nibbled her neck. "'Come live with me, and be my Love,'" he whispered into her ear, "'and we will all the pleasures prove.'"

She let her head fall back against him while he reached around and covered a breast with his palm.

She could never refuse the man when he quoted Christopher Marlowe, but would Leonard value anything he won too easily?

With effort, Amelia pulled away from him and put a few steps between them. However, she couldn't resist turning to look at him. The need in his face lanced her heart.

"Only a few more months, dear. Once Serena is the Duchess of Kent, everything will be different," he said, spreading his arms in invitation. "I promise."

She stepped into his arms and let him take her into his lusty dream. Later, while he lay spent and sleeping, Amelia rose from the bed and moved around the room, blowing out the candles. She wondered if things really would be different once they no longer had to keep their marriage a secret.

Would their love still be this wildly exciting once they didn't have to sneak around? Would Leonard seek a mistress once she no longer served as both wife and light-o-love?

Amelia climbed into bed and curled around his back. *Sufficient unto the day*…She'd worry about that when it happened and cherish the man next to her until then.

❧

Jonah couldn't put his finger on it, but there was a strange air in the great house. He moved through its shadowy corridors, silent as a wraith, his skin prickling with every step. It was something intangible but there, nevertheless. He felt it in heightened senses as he avoided the creaky floorboards and passed noiselessly from room to room. There was a watchful waiting, an expectancy in the very house itself.

If he didn't know better, he'd say someone in Wyndebourne was having "rumple-the-sheets-beyond-recognition-and-smother-your-cries-with-a-pillow" sex.

Perhaps it was only that he hoped he and Serena would be in those happy straits shortly. She wanted new and forbidden experiences, didn't she? He was just the man to give them to her.

It was about bloody time.

If any of the women he'd been with before had heard that Jonah Sharp had been pursuing a certain young lady for as long as he'd known Serena without having taken her to his bed once, they'd have surely laughed.

And wondered if some horrible accident had befallen Jonah's manhood.

Nothing wrong there, he assured himself. His cock had assumed a semi-rigid stance in anticipation. It would only take a whiff of Serena's fragrance to send him into battering ram hardness.

That sounds entirely too military.

Besides, Jonah had no intention of being rough with her. Serena was a virgin. While he hadn't deflowered any in the past, he'd heard a good deal about the proper technique to ensure the young lady was inconvenienced as little as possible by the loss of her maidenhead.

Of course, if the way she practically leaped on him in the stable was any indication, Serena might blossom into the sort who enjoyed a hard swive. For just a moment, he imagined bending her over at the waist so her bum was smiling at the ceiling. Then he'd plunge into her moist pink slit while her fingers were splayed on the floor.

He stifled a groan. A man could lose himself in the heat and friction of a tight fit while he smacked his balls against silken thighs. He drew a deep breath and mentally counted to ten, lest he spend right there in the empty hallway. Blood pounded in his ears so loudly, he was surprised no one else heard the steady drumbeat and came to investigate.

Get a grip on yourself, Sharp.

It wasn't as if this was the first lady's bedchamber into which he'd finessed his way. But this was the first one he was approaching with mixed motives.

Part of him was running on the pure carnal rush of an impending sexual encounter with a woman who'd driven him to distraction. He couldn't wait to claim Serena, to initiate her into the ultimate world of the sensual.

And another part of him, a confused part, wondered if he was just another item to be checked off her confounded list. He wasn't sure why it should be so, but it irritated the fool out of him to think he might be lumped with smoking a cigar. Neither more nor less important, but merely something Serena wished to try.

His reasons for bedding her were still sound. In order to spare his family the scandal Mr. Alcock threatened to rain down on him, Jonah still needed to remove Serena from consideration by the royal duke. But somewhere along the line, Serena Osbourne had stopped being a means to the end for him.

He was beginning to want her simply because of her.

Jonah closed his hand over her crystal doorknob. Did she want him to take her only so she could check off another forbidden pleasure? Or did she want Jonah for himself? Given what she knew about him, how could she possibly?

His cock told him it didn't matter. The growing lump in his chest told him nothing else did.

Coward, he named himself for hesitating. *Get on with it*.

Jonah turned the knob and pushed open the door.

Nineteen

"DAFFODIL: *Perhaps her Ladyship dislikes the opera singers, because they are like fashionable husbands! he! he! he!*

MACPHARO: Like fashionable husbands! How is that, Daffodil? Is it because they are usually accompanied by horns?"

—*from* The Ton; or, Follies of Fashion *by Lady Wallace*

House parties are rife with opportunities for indiscretion. Once the gay Society of London descends upon Wyndebourne, is it possible that the royal duke might sprout the horns of a cuckold even before his match with Lady S. is settled?

From Le Dernier Mot,
The Final Word on News That Everyone
Who Is Anyone Should Know

SERENA SQUIRMED IN THE TUFTED CHAIR BEFORE HER fire, turned to the second page of her friend Lysandra's letter, and held it closer to the light of the candle.

"And so, my dear friend, there is no doubt that the feckless Miss Pinckney finds herself in an

*'interesting condition.' Worst of all, her father has
yet to convince the gentleman responsible—if the
silly chit knows which gentleman that is!—to do the
honorable thing. If the scoundrel can be identified, I
expect it will come to pistols at dawn before a rushed
wedding can be affected. For Miss Pinckney's sake,
let us hope it is soon. Heaven knows, she can only
let out her seams so many times before the gown will
no longer give."*

Serena sighed. "Trust Lysandra to have the most
barbed gossip to share."

There was a time when Serena would have joined
her friend in shaking her head over the foolish
behavior that led to Miss Pinckney's predicament.
They'd have decided the girl deserved the shame
being heaped upon her for giving into her baser urges.

But that was before Jonah made her aware of the
power of those urges.

*"I tell you these things, Serena, my dear, because I
remember how dreadfully obvious Sir Jonah Sharp
was about displaying his interest in you before you
left Town. It's come to my ears that the upstart
baronet accompanied you and Miss Braithwaite
to Wyndebourne and, even more shocking, has
remained in residence there.*

Never say you have encouraged him."

She bit her lip. What would Lysandra say if she'd
seen the way Serena threw herself into Jonah's arms
in the stable?

"At any rate, I shall be there shortly and if I perceive that Sir Jonah has gotten above himself with you, you may depend upon me to deliver him a scathing cut direct!"

A cut direct was the most damning of public censures. It involved looking right through the person to be shamed as if they were not even there at such a time when the action would be seen and marked by the most influential people. It shouted "You are dead to Polite Society and unworthy of the rarified air you breathe" more effectively than a raging scene.

Lysandra was a master of the art.

Serena crumpled the letter without reading the rest. Her father always encouraged her to court the good opinion of the ton, but suddenly what Lysandra and her ilk thought meant less than nothing to her.

How dare Lysandra feel herself above Jonah?

She really knew nothing about him. She had no idea what he'd done for his king and country and how the gravity of that service weighed upon him. She didn't know he was quick-witted and a handy man in a pinch, a situation in which Serena often found herself. Lysandra had no clue that Jonah had not only *not* laughed when he learned about Serena's list of forbidden pleasures, but he'd helped her experience so many of them that she was beginning to lose count.

Of course, Lysandra didn't know about that secret list at all, and Serena was glad she'd never confided in her.

What Lysandra doesn't know won't hurt me.

And most of all, her friend had no idea how Jonah made Serena feel every time they embarked on one of those small adventures together. It was more than just the excitement of exploring the unknown with a knowledgeable guide.

She was safe with him.

He didn't upbraid her for her wants. He took the unruly part of her that longed for the extraordinary and accepted it as no one ever had.

Serena ripped Lysandra's letter to pieces and scattered them on the embers of the fire in the grate. She took grim satisfaction in watching them flare briefly and then curl into gray ash.

"How's that for a cut direct?" Serena said with vehemence.

"Who are you talking to?" came a whispered voice from the dark.

Serena startled, hand to her chest, but when he stepped into the light of the fire, she let out her pent up breath in a single whoosh. "Jonah, you scared the life out of me. How did you manage to enter the room without me hearing you?"

"Practice," he said. "Lots and lots of practice."

Well, an assassin for the Crown would need to be stealthy, wouldn't he?

She shoved that uncomfortable thought away. With any luck, Honeywood was well on his way to locating the unfortunate man Jonah had sought in Portsmouth and would convince the mysterious Sgt. Leatherby to flee before Jonah was forced to kill him.

The sooner Jonah stopped living that shadowy

double life the mysterious Triad required of him, the sooner his soul could heal and he'd be free to live the life he was intended to live.

"What are you burning?" he asked.

She moved away from the crispy remains of Lysandra's letter. "It's nothing. My friend's foolishness upset me. I suppose I should have read it to the end, but I simply lost patience with her."

He snorted. "Remind me not to try your patience."

"Too late for that. You always do."

❧

She hadn't moved toward him, but it seemed as if she leaned his way, as if her weight rested on the balls of her feet and she strained in his direction, merely waiting for the right moment to slip the invisible cord that bound her and launch herself at him.

A man can hope, can't he?

"What am I doing to try your patience now?" he asked.

"Well, for one thing," she said with cat's satisfied smile, "you've been here for more than a minute and haven't tried to kiss me once."

He bounded across the room to her in half a heartbeat and took her into his arms. "Serena, you should know by now that when I decide to do something, I don't try. I do."

Jonah bent to kiss her, but he didn't have far to go. She stood on tiptoe to meet him halfway, her face flushed in breathless anticipation. When his mouth covered hers, it was as if they picked up exactly where they'd left off in the stable, the sudden passion between them flaring white-hot. He knew his kiss was probably bruising her lips, but Serena gave as good as she got, nipping and suckling.

He should've known she'd never do anything by halves.

Jonah kissed along her jawline and down her neck. He sucked at the tender skin below her ear for a moment. "Lord, you taste so good."

She tipped her head back, giving him better access, and murmured incoherent little nothings that went straight to his groin. He fisted her hair to hold her still as he kissed along her collarbone, parting her wrapper and shoving the silk off her shoulders. She whimpered when he trailed his tongue along the lacy top of her night rail. Then she threaded her fingers through his hair, kneading his scalp in encouragement.

Even though the room was dim, the dark shadows of her nipples showed beneath the thin muslin. Jonah wasn't going to settle for suckling her through the fabric this time. He tugged the ribbon that held her bodice closed with his teeth. The knot gave and the fabric fell away, baring the curves of her breasts.

He parted the front of her night rail and looked down at her. Her breasts weren't overly large, but they were perfectly sized to fit the palm of his hand. He cupped them both. Her hot, hard nipples fairly scorched his palm.

He bent and took one into his mouth, sucking hard. The tip was sweet and felt so good between his lips.

"Oh, Jonah, what are you doing to me?" she murmured. She grasped his shoulders and hooked one leg around his to steady herself.

"You tell me." He brought his teeth down on the taut bud in a sharp love nip. She rewarded him with a gasp. "How do I make you feel?"

"Wild and out of control." She gave a shuddering breath and rocked herself against him. "More than a little wicked."

"If there's wickedness done tonight, let it be on my head." Jonah straightened and ran his hands down her spine. Then he cupped her bum and pressed her against his hardness. "I'll answer for it."

Serena reached up and stroked his cheek. "I want you here, Jonah. This is my choice. If there are consequences, they are my consequences too. Only..."

"Only what?"

"Only a woman's consequences are always more serious than a man's." She unhooked her knee from around his leg and settled her foot back on the floor. "I supposed it's my friend Lysandra's letter that's making me fret. She wrote me about a mutual acquaintance of ours who now finds herself with child while she is yet unmarried. A consequence which is unthinkable to me."

She worried her lower lip, and Jonah felt the tension roiling off her. She wanted two things at once—both sensual adventure and safety. Just because she was passionate didn't mean she'd checked her sense of self-preservation at the door to possible ruin.

"Is there a way, Jonah...I mean, is it possible...for us to please each other without me losing..."

He put a finger to her lips to stop her. She didn't mean to surrender her maidenhead to him after all. To his very great surprise, he was relieved. Not that he didn't long to bury himself in her, to feel her engulfing him completely. And not that he didn't need to claim her virginity in order to satisfy Mr. Alcock's demands.

Serena had led him a merry chase. But if he took her this night, the hunt would be over. He'd have finished his commission, spoiled any chance she had to become a royal duchess, and she would hate him for it once she realized why he'd done it. He was fully prepared to fight with her, to argue with her over her list, or to protect her from herself when she insisted on doing something dangerous.

But he wasn't ready for her to hate him. If she did, what would become of that hot lump in his chest?

"You are going to be closer to me tonight than you've ever been to another human being since the moment of your birth," Jonah said. "Trust me, Serena, I'll see to it nothing we do together will cause you shame. But I have to know something."

"What?" she asked as she sagged against him.

"Is this just another item from your list?"

⁂

He looked down at her with such an earnest, hungry expression, his brows drawn together, his mouth tight. It seemed terribly important to him that this night wasn't about her list. Yet she couldn't find it in her to tell him a soothing lie.

"This is a forbidden pleasure I didn't dare write down. But yes, it's on the list." She grasped the lapel of his banyan and tugged him closer, willing him to understand. "I know if I marry the royal duke, I can't expect a love match. I can't even expect tenderness." Tears pressed against the back of her eyes, but she blinked them away. She didn't want anything to mar this night. "Even so, I know I'll have to give myself to my husband and he may use my body as he will. But at least once in my life, I want to lie with a man of my choosing."

She unbuttoned her night rail to the waist, slipped it off her shoulders, and let it fall to the floor. She was more than naked before him. Her heart was naked too, and surprisingly she felt no shame.

"I choose you, Jonah."

❦

"You're so beautiful," Jonah said softly. He was half-afraid he was dreaming and might wake himself if he spoke too loudly. She lifted her chin and rewarded him with a smile that melted something inside him.

His hot gaze traveled over her flawless skin, her rose-tipped breasts, and the soft-looking triangle of curls at the juncture of her legs. The cinch of her waist and the flare of her hips were in perfect proportion. His mouth sagged a bit in speechless awe of her.

Then he realized she hadn't really said what he was hoping to hear.

Fool, he named himself. *Did you really think she'd toss away a chance at a crown for the likes of you?*

But it was close enough. Serena wanted him. She'd chosen him. She was prepared to trust him with herself.

An old soldier had given him a piece of advice once that had stood him in good stead no matter how unlikely the situation to which he applied it. *When in doubt, son, always eat.*

Jonah would revel in the feast set before him and try

not to wish for the more nourishing fare of a declaration of love everlasting.

As if such a thing truly exists.

He began to wonder what was happening to him. As little as a month ago, such thoughts would never have occurred to him in the presence of a willing naked woman. He must be going a bit soft in the head.

But he was definitely not soft anywhere else. Jonah started to untie the belt at his waist.

"No," she said. "Let me. I've never undressed a man before."

Jonah let his hands fall to his sides. "If that's another thing on your list, far be it from me to disappoint you."

She flashed him another small smile, this time one that seemed unusually shy from a woman who'd just peeled out of her night rail and was as bare as God made her. Then she tugged at his belt and parted the silk sleeping robe. Her eyes flared as she looked him over. His cock twitched as if she'd stroked it.

"Oh, no, Jonah. You never disappoint."

Then, blessed woman, she did stroke it. Her cool fingertips brushed over his full length from root to tip. He gritted his teeth to keep the pressure from rising in his shaft.

"I'm still dressed," he reminded her.

"Oh, so you are." She tore her gaze away from his groin and pushed the banyan off his shoulders. Serena trailed the silk with her palms as it slid down his arms and then joined her night rail and wrapper in an untidy pile on the floor. "How's that for my first time undressing a man?"

"Incredible," he assured her. "However, I must

warn you not to get puffed up about your accomplishment. There is no wrong way to do it."

He reached for her, but she straight-armed him and took a leisurely stroll around him, perusing him as if he were da Vinci's *David*. Except that no self-respecting docent would allow her to trail her fingertips along the statue's waist or trace the creases beneath his buttocks. His breath hissed in over his teeth in surprise at her audacity.

"So a woman may undress a man in any way she wishes and he'll be pleased?" she said when she'd completed her short trek and stood facing him once more.

"And touch him any way she wishes."

"Good to know." Serena ran her fingertips up his thighs and around his scrotum, setting all the wiry hairs on end. Then she cupped his balls, fondling the sack.

Jonah's eyes nearly rolled back in his head. It took all his self-control not to spend in her hand like a randy boy.

"Of course, you must realize that a man can only take so much."

Serena grasped his shaft and squeezed. "What happens then?"

Twenty

On January 3 of this Year of Our Lord 1818, astronomers tell us that the planet Venus and the giant planet Jupiter fell into rare alignment so that the much smaller Venus eclipsed the larger body. Such a thing does not happen often, and, if one puts stock in such things as mathematics, clever fellows from the Academy of Science have determined that the occurrence will not repeat itself until the distant year of 2065!

However, this celestial event serves to remind us that every once in a while the dainty goddess of love trumps the larger bodies of marriages of convenience and political expediency.

It happens, of course, but so rarely it's hardly worth mentioning.

From Le Dernier Mot,
The Final Word on News That Everyone Who Is
Anyone Should Know

JONAH DIDN'T ANSWER IN WORDS. INSTEAD, HE MADE A sound in the back of his throat that greatly resembled a growl. Then he picked her up and carried her to the waiting bed before she could protest.

Not that she felt like protesting. Serena was still tingling with feminine power over driving him to such feral extremes. He laid her out on the counterpane and bent over her, supporting his weight on his knuckles while he ravaged her mouth. Then he pulled back and straightened upright.

"Serena, I've been thinking…"

"That sounds ominous." She tried to keep her voice light. Seeing his long, lean frame licked by the flickering firelight left her breathless and dry-mouthed. She ran her palm up his hard thigh. How could the man think about anything when all she wanted to do was feel? "What about?"

"About us."

"There's so precious little of 'us' to contemplate, I can't imagine what you're thinking on," she said. "Doubly ominous then."

"I don't mean it to be." He settled a hip on the bed and leaned over her, focusing his attention on her face.

Serena forced her gaze away from his mesmerizing eyes. His mouth was wide, his lips full, slightly parted, and firm. Just looking at them made her ache to feel those lips on her, trailing over her hills and valleys, on any bit of her he chose to kiss. The thought brought fresh blood to her cheeks, but she wouldn't unthink it. If she was going to lie with a man, she wanted as much of the adventure as a maiden could have and still remain a maiden.

A crisp mat of dark hair whorled around his nipples, and the thin strip of hair that started beneath his navel broadened to nest around his astonishing maleness.

She itched to run her fingers through that hair, but

before she could, he caught up both her hands and pinned them above her head. Somehow, the fact that she couldn't touch him then made her want to do so all the more.

"I've been thinking you're right," he said.

She shook herself, sure she hadn't heard him properly. She scarcely remembered a conversation with Jonah when they weren't at loggerheads at least part of the time. "About what?"

"About making sure you're pure for your duke," Jonah said. He bent down and nipped her breast, sending a fiery message to her lower belly that was anything but pure. "I understand why you wouldn't give up the chance of a crown for someone like me."

Serena wrested one of her hands free and laid her palm on his chest, feeling very tender toward the steady thump of his heart beneath it. "Jonah, it's not like that."

He ran his thumb along the curve of her cheek, down her neck, and then around a breast in ever smaller concentric circles. Would she be able to remember to keep breathing if he kept touching her like that?

"I tried to imagine what I could bring to you that might make you think twice about the Duke of Kent. I realize now that's foolishness. I could never deserve you, Serena." The words came out haltingly. "If I had any courage at all, I'd walk away right now."

"Jonah Sharp!" All the tender feelings he'd evoked in her were suddenly smothered by indignation. After all he'd dared in defense of the Crown, he had more courage in his little finger than most men had in their whole bodies. "Don't you dare go. You can't make me ache for you and then leave me."

She wrapped her arms around his shoulders and pulled his head down so she could kiss him hard on the mouth.

"Do you think I care two figs for the Duke of Kent? Not even a little," she said when she finally pulled back from him. She took his hand and pressed it against her breastbone so he could feel her heart pounding. "Whether I end up as his wife is not about caring. It's about political wrangling and the weight of history and all that rot my father cares so much about."

"By those lights, you deserve much more than the duke is offering as well," Jonah said gruffly.

"Jonah, please. Don't make me think. Don't ruin this for me. All I want to do is feel." She sat up and palmed his cheeks, the prickly stubble of a day's growth of his beard nicking her skin. She searched his face, noting the little scar in his eyebrow, pale in the firelight, the fine lines at the corner of his eyes, the deep sadness in them. Didn't he know she was storing up all the small details, learning every bit of him by heart, so she could pull the little treasures out and use them later to console herself when she was trapped in a cold marriage?

"Don't you realize tonight is all I may ever have?" A suppressed sob made her voice break.

"It doesn't have to be."

"What are you saying?" Was he offering marriage? Her heart leaped like a springer spaniel at the thought.

"Just that...I know you've turned down other proposals. You don't have to accept the Duke of Kent's suit."

Her belly spiraled downward. If he'd asked her, she

might well have said yes. But now she lifted her chin so he wouldn't sense her disappointment. "Do you think it sensible to hold out for a *better* offer than one from a son of the king?"

He took her shoulders and gave her a small shake. "You should hold out. You deserve better. You deserve…"

"What, Jonah?"

His fierce expression softened and he lessened his grip on her shoulders. "Love, Serena. You deserve to be loved."

Was he trying to say he loved her in some cryptic roundabout way? Normally Jonah said what was on his mind in a straight, no-nonsense manner.

Maybe he was having trouble saying what was in his heart.

Serena could have swatted herself on the nose for nursing such a ridiculous hope, but the yearning to hear him declare himself wouldn't go away.

Say it, Jonah, she urged silently. *Speak the words and watch how the world will change.*

But he didn't.

"Just promise me you'll think twice if the duke offers for you," Jonah said as he took both her hands and bent to press his forehead to hers in a surprisingly tender gesture.

"All right. I promise." She squeezed his hands. "We have this time together now. Please don't let what might be spoil what is."

❧

Damn, what's wrong with me?

He clamped his lips shut and stretched out beside

her. No good could come from talking. She didn't want to hear him. All he could do was give her what she wanted—a night of passion to remember. A way to tick off another item on her list with a big red check.

And what else could you give her, Sharp?

If they married, she'd be simply Lady Sharp with no title to pass on to her sons. He could offer her a more than comfortable living, a town house in London, and a charming country place. His income from investments and property far exceeded that of many titled gentlemen, but compared to the bottomless purse of a prince, Jonah was a pauper.

He rolled toward her and covered her mouth with his, pouring all his longing, all his frustration into the kiss. Then it occurred to him that he could give her love.

Love. What a fool's game.

How did a man know if he loved a woman?

He knew he loved the way she melted into him, the soft, needy little sounds she made. And those tiny goose bumps that shivered over her skin when he touched her, he loved those too.

He rolled on top of her and began to kiss down her body, lavishing her breasts with his tongue. He loved the soft indentations between her ribs.

"Oh, careful there," she said with a giggle. "I'm ticklish on that side."

He loved that too. "Could be useful information." He stroked her ribs again for the pleasure of watching her squirm.

"Not fair. I don't know where you're ticklish."

"I invite you to find out for yourself later."

He nuzzled her navel and she writhed under him as he spread her legs wide. Her fingernails raked along his back, but the slight pain only added to the pleasure of having her opening to him. She smelled wonderful, all musk and warm woman.

He had no idea why she wasted good money on perfume when the fragrance of her arousal was sweet enough to almost shove him over the edge.

There was tension in her thighs and she started to bring her knees together.

"Lie still," he commanded and was pleased, and more than a little surprised, when she obeyed. He dropped a row of feathery kisses along her inner thigh and she groaned. He nipped and licked at the edges of her triangle of curls.

Delicious.

Serena was all things adventurous, all things forbidden. She was his ruin and his atonement. He couldn't imagine life without her. Given the difference in their stations, he couldn't imagine a life with her. But did that mean he loved her?

And if he did love her, what then?

❧

Every fiber in Serena's body was on high alert wondering what Jonah was going to do next. She'd given up trying to beat back the pounding ache *down there* or wondering how to still the throbbing in her nipples. They were only a few things in the long list of pleasurable torments Jonah was inflicting on her. Even the tickling was its own brand of helpless delight. She was stretched out on a rack of exquisite agony.

But she wouldn't stop him for worlds.

She raised her head from her pillow and looked down at him. He was kissing her belly and running his tongue along the seam between her thigh and her private folds. With each pass he drew closer to her most sensitive place. She wished she could be embarrassed over how badly she wanted to feel his mouth on her there, but the wanting so totally eclipsed shame, it was of no consequence.

Surely, he's not going to…he wouldn't…

Then he did.

The tip of his tongue parted her folds and sent her into a quaking frenzy. Sneaking a glance at him from under her lashes, she saw him look up at her, a look of possessive pride on his face. He knew she was his to do with as he pleased.

As his breathing became short and ragged, the ache building inside her turned sharp-edged as well. His blessed mouth played a lover's game on her sensitive flesh. She moaned when he stopped and started to withdraw, and then moaned louder when he resumed his gentle assault. She seemed to have grown a second heart. Serena felt the new one pounding between her legs.

She begged him to stop. She urged him to go on.

This must be what madness is. Meaningless sounds escaped her lips, but she was powerless to control them.

She was on a journey. A quest. She drew perilously near her destination once or twice, enough to feel herself start to spiral downward, but then the elusive goal retreated before her in a maddening game of hide-and-seek.

Then Jonah tongued her more deeply, and without warning, a sun burst forth in her secret place, sending warmth and light to all her limbs. Deep bliss radiated from her womb in concentric spasms and her whole body bucked with the force of it. The rhythmic joy was even more intense than the release Jonah had given her in the hunting lodge.

Serena squeezed her eyes shut, and pinpricks of stars wheeled drunkenly on the back of her eyelids. If the heavens had parted and she caught a glimpse of Glory itself, she would not have been the least surprised.

"Well," she said when she finally found her voice and the will to form a coherent thought, "that settles it."

Jonah moved up to lie beside her. She was achingly aware of the hot length of his maleness pressed up against her thigh. Even though she was still boneless and sated, there was a sense of being unfinished, of a new longing that was ready to begin tormenting her.

He covered her mouth with his own in a gentle kiss, then laid his head on the pillow beside hers. "That settles what?"

"I won't be writing any instructional pamphlets about this."

He chuckled and she felt his belly shake against her hip. "Too wicked for you?"

"No, too wonderful to be believed. I would be accused of writing fiction instead of educational self-help."

He took her mouth then, ravaging and demanding. The ache she'd thought was stilled began again and she met his kiss with need of her own.

His hands were restless wanderers. He couldn't seem to keep them still. They roved over her shoulders and down her arms to entwine his fingers with hers. A light brush down her spine, a gentle squeeze at the curve of her waist, relentless strokes on the underside of her breasts, his hands made her come alive again with a freshly throbbing batch of needs.

"Oh, Jonah, are we never to have a little peace together?"

"We will, sweetheart. As much as you wish," he murmured into her hair. "But now we'll have a bit of what I wish."

He covered her mound with his hand, sweetly invading her secret place with his fingertip. She was still hot and wet, and her insides convulsed once more in answer to his finger's nearness.

She gasped at how quickly he sent her spiraling back into that hot, dark place. "What are you doing to me?"

"Loving you," he said as his fingers found her particularly sensitive spot. He flicked it lightly and buried his nose in the curve of her neck. "Do you want me to stop?"

"Lord in heaven, no," she said as his lips brushed her temple, her closed eyelids, and down to the hollow of her throat. He sent her into a second sheet-fisting climax after only a few skillful strokes.

Serena gulped air, her breath catching in the glow of tiny after-shocks. He gave her sensitive spot one last stroke and pulled his hand away as she floated in the aftermath.

He could do anything with her now and she hadn't the will to resist. But Jonah only lay beside her, his head propped on his hand as he watched her struggle to come back to herself. A self-satisfied grin lifted the corners of his mouth.

Then he rocked against her hip. His thick hard length was so hot, feverish almost.

"Oh, yes," she said, amazed to feel the yawning emptiness inside her again where only a moment ago all had been light and peace. The ache roared back to life once again. She turned to face him and took his shaft in her hands. "Now what about you?"

She met his gaze squarely. Her eyes glowed with a soft light that was more than just the aftereffects of two bone-jarring climaxes. She seemed to see into his very soul, but he didn't shrink from her intense scrutiny. He read acceptance on her face.

For all of him.

She began exploring his cock and discovered the sensitive bit at the base of its head when his breath hissed in over his teeth.

"Oh, so that's it," she said knowingly and began to tease that susceptible spot.

Before she could reduce him to helpless pleading, he showed her how to stroke his full length, how to vary the speed and tighten her grip.

"I won't hurt you if I'm that rough?" she asked.

"I invite you to try," he said through clenched teeth as he rolled onto his back. "Harder."

Even though she was inexperienced, he gave himself over to her hands willingly. All he was, good and bad, Serena was welcome to know, to handle. He'd let her push his flesh to the limit and his spirit to the farthest edge it could reach.

A muscle ticked in his cheek when she chanted his

name softly. Having her call to him released him. A deep groan tore loose from his throat, and his seed pulsed onto his belly in hot spurts.

It wasn't the same as coming inside her would have been. If they'd been joined, he'd lie still and will himself to remain erect as long as possible so that they didn't need to separate. A spending on his own belly was a pale shadow of that greater joy, but he'd come with her beside him, with her sweet hands urging him on, and that was something.

He'd made himself vulnerable to her in those moments of madness. It was like offering his unprotected chest to an enemy's pistol ball. The way she kissed him as she cupped his balls was a direct shot to his heart.

He swung his legs out of bed and strode back to his discarded banyan.

"Where are you going?" she asked, her voice small.

"Nowhere." *Truer words were never spoken*, he thought ruefully. He didn't see any outcome for them that didn't end in disaster all around.

He snatched the handkerchief out of his pocket and cleaned himself off. If he wasn't going to ruin her—and he was determined not to taint this night with betrayal—he couldn't leave any stains on her linens.

Then he returned to the bed and gathered Serena into his arms, snuggling her so close no one could have fit so much as a farthing between them. She sighed and laid her head on his shoulder while he traced lazy circles on her bare bum. She didn't move a muscle. Evidently, she wasn't willing to separate from him yet either.

At least, that's what he thought till he heard a soft snore.

"That's all right. Sleep, Serena. I've got you," he whispered. Then when she didn't stir, he felt safe to go on. "I do love you, you know. No matter what happens, I'll love you till my last breath."

Twenty-one

Scholars tell us that from time immemorial, humans have been social creatures, relying on the safety of greater numbers for protection. Acceptance by Society, even of the primitive variety, was mandatory for survival.

In these modern times, it is astonishing how many seek to flaunt Society's rules by going their own way and still expect others to continue to approve them. Many have been astounded to find themselves outside the shelter of Society's communal fire of acceptance.

Be forewarned. The ton is an unforgiving circle. And it seems the higher one's star is in ascendance to begin with, the more Society delights in seeing its luminaries tumble to earth.

From Le Dernier Mot,
The Final Word on News That Everyone
Who Is Anyone Should Know

JONAH JERKED IN HIS SLEEP AND STARTLED HIMSELF awake. His heart was pounding like a coach-and-six. He'd had the dream again, the one where he was falling into a black abyss. Then just before he struck the jagged bottom, he always woke up.

He wondered what would happen if sometime he didn't.

If he died in his dream, would his soul fly from him in waking life?

But at the moment, he had more immediate concerns, chief among them was not being caught in Serena's bed. She mumbled something in her sleep and rolled over, turning her back to him. He longed to trace the sweet indentation of her spine, but he didn't want to wake her.

He slipped out of bed, put on his banyan, and walked over to look out her window. The eastern horizon was brightening to pearl gray. Time to make his way back to his chamber before the maids, whose job it was to scrub the hearths every morning, started their rounds.

He should probably just slip out without a good-bye. If he kissed Serena, he'd be tempted to stay for more. He knotted the belt at his waist with the best of intentions, but try as he might, he was drawn inexorably back to the side of her bed.

Serena's hair was spread over the pillow and half obscured her face. Her lips were parted in the relaxation of sleep. One of her hands rested on the counterpane.

Though he ached to kiss her mouth, he settled for lifting that hand to his mouth and brushing her knuckles with his lips.

"Jonah," she said, her voice warm and drowsy, redolent with the remnants of a night of satisfaction. "Come back to bed."

"It's nearly dawn. If I don't go now…" He let the thought dangle in the air. What if he were discovered there? It would settle once and for all any question of a match with the Duke of Kent. Of course, they'd face some public censure if the tale spread beyond Wyndebourne, but surely by now she knew he'd do right by her.

She pushed a wayward lock of hair off her forehead and out of her eyes, which suddenly lost their hazy look as she came fully awake. "I understand. I'll see you at breakfast then."

He'd have stayed if she'd asked, bedamned to the rest of the world. Jonah tamped down his disappointment. He backed away from her, still holding her hand. She stretched with him till just their fingertips touched. Then the space between them exceeded the length of Jonah's reach and the connection was broken.

He slipped out of Serena's chamber and made his way back to his own, cursing himself for a fool with every step.

❧

Serena didn't come down for breakfast. Instead Jonah found the marquis there. He'd arrived late the night before after a difficult journey from Town, but sleeping in his own bed had evidently allowed him to shake off any ill effects from the inconveniences of travel. Lord Wyndleton was full of good humor. Negotiations with the royal duke's factor were at a critical juncture, he confided, but going well.

It was enough to put Jonah off his feed and make

him go out of his way to avoid his host for the rest of the day, lest he be forced to listen to more of the marquis's plans for Serena. Fortunately, Wyndebourne was large enough for Jonah to be a recluse without being obvious about it.

He took Turk out for a punishing ride to the castle ruins and back, hoping to find Serena there again because her usual mount was missing from the stable. But when he returned to Wyndebourne, he discovered Miss Braithwaite riding Serena's mare at a sedate walk alongside the marquis. The daughter of the house was either closeted with the under-butler, flustered with the final plans for the house party and ball, or she was avoiding him.

The carriages began arriving in the late afternoon. There was a steady stream of coaches, elegant barouches, and more than a few sporty gigs driving down the tree-lined lane that led to Wyndebourne's impressive front doors. The ton had come to the country, and they'd come to play.

Jonah watched their relentless advance from the window in his chamber, feeling as if time had slipped away from him. Or maybe it was only Serena who was slipping away, moving back into her accustomed orbit with the glittering people of much higher rank than he.

Such things had never bothered him before. They rankled his soul sorely now.

For some reason, Mr. Honeywood seemed to be absent from the estate. The usually well-organized army of servants was in mild disarray as they ported in trunks and escorted the overdressed visitors to their guestrooms. Jonah was gratified to see that no carriage with the royal insignia made its way up the long drive.

So far, the Duke of Kent had been content to woo Lady Serena from afar through intermediaries. Jonah hoped that state of affairs continued. If the paunchy, balding royal ever got a chance to truly know Serena, he'd forget about that German princess in a heartbeat.

Jonah's own heart felt tight, as if his ribs were constricting on it.

What are you doing, Sharp?

He strode away from the window, grinding a fist into his other palm. He shouldn't have wasted the day watching from the fringes while Serena's guests descended upon Wyndleton. He ought to have gone back to Portsmouth to try to find Leatherby again. But he couldn't bring himself to leave now.

Somewhere deep in the great house, a bell tolled. It was a warning. The assembled guests had only sixty minutes in which to array themselves in their most impressive finery before supper would be served in the sumptuous dining room. The upstairs servants likely felt they needed six hands each in order to meet all the demands for assistance in dressing hair and last-minute shaves.

Jonah merely washed his face, combed his hair, and donned his best suit of clothes. He'd make a somber showing in all black, a crow amid a flock of showy roosters. His wrist studs were silver instead of gold, and he didn't possess any flashy brocade waistcoats. Unlike his friend Nathaniel Colton, who was something of a sartorial peacock, Jonah always measured a jacket's worth not by its cut or the fineness of its fabric but by how well he could swing his sword arm in it.

He found himself wishing he had a saber at his hip and that he'd find a reason to use it. A man could lose himself in parry and thrust, footwork and strategy. If impending death was singing in the wind, it only served to make him feel more achingly alive.

Jonah had few equals when it came to swordplay. He was much less adept at the verbal sparring that was as much a part of an upper crust dinner as a dowager's ostrich-plumed turban.

He waited another thirty minutes, then squared his shoulders and strode out of the room like a man destined for the rack.

❧

"Of course it's true. *Le Dernier Mot* wouldn't print it if it wasn't," Lord Boswell said as he scraped the last of the lemon trifle from his dessert bowl.

Jonah half-expected the garrulous fellow to lick the bowl clean. Even though there were a dozen guests around the table, the man had monopolized the dinner conversation with mindless drivel. If he was that starved for attention, why wouldn't he be greedy for every last bit of his dessert as well?

"Besides," Lord Boswell continued, "if the Lady Patronesses at Almack's wouldn't make an exception for the Duke of Wellington, they surely wouldn't make one for Lord Talwin. Rules are rules. If a gentleman wishes to be admitted, he must wear knee britches."

"Still, one wonders why he refused to honor the dress code," said Lady Lysandra with a malicious grin. "Could it be he didn't wish to wear the white stockings? I've heard some gentlemen are horribly spindle-shanked."

Lysandra Grey might be Serena's friend, but Jonah wasn't disposed to like her. With her long neck and longer than fashionable nose, she reminded him of a coursing hound he'd once owned. It possessed beautiful conformation and impeccable bloodlines, but it was also nervously vicious. Every chance it got, the damned bitch bit him.

Lord Boswell returned Lady Lysandra's sly smile. "Perhaps I should suggest Lord Talwin try slipping some wooden falsies into his stockings."

The lady tittered in mock outrage. "Lord Boswell, such talk! You are desperately wicked."

"Not quite desperate, but I cannot deny the wicked," he quipped.

Jonah was relieved when Lord Wyndleton rose from his place at the far end of the long table, signaling that the interminable supper was over.

"Gentlemen, shall we adjourn to the smoking room?" the marquis said. It was phrased as a question, but everyone knew there was but one answer.

Everyone except Serena.

"Oh, father, not tonight, please," she said, her gaze sweeping around the table. Jonah thought her gaze rested for a bit longer on him than the others. Or maybe it was only that he wanted it to. "Instead of splitting up this evening, I was hoping we might all remain together and adjourn to the parlor to play games."

The marquis's lips drew downward into an inverted smile, but he nodded grudgingly. Evidently, he had as much trouble saying no to his daughter as Jonah did.

The company rose as one, and pairing off, they all followed Serena out. Lord Boswell had abandoned Lady Lysandra in order to scurry to the end of the table to offer his arm to Serena. Jonah found himself escorting Miss Braithwaite somewhere in the middle of the press.

"Is something wrong, Sir Jonah?" Amelia murmured as they processed in queue from the grand dining room to the equally grand salon. When a family had been wealthy as long as Serena's had, their entire home took on a patina of opulence. From the carefully chosen furnishings to the exquisite *objets d'art*, every chamber in the great house proclaimed the exalted state of the Wyndleton name more effectively than a trumpet fanfare. "I must say, you don't seem to be enjoying yourself."

"What makes you say that?"

"You didn't contribute much to the general conversation at supper," Miss Braithwaite said.

"I don't think the ton cares what I have to say about its fashions or follies, and no weightier topics were offered."

"Of course not. Weighty topics are bad for the digestion," she said. "And I didn't see you chatting with either of the ladies seated at your sides beyond a few words. Miss Bianca Dobby seems quite taken with you, and it wouldn't have cost you a thing to make polite conversation. I do wish you hadn't ignored her like that. I wouldn't have thought you the type to play cruel games."

Which of the two shy ladies on either side of him was Bianca Dobby? He really ought to have paid better attention when introductions were made before dinner. He'd been listening with half an ear for Serena's voice in the midst of so many mingled conversations and didn't remember most of the people he'd met that evening.

"I'm not one for game playing of any sort," he said gruffly.

As they entered the salon and found seats, Jonah noticed that Miss Braithwaite's gaze tracked the movements of the marquis as he escorted the widowed Baroness Godfrey to a comfortable chair near the fireplace.

It occurred to Jonah that he and Miss Braithwaite had a great deal in common in this company. As a baronet, he occupied the lowest rung of the social ladder. As a governess, neither officially a servant nor one of the family, she wasn't even permitted to steady the ladder.

Yet if that entry in the Portsmouth church register was to be believed, Miss Braithwaite was, in reality, the highest ranking woman there. Yet for Serena's sake, she was prepared to be the lowest.

What nonsense there is in the world. It sickened him. Jonah was seized by the almost uncontrollable urge to grab Serena and carry her off till they were someplace free of the insanity of Society and its expectations of them.

The only thing wrong with that plan was he had no idea where that would be.

"Now, what shall we play?" Lady Lysandra clapped her hands together. "What about the Minister's Cat?"

"Begging your pardon, milady, but the Minister's

Cat is for dowagers and dotards," Lord Boswell said, stifling a belch by pressing a fist to his chest.

"How about Sardines?" someone suggested.

"There are plenty of places to hide in Wyndebourne, but I think Sardines might be more fun once you all learn the lay of the house more completely," Serena said. "We don't want to lose anyone on the very first night."

"Getting lost is the whole point," Lord Boswell said with a wink. "Provided you get lost with the right person."

The under-butler appeared in the doorway and sidled haltingly toward the marquis. He spoke softly enough for only Lord Wyndleton to hear him. The marquis rose immediately.

"Pray, excuse me," he said. "A matter has arisen to which I must attend. Good night all."

His glance darted briefly at Miss Braithwaite and then he strode from the room.

Once Wyndleton was gone, Lord Boswell slapped his thigh. "I have it. What about Hot Cockles?"

"An unusual name. How is it played?" Miss Braithwaite asked, dragging her gaze from the door through which Lord Wyndleton had just disappeared.

Lord Boswell grinned. "Easy. We blindfold a fellow. Then we spin him around a bit and when he's good and woozy, we lay his head in one of you lovely ladies' laps. While he's trying to figure out whose lap he's in, the rest of we gentlemen will take turns whacking his bum with a cricket bat."

"The game has the benefit of novelty. That's for certain." Lady Lysandra arched a skeptical brow. "And how does one win this game of Hot Cockles?"

"Well, there are those who would say that merely being able to rest one's head on feminine satin is winnings enough," Lord Boswell said, waggling his eyebrows.

Jonah wondered how much wine the man had consumed at supper. He might be an earl, but his speech and behavior were as loutish as a dockworker's.

Why am I the only one who can see it?

"But in order to be declared the winner, the blind-folded fellow must correctly guess the identity of both the gentleman who's whacking his bum and the lady whose lap he's sniffing—I mean, resting upon."

He giggled nervously as silence descended on the room.

"A lady's scent is really the only thing to go by since the blindfolded fellow ought to have his hands bound as well. Otherwise, he might be tempted to try to identify the lady based on a flounce around her hem or a well-turned ankle if his hand should happen to slip under skirt," Boswell rattled on. "I'll go first. Have you a cloth for a blindfold, Lady Serena?"

"If it's a beating you're wanting, Boswell, I'll oblige you," Jonah said, rising to his feet. He'd be damned before he sat by and watched while Boswell laid his head on Serena's lap, or on any of the other women present, come to that. The man was nothing but a swine dressed in a Saville Row ensemble. "And since I won't be using a cricket bat, you won't need a blindfold."

Miss Braithwaite raised a hand as if she'd admonish him but then thought better of it and lowered her palm to her lap.

Lady Lysandra rose to her feet, glared directly at

Jonah, and then sniffed and looked away. "I'm so glad we are among sophisticates who understand that a game is just a game. Since I heard no objection raised, certainly not by anyone of import, I think we should play Lord Boswell's game." She pulled an embroidered handkerchief from her sleeve. "This should do for a blindfold, I believe, though I fear some of my perfume may linger on it."

"In that case," Lord Boswell said, "I shall count myself extremely fortunate to be awash in your scent, dear lady, even if it makes something harder."

Lady Lysandra's brows shot upward. "Something?"

"My task, of course." Lord Boswell waggled his finger at her. "You naughty girl, what were you thinking?"

The rest of the assembly tittered uncertainly at this. From the corner of his eye, Jonah saw that Serena's face was drawn taut as a bowstring. Boswell was well on his way to hijacking the house party, but as an earl and the reputed intimate friend of the Prince Regent, he could evidently do no wrong. He stooped before Lady Lysandra to allow her to fasten on his blindfold.

"Now all we need is a cricket bat," Lysandra said. "Serena dear, should you ring for a servant? Oh wait, perhaps there is someone here who doesn't belong in our company but is probably equal to the task fetching and carrying for his betters." She riveted her gaze on Jonah. "At least, one hopes he's bright enough to serve such mundane purposes."

Jonah gave a curt bow in Serena's direction. "I believe I've had all the frivolity I can stand for one evening, my lady. If you will excuse me."

He didn't wait for a reply. Jonah turned on his

heel and stalked out of the room, thinking that Lady Lysandra had better hope he wasn't really going to fetch a cricket bat.

Twenty-two

From cradle to grave, one's place in Society is settled by the question of birth and breeding. Unlike the American upstarts who tout their "self-made man," we know Society has made us what we are and if we are wise, we are properly grateful.

It's a canny man as knows his place. To change it would require changing not only the man. It would mean upsetting the order of the entire world.

From Le Dernier Mot,
The Final Word on News That Everyone
Who Is Anyone Should Know

JONAH RIFLED THROUGH THE LIBRARY SHELVES, looking for something—anything—to take his mind off the lascivious game Serena's houseguests were playing. Of course, if he were honest, a few weeks ago Hot Cockles would have sounded like a grand time to him. Now the thought of another man being that close to Serena made a red haze descend on his vision.

If Jonah were the one wielding the cricket bat, he'd

knock the bum of any man who dared lay his head in her lap into next week.

He wanted to hit something, preferably something that could hit back. But fisticuffs were frowned upon in Polite Society, and the drawn look on Serena's face when he left the salon told him he'd mortified her enough for one evening.

He fingered the spines of DeFoe and Keats and Sir Walter Scott tomes. None of the titles were dark enough to suit his mood.

Perhaps Dante's Inferno?

The door to the library creaked open behind him and then slammed shut with a resounding thwack. He turned to see Serena framed by the lintel.

"Well, I hope you're satisfied," she said, her hands fisted at her waist. "You made a fool of yourself."

"Me? I'm not the one who wanted my arse whacked in public."

She heaved an exasperated sigh. "Jonah, don't you see? You can't go around insulting an earl to his face and expect others to sit by and—"

"I don't care if he is an earl," he said with a snort. "I'd have said the same if Boswell was the bloody King of Siam."

She shook her head slowly. "I believe you would. But Society will not allow it."

"Seems to me they all did." His shoulder lifted in a shrug. "Except for your friend, Lady Lysandra. I suppose in the language of the ton, she feels she skinned me rather efficiently, doesn't she?"

"She does. And to be honest, you deserved it." She crossed the marble expanse of the library floor, her arms resignedly at her sides now. "You were doing so well at dinner. Why did you have to say anything in the salon?"

"Because no one else did. Serena, if you think I'd stand by and watch while that"—he searched for a sufficiently vile term for Lord Boswell that wasn't too shockingly vulgar for mixed company and came up empty—"that…waste-of-skin that answers to the name of Boswell came anywhere near you, you don't know me very well."

"That seems to be the general consensus—that I didn't know you before this house party and the only reason you're here at all is because of the marquis's whim," she said with another sigh. "Please, Jonah, behave yourself. I'm so tired of trying to defend you."

"I don't need you to defend me."

"Yes, you do, whether you realize it or not. Once you left, the whole company was clamoring to know why you were invited to Wyndebourne."

"The whole company?" According to Miss Braithwaite, Bianca Dobby, at least, should have been on his side.

"Well, maybe not everyone, but those with the most strident voices, that's for certain. Even the ones who agreed with you about Lord Boswell's game couldn't support the way you insulted him."

If they'd had an inkling of what Jonah would really have liked to do to the man, they'd have realized an insult was letting him off easy.

"The man spends his summers in the Prince Regent's Brighton palace, for pity's sake. He entertains royalty with the very sort of game he suggested for us." She paced before him like a caged lynx. "Do you know how difficult he could make your life if he wished?"

Evidently, she'd forgotten how difficult Jonah could make it for the earl to simply breathe if he wished.

"I can't tell you how relieved I was when Father returned and insisted on breaking up the party to share a new shipment of port with the gentlemen," she said. "Believe me, I made no objection this time when he led them away."

If her father had been in the parlor the whole time, Jonah doubted Lord Boswell would have felt bold enough to suggest Hot Cockles in the first place. The marquis didn't suffer fools gladly. Certainly not ones he outranked. Jonah only hoped Miss Braithwaite would give Lord Wyndleton a fair version of the incident later.

He'd seen them riding together earlier. Surely the secretly married couple had some way of spending time together out of the public eye, even when Wyndebourne was filled with guests.

"Are you listening to a word I'm saying?" Serena's voice interrupted his thoughts. Her fists were back at her waist and her eyes were spitting blue fire.

He nodded slowly but didn't really have a clue. Her angry words had trickled past his ears and spilled off his shoulders like water over a dam.

"What did I say?" she demanded.

He decided not to play fair. Jonah caught her into an embrace and pulled her close. "You were saying that you're glad all your other guests have toddled off to their beds because that means you and I can be alone now."

"I did not." She punched his chest with her fist

once, but didn't try to pull away. "I said I had to plead a headache in order to escape the women and come looking for you."

"So even though you're angry, you *were* looking for me," he said, his chest warmed by the knowledge. He bent and gave her a lingering kiss. "What did you intend to do once you found me?"

"That depends," she said, a sly grin lifting the corners of her mouth. "Did you find a cricket bat?"

He gave her bum a playful swat. "Jezebel!"

She reached around him to whack his right back. "Cretin!"

Jonah pulled her close for a deeper kiss while he cupped her bum and lifted her against him. She tilted herself into him with a deep groan.

"Lady Serena!" The shocked voice belonged to Amelia Braithwaite.

Serena tore herself out of his embrace as if he were on fire and put several arms' lengths between them. "Amelia, this isn't what it looks like," she said.

"And what do you think it could possibly look like other than what it is?" The older woman moved smoothly into the room, letting the door close softly behind her. Only the twin splotches of red on her cheeks betrayed the fact that she was quietly livid. "I know Sir Jonah is here to inspect the horses, but I hardly think he needs to check *your* teeth." She flicked a cold glance at him. "If you'd be so good as to leave us, sir."

"No." He was already in trouble for behaving boorishly this evening. He wasn't about to add to his list of sins by being a lout and letting Serena face her mentor alone. "I won't."

Serena cast him a pleading look. "Jonah, don't be difficult. You'll only make things worse."

"I'm not being difficult." He moved to place himself between Serena and Amelia. "I simply need to speak to Miss Braithwaite. Alone."

"Oh, I think you've already spent enough time alone with the women of this household," Amelia said through clenched teeth.

"It's important that I discuss my recent trip to Portsmouth with you, Miss Braithwaite. Once you hear about where I went, I'm sure you'll agree."

"Where you go when you gad about the countryside is none of my concern."

Amelia tried to peer around him to glare at Serena, but he sidestepped to keep the two women apart. With both of them circling and Jonah shifting to maintain his position between them, it was the oddest dance he'd ever been a party to.

"You'd be surprised at what might concern you," he said. "I certainly was when I visited the parish church and looked through their marriage records."

Miss Braithwaite's eyes flared with sudden alarm, and Jonah gave her an almost imperceptible nod.

"Serena, go to bed," Amelia said in a clipped voice.

"Now, wait a moment." Serena ducked under Jonah's arm and pushed past him to face her governess. "What are you and Sir Jonah talking about? And besides, the time is long past when you could send me to my room."

"Would you prefer that I call your father here and describe to him the state in which I found the two of you?"

Serena frowned like a Kraken, but Amelia Braithwaite didn't turn a hair. Finally, Serena gave an exasperated growl and stormed out, making the door rattle against its hinges behind her.

Jonah grinned after her. Serena was intriguing when she was curious, but she was magnificent when she was angry. "She does have a temper, doesn't she?"

"She also has a family that loves her very much." Miss Braithwaite laced her hands before her trying to project a calm image, but her knuckles went white from the tightness of her grip. "Now, tell me, Sir Jonah, what is your price?"

"My price?"

"For your silence. You wouldn't have brought up the church register unless you meant to blackmail the marquis and me," she said with a surprisingly even tone. She might have started in this household as a governess, but her manner was as haughty as any marchioness ever thought about being. Then her eyes narrowed. "But you should be aware that you will be making a powerful enemy. There is not enough coin in the realm to shield you from the hailstorm you'll find raining down upon you once his lordship learns of your extortion."

Jonah shook his head. "I'm not going to blackmail you. What do you take me for?"

Amelia's hands relaxed slightly. "You're not?"

"Of course not. I only brought it up because I wanted to talk to you without Serena around and figured that was the best way to convince you to let her go without a dressing down. She doesn't deserve it.

Whatever fault there may be with what you witnessed here this evening lies with me," he said. "But back to you and the marquis. I assume Serena doesn't know about your...arrangement with her father."

"No, though we intend to tell her when the time is right," she added quickly.

"Soon, I hope. Like week-old fish, this sort of news doesn't improve with keeping."

"I know, but it can't be helped. To be honest, Sir Jonah, it's something of a relief to be able to talk with someone about it." Amelia walked across the room, tension draining from her like a lubberly coracle with the wind spilt from its sails. She sank into one of the Sheraton chairs near the burled oak desk. "As soon as things are settled with the Duke of Kent and Serena is safely wed, Lord Wyndleton feels it will be the right time to announce the truth about our marriage, to his daughter first and then to the world."

"And what if the duke doesn't offer for her?"

"He will," she said vehemently, as if her fervor would make it so. "There's a great deal of pressure on Kent from the House of Lords not to wed Prince Leopold's sister. Our alliance with Saxe-Coburg-Saalfeld is strong enough without it. England wants an English princess, my husband says, not one who speaks German."

Jonah came over and sat in the chair opposite her. "What if Serena doesn't want to marry Kent?"

"She does. She must." Amelia scrunched the fabric of her skirt between her fingers. "Her father is counting on it."

"What if she doesn't?" Jonah repeated.

"Why would she refuse him? Are you saying that…" Amelia's eyes widened. "Have you proposed to her? Tell me you haven't done anything so foolish."

"No. I haven't."

But he almost wished he had. Marriage was no longer the unthinkable proposition he'd always considered it to be.

"Good. Please don't—oh!" One of her pale eyebrows arched and her expression softened. "I just realized. This is no rake's game to you. You love her, don't you?"

He leaned forward, resting his elbows on his knees, and studied the tips of his Hessians, wondering what had given him away. "It's that obvious?"

"No, it wasn't, but now that I've taken the time to consider, to notice the look in your eyes when you speak of her, I can't think how I missed it before." She laid a hand on his forearm and gave it a gentle squeeze. "I'm so sorry, Sir Jonah. This cannot be easy for you."

"I don't expect pretending to be a governess when you're really the lady of the house is easy for you either."

She turned her lips inward for a moment. "No, it's not. But I do it willingly for my husband's sake. And Serena's too."

"Then I hope you'll do something else for her." Jonah reached over and took both of Amelia's hands in his. "Don't let the marquis force her. If she refuses the duke, convince her father to accept Serena's decision with good grace."

"How can he accept that? It would be the match of the century. You don't know what you're asking."

"Yes, I do." He squeezed her hands, willing her to understand. "You and Lord Wyndleton should know better than most that we can't order passion. It comes where it will. I want Serena to be free to choose whether or not she accepts Kent."

"Then Serena loves you too."

He wished. "She has not said so."

Amelia looked thoughtful for a moment. "Have you declared your feelings to her?"

"Not in so many words—"

"Then don't. If you are sincere in wanting Serena to have a free choice about the Duke of Kent, she must not have any other considerations muddling her decision." When he started to protest, she raised her hand to stop him. "Love is not love if it is not willing to sacrifice itself. If you love her, you know you must not interfere."

Jonah wouldn't have given weight to that argument from anyone else, but Amelia was the embodiment of what she preached. Her own sacrifice was etched on her taut features.

"What would you have me do?" Jonah asked.

"You are not to speak to her either of love or your intentions until she has made her decision about the royal duke. That is the price of my help with Lord Wyndleton should the need arise." Amelia skewered him with an intense gaze. "Do we have an accord?"

In some ways, it made sense. If he tried to force the issue now, Serena might agree to become his wife in the heat of passion. But in the years to come, she might well resent the fact that she could have been royal if only she'd waited.

How would he ever know if she'd truly choose

him unless she had the freedom to decline becoming royal first?

"You have my word," Jonah said solemnly. "I will not tell Serena I love her or ask for her hand until after she refuses the duke."

"You mean *if* she refuses him."

"If," Jonah said with a nod. A world of possibilities lived in that small word. Not all of them good. But this was the best bargain he could hope to strike with Miss Braithwaite at the moment. And at least he'd distracted her from the fact that she'd caught Jonah kissing her stepdaughter senseless. "We have a deal."

"And I'll have your promise to stay away from her as well."

"No, you won't." These next few days might be all he'd ever have with Serena. He wouldn't surrender a moment of it now. He'd already decided to let Mr. Alcock's plans slide by the wayside. Surely he and his friends could find Sgt. Leatherby and settle their problems in France with his testimony, even if they had to force it from him.

No matter what, Jonah wasn't about to ruin Serena Osbourne. He loved her. Hearing Miss Braithwaite say it out loud made it more real somehow. He even loved her enough to let her make her own decision about the Duke of Kent, but he'd spend as much time with Serena as she'd allow in the meantime.

Jonah stood and gave Amelia a quick bow, then he strode toward the library door. Once it closed behind him, he murmured, "I can't leave Serena alone. I'd sooner give up sunlight and air."

Twenty-three

So many couples operate at cross purposes with each other, even when they have the best of intentions. Missed train connections, an undelivered letter, even a mistimed turn around a ballroom can make a lifetime of difference. Whether from lack of communication of their wishes or plain misunderstanding, romantic tragedies abound.

Robert Burns was right:

"The best-laid schemes o' mice an' men Gang aft agley."

From Le Dernier Mot,
The Final Word on News That Everyone
Who Is Anyone Should Know

"AND SO, MY LADY, YESTERDAY I SAW SGT. LEATHERBY and his goodwife board the *Matilda Anne*, bound for Boston and, if I may add, blessing the name of their anonymous benefactor as they did so," Mr. Honeywood said, finishing his report on the special task Serena had laid upon him.

Eating a late breakfast by herself in the cavernous dining room, Serena sipped her hot chocolate. She'd sat up till the wee hours of the morning, watching the fire in the grate wind down its flickering dance and hoping that Jonah would come to her. When she finally dropped off to sleep in her chair, she realized he was wise to stay away after Amelia had caught them together in the library. Her governess was likely to be extra vigilant about late-night wanderers and it wouldn't do for her and Jonah to be found together in an even more compromising position.

But that didn't lessen her disappointment one jot.

Mr. Honeywood lifted the chocolate pot and topped off her cup with the sweet, fragrant cocoa.

"Excellent work, as always, Mr. Honeywood." Her insides warmed with the knowledge that she'd saved not only Sgt. Leatherby, but Jonah as well. If he couldn't find the man, he didn't have to stain his soul with one more assassination for the Crown. "You certainly wasted no time persuading the Leatherbys to emigrate."

"Surprisingly enough, it was very little trouble to convince Sgt. Leatherby that he was in some sort of danger. Another fellow had been searching for him a few days earlier. Leatherby's friends in town colluded to hide his whereabouts from some big chap who was asking about him." Mr. Honeywood shrugged. "Evidently, no one finds me the least threatening and it did not hurt that I am known to be in the marquis's employ. The people of Portsmouth owe a good deal to Wyndleton. I didn't even need to give Leatherby all the funds your emerald choker fetched. Here are the remaining moneys, along with a strict accounting of my expenditures."

He laid a leather-bound packet on the table beside her plate of buttered scones.

"Thank you," she said. "I trust this is the end of the matter and we will not need to speak of it again."

"Almost." Mr. Honeywood replaced the chocolate pot on the sideboard. "While I was searching for the sergeant, it came to my attention that two more gentlemen were looking for him as well."

"Oh?"

"I thought you should be apprised of it since their names appear on the guest list for the ball tomorrow evening."

Her brows shot up. "Who is it?"

Mr. Honeywood nodded. "Lord Rhys Warrington and Lord Nathaniel Colton. Friends, I believe, of Sir Jonah Sharp."

She remembered that in his note, Lord Rhys had mentioned that he and Colton were attending the ball. "I didn't send them invitations."

"No, milady. Mr. Brownsmith did, on the marquis's orders. Both gentlemen are well-connected and from prominent families."

And evidently part of the Triad's shadowy network, Serena thought, running the contents of the note she'd intercepted through her mind. Warrington seemed even more interested in the whereabouts of Sgt. Leatherby than Jonah was.

"Do you think they knew you were looking for the sergeant?" she asked.

"No, milady. I paid all my informants with a liberal hand to ensure their silence. Since the inhabitants of Portsmouth live in Wyndebourne's shadow, they know better than to act against the interest of this house."

"Good," she said. "Inform me when those two gentlemen arrive."

"Lord Rhys and Lord Nathaniel are already here. They arrived while the rest of the household was at breakfast." Mr. Honeywood implied no censure for her sleeping late. It was merely a statement of facts. Honeywood would have no more dared to even think a criticism of his mistress than he'd have attempted to fly from Wyndebourne's slate-tiled roof. "The gentlemen presented themselves without their wives, which might be expected since they apparently came directly from Portsmouth instead of London. However, I'm given to understand the ladies are expected this afternoon. We have situated them in the Gold and Blue rooms respectively."

It occurred to Serena that she might learn more about the Triad and its interest in Sgt. Leatherby if she rifled through the visiting lords' personal effects. "It appears I've been remiss in greeting new arrivals. Do you know where the gentlemen are at present?"

"I believe they have gone riding with Sir Jonah. A mention of the castle ruins was made over breakfast and the three of them set off almost at once."

Serena considered a quick search of the Blue and Gold rooms afresh, but decided against it. If she was seen entering or exiting those chambers, even by a member of the staff, it would cause unwanted speculation.

However, if Jonah and his friends were at the castle ruins, they might be speaking freely. And they might not be aware of the tricks tumbled stone played with sound, making some whispers echo as loudly as a shout.

❦

"The pair of you aren't any prettier without those false beards and mustaches," Jonah said to his friends.

"You didn't like our highwaymen disguise?" Nathaniel Colton sketched a mocking chevalier's bow. "The little maid seemed to find us quite dashing."

"Perhaps because you only pilfered *my* things."

Rhys Warrington fished in his waistcoat pocket, came up with Jonah's wrist studs, and returned them to him. "You needed a new shaving kit in any case. But we have bigger problems at the moment. You didn't find Leatherby, and you haven't done Alcock's bidding either."

Warrington raked a hand through his hair as he paced along the crumbling parapet of the castle's remaining curtain wall. They'd waited to discuss anything about the elusive sergeant until they were well away from Wyndebourne and had done a thorough reconnoitering of the ruins to ensure their privacy.

"Stay out of it," Jonah said testily. The fact that they were friends didn't mean he wouldn't blacken Warrington's eye if he deserved it. And Rhys was fast on his way to earning a shiner. The pair of them lined up nearly nose to nose. "You didn't see me racing up to the Lake District to make sure you were toeing the line with your virgin, did you?"

"Easy now," Nathaniel Colton said, stepping between them. "We're all on the same side here."

"The hell we are," Jonah said through clenched teeth.

"What's that supposed to mean?" Rhys demanded.

"Just that the pair of you got off easy. You're done with Alcock," Jonah said. "Even if we never find

Leatherby, you'll just return to your wives and your lives and—"

"That's just it," Nathaniel said, smacking his hat against his thigh. "We're not going to find Leatherby. He took ship for Boston and someone else—we weren't able to determine who—paid for his passage."

Jonah sank onto the cold stone, his last hope of removing the taint of Maubeuge and regaining his honor fading like mist in the morning sun. The one man who could put an end to the whispering accusations about Jonah and his friends and the disastrous defeat in France had sailed out of their reach. If he ever discovered who paid for the man's passage, he'd cheerfully strangle them bare-handed.

"Without Leatherby's testimony clearing us once and for all of wrongdoing at Maubeuge, we're all in jeopardy. And more importantly, so are our families. Olivia and I are going to have a child." Rhys clenched his fists at his side. "If it were only my name sullied by Alcock's accusations, it wouldn't matter so much. But if we're brought up on charges of treason, it could ruin my son's life before he's even born."

"Cheer up, old man," Nathaniel said, trying to lighten the mood by slapping a hand on his friend's shoulder. "It could be a daughter."

Rhys shrugged him off angrily. "There's no laughing this off, Colton." He turned back to Jonah. "So you see, you're down to only one choice now, Sharp, or we're all in for it. I won't let you shirk your duty."

"When have I ever?"

"You seem rather negligent about it now, friend."

Rhys stood toe to toe with him again and growled out "friend" as if it were a curse. "What's keeping you?"

Just because Jonah wouldn't debauch a virgin and trumpet his dubious achievement to the world, Rhys was ready to throttle him. The three of them had strayed a long way from the young fellows who rode blithely off to war together, ready to die for king and country. And each other, if needs be.

"I think we both know who'll win if you start a fight, but I give you leave to try." Jonah pushed past him, stomping toward the stone steps leading downward.

"Wait, Rhys." Nathaniel stopped Warrington with a hand to his chest when he would have followed Jonah. Apparently, Colton valued Rhys's skin more than he did. "Sharp, there is another way, you know. You could marry her."

"I can't ask her."

"Why the hell not?" Rhys demanded.

Jonah wasn't about to admit that he'd promised Amelia Braithwaite he wouldn't. His friends would think him as mad as King George.

"You must love her," Nathaniel said, "or you wouldn't—"

"You don't know that. No one has a window to my soul." If they did, they'd find it too dark a place for comfort and flee immediately. He'd never told his friends about his work for the Triad, and he wasn't going to start now. Bad enough that Serena knew.

And yet she hadn't turned away. The knowledge gave him both more hope and more despair than he'd ever known.

"Then if you won't wed her, you know what you

must do," Rhys said. "You agreed. Hell, we all agreed to Alcock's terms."

"I know. But I cannot do it. I won't. Now unless either of you have a bright idea for intercepting a ship at sea and dragging Leatherby back to testify, we're done here," Jonah said as he tromped down the stone steps and mounted Turk without waiting to see if the others followed. He didn't say what was in his heart— that the three of them were done as well. How could he remain friends with Warrington and Colton when they urged him to publicly ruin the woman he loved?

Yes, he'd agreed to Alcock's unholy bargain in the beginning. He wanted to spare his father and brother from his shame if he could. What man wouldn't?

But that was before he knew Serena. Before he'd fallen in love with her liveliness and daring and her quirky list of forbidden pleasures.

And for the way she took away the blackness in him and filled those dark places with light. She was like no one he'd ever known.

No one he ever would know.

And there was only one chance for him now. Somehow, without a word of love or a declaration of intent from him, his whole world hinged on Serena turning down the match of the century.

Jonah didn't much like his chances.

❧

Serena stayed in her hiding place until she was sure the three men had gone. In all her imaginings as a child, the only time the mythical Visigoths defeated the Wyndleton defenders was when she pretended the villains made themselves temporarily small as brownies by some dark art. Then in that scenario, they crept in through the drainage system that ran from the curtain walls, through the now dry moat, and into the surrounding woods. All that was left of the drains were broken clay pipes that wouldn't hold water, but they were still fully capable of bearing conversations from the top of the wall to her ear at the end of the line behind a ponderously large oak.

"Men must speak in their own sort of code," Serena fumed as she mounted her mare. There was much she didn't understand about the overheard conversation. She was incensed over the fact that Jonah and his friends had staged their run-in with the highwaymen on their way to Wyndebourne. He'd meant to spirit her away to that hunting lodge. That sensual interlude that had so changed her world hadn't happened naturally.

Jonah had arranged it all.

She felt dirtied somehow, but she knew she couldn't confront him about it without admitting to eavesdropping.

Then the men's topic of conversation flitted from Leatherby to someone named Alcock to virgins and Jonah asking someone to marry him, albeit as some sort of last resort.

They hadn't mentioned any names, but surely they meant her. What other woman had Jonah been spending any amount of time with of late?

He wouldn't ask her to marry him, he'd said. Her chest constricted, but she shoved that thought aside, just as Jonah had.

When one of his friends accused him of loving her, what were the words he used?

"You don't know that."

Neither did she. He'd certainly never said he loved her. Not once.

But as much as Jonah's apparent coldness toward her stung, her conscience stung her even more. She'd totally misconstrued Jonah's intentions toward Sgt. Leatherby. He didn't want to hurt him. He and his friends *needed* the sergeant. Badly, it would seem.

And she was responsible for making sure Leatherby was out of reach.

She kicked her mare into a canter and sped through the forest, ducking low-hanging branches and swerving around saplings. One of the supple new growths whipped her cheek and brought hot tears to her eyes.

There was no undoing her meddling with Sgt. Leatherby.

If Jonah found out, he not only wouldn't love her, he'd never forgive her.

Twenty-four

"Waltz—Waltz alone—both legs and arms demands,
Liberal of feet, and lavish of her hands;
Hands which may freely range in public sight
Where ne'er before—but—pray 'put out the light.'
Methinks the glare of yonder chandelier
Shines much too far—or I am much too near;
And true, though strange—Waltz whispers this remark,
'My slippery steps are safest in the dark!'"
George Gordon, Lord Byron

If the morally ambiguous Byron had those scathing words to say about the waltz, need we, who are decidedly unambiguous, say more?

From Le Dernier Mot,
The Final Word on News That Everyone
Who Is Anyone Should Know

"OH, MILADY, YOU'RE A LOVELY SIGHT, YOU ARE. IF only His Royal Highness, the duke, could see—"

Eleanor dropped the hairbrush she'd been wielding

and slapped a hand over her mouth. The fact that the Duke of Kent had not deigned to make an appearance at the Wyndebourne ball to benefit the Orphans of Veterans of Foreign Wars was a sore spot to Serena's father. It was a source of worry for the servants who feared their preparations had been found wanting. And the apparent royal snub was too juicy a tidbit for the gossipy ton to refrain from sucking dry.

More carriages rolled up the long drive to Wyndebourne and deposited more glittering people into the great house. Every guest chamber was pressed into service to accommodate the wellborn visitors who would be staying since Wyndebourne was too remote for them to do otherwise.

The lack of a royal presence was topmost on everyone's mind. It seemed whenever Serena joined a group of her guests that afternoon, conversation ground to a sudden halt. She caught more than one look of pity directed her way.

Lysandra, however, was not silent and didn't hesitate in telling Serena where she went wrong.

"I knew removing yourself from Town was a bad idea. Since you weren't there to be seen out and about in Society, the tabloids have had to make up things about you." She'd rolled her eyes and affected an injured sniff. "At least I hope to heaven they were made up and you haven't really been seen consorting with gypsies. However, I couldn't swear to it either way. You never tell me anything anymore."

With good reason. Serena had pled yet another headache and avoided Lysandra for the rest of the day. Now she met her maid's gaze in the mirror.

"It's all right, Eleanor." She punctuated the statement with a curt nod, which set the gemstones threaded through her tresses sparkling in the candlelight. If she wasn't going to host royalty, at least she was making a good show of looking the part herself. "You've done a wonderful job with my hair. If the royal duke isn't here to see your handiwork, it's his royal loss."

"Don't let the marquis hear you say such things." Amelia draped the ruby pendant over Serena's head and fastened the clasp at her nape. "He won't be pleased."

"I'm not entirely pleased myself about a number of things. For example, it's ridiculous of Father to exclude you from the ball," Serena shot back. "You love to dance and you know it."

"That's of no import," Amelia said, looking a little bedraggled in her serviceable gray serge. She'd been as occupied as Eleanor with preparing Serena for the occasion and hadn't spared a moment for herself. "Besides, you know someone in my position is only welcome at this sort of occasion if there is an imbalance between male and female guests. Since Mr. Alcock arrived with his wife *and* a marriageable daughter in tow, we have more need of spare men than women."

The name pricked Serena's ears. "Alcock? Who is he?"

"A Member of Parliament. I forget which borough he represents, but it's probably one of the little old ones with only a handful of voters," Amelia explained as she smoothed down the drape of fabric attached to Serena's shoulders. It flowed down her back in a waterfall of silk that would have looked quite at home on a Roman goddess. "It makes Mr. Alcock almost impossible to unseat, which means he's likely been in Parliament forever and amassed his own network of cronies and allies. Because of that, unfortunately, the marquis has to give his ilk more attention than he would normally warrant."

It surprised Serena that Amelia knew so much about the inner workings of Parliament. She must have been attending more closely than Serena did when her father began to wax political over the supper table.

From what little she'd been able to glean from the cryptic conversation at the castle, the Member of Parliament seemed to have some sort of hold over Jonah and his friends which required them to do his bidding in a mysterious matter.

"And Father has doings with this Mr. Alcock?"

"Evidently," Amelia shrugged, "or the man wouldn't be here."

From a story down and a wing away, strains of the string quartet warming up wafted toward them. Someone repeatedly struck the A on the piano so the musicians could tune their instruments. Serena smiled. The pianist was sober enough for one note at a time, at least. She wondered if she'd ought to mention to Amelia that he shouldn't be served any punch that wasn't watered down, but then decided she had enough on her own plate without worrying about someone else's.

In another moment, a sprightly Purcell tune tickled Serena's ears.

"It's begun," Amelia said. "The marquis will be waiting for you at the head of the staircase. He wants to walk you down. Now let me look at you one last time."

Serena rose and gave a graceful twirl, feeling a bit like an overdressed marionette, minus the strings, but still ready for a play.

It would have to be a farce, she decided. No royal duke was coming for her to make her father proud. Jonah had manipulated events to spend unchaperoned time with her but didn't seem to want to swoop in and snatch her away in any respectable manner. Her heart still beat regularly in her chest, but it ached all the same. For Amelia's sake, she pasted what she hoped was a bright smile on her face.

"Oh, you are beautiful, my dear," Amelia said, her eyes shining. "Your mother would have been so proud."

Would she? Her mother had always admonished her to be herself. After being powdered, pressed, and poked for hours, Serena felt like someone else entirely. She suspected Miranda Osbourne would have been more likely to advise her to do the unexpected and have a little adventure. No staid and respectable garden for her. Serena's mother reveled in vibrant chaos.

I wish I could ask her what to do. Then maybe she'd have the courage to pull off her gem-encrusted slippers and spend the night dancing barefoot on the new spring grass under a star-spangled sky.

Or maybe her remembrances of her mother were tainted with wistfulness and yearning for more time with the parent who'd been snatched from her too soon. Her mother surely couldn't have been as unconventional as Serena remembered her or the staid marquis would never have chosen her.

Amelia gave her a quick hug. "Hurry, my dear. Your father will be waiting."

Eleanor scuttled over to hold the door open and Serena floated through it, her gown's many diaphanous streamers fluttering in her wake. Her modiste had gone a little wild in her quest to recreate the glory of the classical age. But then, from the corner of her eye, Serena caught her reflection in the long looking glass at the end of the hallway.

When the gown was in motion, the effect was ethereal. She looked like a young Daphne fleeing from her lover. Just the sort of image that made a man want to pursue, she realized.

The new style had cost the earth, but it appeared she hadn't paid the modiste enough for the gown after all.

When she rounded the corner and met her father at the head of the grand staircase, the expression on his face cemented that thought in her mind. His eyes misty, his smile broad, he'd never looked more pleased with her.

Which was strange considering she'd failed to bring down the biggest trophy of the Season—a royal buck.

The marquis gave her a deep bow and pressed a kiss to her gloved knuckles.

"How like your mother you look tonight," he whispered. Then he offered her his arm and they began to descend.

"Father, I know you're disappointed. I'm sorry things did not work out the way you wanted with the

Duke of Kent," she said softly. If she didn't say it now, there'd never be a better time.

"Who says they haven't?" her father answered in hushed tones. "Not all is as it seems, my dear. You'll see. Now, don't worry a particle about anything. All I want you to do tonight is enjoy yourself. I know Society can be cruel during unsettled times, but take note of any who laugh at your expense. Trust me. You will have the last laugh."

The marquis patted her hand and Serena basked in this unexpected moment of fatherly approval. Then he escorted her into the ballroom and partnered with her for the cotillion.

After that, Serena's dance card was fairly full, but she never had to consult it because as soon as one musical piece was done, another elegantly dressed fellow presented himself before her for the next dance. She snatched occasional glimpses of Jonah, looking dark and dashing in his simple but perfectly tailored ensemble. But it was always a fleeting glance between other dancers, and she never caught him gazing back at her. Finally, she begged off when Lord Nathaniel Colton arrived to claim her for a reel.

"Of course you'll be wanting a rest, milady," he said smoothly as he offered her his arm to escort her from the dance floor. "It will afford me the opportunity to introduce you to my wife, Lady Georgette. I don't believe she's had the pleasure yet. But be forewarned. She's a bit of a crusader, and while she heartily approves of your generosity toward orphans, she's likely to try to recruit you to help with her work among the 'soiled doves' of Covent Garden as well."

Serena was charmed by Lady Georgette who, as Lord Nathaniel predicted, did try to enlist Serena's support for her academy for former prostitutes, and also introduced her to her friend Lady Olivia and her husband Lord Rhys Warrington.

"You dance beautifully," Lady Olivia said to Serena. "I'm terribly jealous. My husband," she gave Lord Rhys a playful swat on his lapel with the back of her hand, "keeps insisting that I should sit about like an old woman simply because I'm in…an interesting condition. Honestly, it's such early days no one would even know if he didn't trumpet the news about like a rooster who thinks he made the sun rise."

The married ladies enjoyed a hearty chuckle at Lord Rhys's expense.

"I merely wish to make certain you don't tire yourself, my dear," her husband explained stiffly.

"Oh, pish! If I get any more rest I'm likely to start hibernating," Lady Olivia said, her eyes dancing and her feet tapping to the music. "Oh, Rhys, it's a waltz. Take me out onto the dance floor this minute or…"

"Or what?" he asked with a lift of a dark brow.

"Or I'll run off and dance with the gypsies." Lady Olivia cast her husband an impish smile and Serena decided she liked the woman very much indeed. "I've heard Lord Wyndleton shelters a troop of them on his land hereabouts."

"He does," Serena confirmed. "Lord Rhys, I suggest you waltz with your wife. She'll be much safer here than traipsing around a campfire."

The Warringtons took to the floor and began the intimate dance.

"Please, join your friends, if you like," Serena said to Lord and Lady Colton. She pretended to consult her dance card, but she knew there was no name penciled in beside the waltz. Even though she wondered what it would be like to try the dance, she wouldn't dream of doing so with a man in public. It would be a surefire scandal.

"If you're sure—" Lady Georgette began, but her husband waltzed away with her before she could finish her thought. From the practiced way they moved together, sinuous and graceful, Serena gathered this was not their first waltz.

She watched the handful of couples brave enough to attempt the sweeping steps around the floor with barely concealed longing. There was something magical about the way the gentlemen gazed down at their ladies, something intimate and precious. It made her wish Jonah's name had appeared on her dance card for this tune.

"Serena, what on earth?" Lysandra came up to her and hissed into her ear. "You ought to give the dancing master the sack with no character."

"It's not his fault."

"Then who was daft enough to put a waltz on the dance program?"

"I was," she confessed.

Lysandra's eyes went round as an owlet's. "But once word of this outrage gets back to the Duke of Kent—"

"The waltz will be over and it will be of no consequence." Why couldn't Lysandra just enjoy the way the music washed over them, languid and yearning? Music was a vapor. A will-o'-the-wisp. Once the piece was done, there was nothing to prove it had ever existed except in the memory of the way the lush chords shivered over her skin. "Besides, it's not as if I'm—"

Suddenly Jonah was standing before her, bowing over her hand. He straightened and looked down at her, his manner so formal, she hardly recognized him. "May I have the honor of this dance?"

"Serena," Lysandra whispered. "You mustn't."

That settled it. She simply must. She squeezed Jonah's fingertips and sank into a low curtsey. "The honor is mine."

Twenty-five

To dance with someone is to perceive their estimation of their own worth. The care with which one places a foot in order to achieve the best affect can reveal a good deal about the dancer. How one comports oneself on the ballroom floor mirrors one's station in life.

To waltz with someone, on the other hand, is to realize that the eyes are indeed the window to the soul and unless one is very careful, one is likely to tumble hopelessly through the open sash.

From Le Dernier Mot,
The Final Word on News That Everyone
Who Is Anyone Should Know

"I MUST THANK LADY LYSANDRA SOMETIME," JONAH said as he led Serena onto the floor.

"Why? She doesn't like you a bit, you know."

"That much is obvious. But I wasn't sure you'd accept my invitation. Telling you that you mustn't dance with me was the best way to ensure that you would."

Serena laughed as he folded her into the promenade

position so that they were joined hip to hip. Even in this hold, the waltz required them to maintain eye contact. "You obviously know too much about me."

"And yet not as much as I'd like." He'd sounded so cold toward her at the castle ruins. There was plenty of heat in his gaze now.

Which was the real Jonah?

"I didn't know you could dance," Serena said, a little breathless at being so close to him in public. Surely the other guests could hear her heart pounding and sense the way her insides cavorted about like a drunken faery.

"I can do many things that you don't know about." His voice rustled over her, deep and stirring with promise. He led her through an under arm–turn and snuggled her against his hip again, though this time they faced opposite directions. They moved slowly, one step per measure in a small circle. "Where did you learn to waltz?"

"At school after the headmistress called for lights out. Though I must confess when I danced it with Lysandra, there was a good deal more giggling involved."

He smiled down at her. "I imagine there was."

The man had seen her naked and yet she'd never felt quite so bare before him as she did now when she was required to look into his eyes without respite before a roomful of people. Jonah turned her in his arms and they began the slow circles facing each other. The ballroom became a blur of color at the edges of her vision. The many candelabras turned into vibrant pinwheels of light.

Every bit of her was intensely aware of each place

their bodies touched. The brush of her breasts against his chest set the tips aching. His hand at her waist was so warm, she felt the heat of him through the layers of fabric separating them. They moved together to the music and it reminded her of how they'd moved together in other more intimate ways. His lead was so firm, she had no chance to stumble or mistake where the dance was heading. He turned her as he willed, and she melted in his arms.

And always there were his eyes—those deep green eyes. They were flecked with gold, she realized, and fringed with lashes as dark as his brows. And behind them, there was the man.

His eyes were saying what his lips never had.

He wanted her. That wasn't in the least doubt, but there seemed to be more there as well.

Was that love in his gaze? Surely it was. She couldn't be imagining it. There was such tenderness on his features, much more than she'd have expected of someone who'd led such a life as his, one devoid of any softness or ease. And she seemed to hear a question he hadn't given voice.

Couldn't, he'd said at the castle.

Why ever not? she wondered. Serena had received plenty of proposals during her first Season and they weren't all from men the ton considered eligible. Was it only the difference in their stations that kept Jonah from asking for her hand?

"I was thinking today of an old saying," she began.

"Let me guess." The warmth in his gaze was replaced by an inquisitive glint. "'A bird in the hand is worth two in the bush'?"

"No." She hadn't intended to turn this into a guessing game. "It's—"

"'Don't count your chickens before they hatch.' Funny that so many old sayings involve feathers, isn't it?" There was no need for him to whisper. It wasn't as if they were saying anything that shouldn't be over-heard, but something about the intimacy of the waltz seemed to require it.

"No, that's not it," she hissed in frustration. He was completely spoiling the romantic mood of the dance. "And in any case, I don't mean for you to guess."

"Oh. My apologies. Perhaps you'd better tell me then." This time he bent his head so he could whisper directly into her ear. His warm breath washing down her neck sent shivers of wicked sensation over her skin. The romance was definitely back. "What were you thinking?"

She leaned into him a bit as they executed another turn. "I was thinking about how a 'cat may look at a king.'"

He raised his head and frowned down at her. "And you're the cat in this scenario."

Drat. Well, she supposed she could see how he might have thought that, seeing as how a royal duke was only a few heartbeats from being a king. "No, I'm not the cat."

"Am I the king then?" he asked with a beaming smile.

She wanted to tell him it didn't matter who was the cat or who was the king. The saying meant that in some instances, differences in station truly made no difference at all. That if he were hesitating because she was the daughter of a marquis and he a mere baronet, he should realize it didn't matter to her a snippet. If he asked her, she'd say—

"Well, am I?" he prompted. "Or does the proverbial cat have your tongue?"

She rolled her eyes at him. "Yes, Jonah. You're the king."

"Good. That's all I wanted to hear."

She clamped her lips shut.

"You're upset," he guessed, an amused grin still tugging at his mouth. "Why?"

"Because you're being purposely silly and this is not the way a waltz is supposed to be."

"All right. Since we've exhausted all other possibilities, in this metaphor you must have considered yourself the king and me the cat. And as far has how a waltz is supposed to be…" His smile faded and a smoldering look replaced it. "Would you rather hear how I want to pull out all your pins and shake the stars from your hair?"

She sucked in a quick breath as she imagined him doing just that.

"Or how I'd love to take my time peeling off all the layers of your clothing till you're standing before me in naught but your skin?"

Her skin prickled rosily at the thought.

"Do you want to hear how your scent is making me crowd my trousers?"

She stumbled and missed a step, but he waltzed on, carrying her with him, his glorious male hardness brushing her belly with each turning dip.

"How I want to taste and touch and torment every inch of you?"

She seemed to feel his mouth on her, licking the crease of her elbow, the curve of her breast, the dimple on her knee. Her cheeks were so hot, she was sure the entire company must be able to see her blush and wonder what he was saying to cause it.

"Do you want to hear me say I love you, Serena?"

Yes, God in heaven, yes, she wanted that. She'd never wanted anything more, but her tongue seemed stuck. She couldn't speak a word. The way one of the muscles ticked in his cheek was a warning she couldn't ignore.

Then suddenly she realized the music had stopped and she and Jonah coasted to a graceful halt as well. He made no move to release her from the dance hold.

"Sometimes, my lady," he said softly, "a cat doesn't dare look at a king. And not because the cat doesn't wish to, but because he mustn't. Good evening."

He executed a perfectly correct bow and turned and left her standing on the dance floor.

"The evening went incredibly well," Amelia said as she and Eleanor fluttered around Serena, two busy bees trying to prop up a drooping blossom. The maid plucked out the gemstones from Serena's coiffure while Amelia counted them and stored them back in their velvet-lined case. "As well as could be expected, in any case."

Since the royal duke wasn't here hung unspoken in the air. Serena sighed at her reflection in the vanity mirror and stifled a yawn. It was nearly half past two in the morning and she was far too weary to fret over the Duke of Kent. She was more upset about Jonah's abandonment on the dance floor. And his cryptic turnabout of the cat saying…what on earth was that about?

Not because the cat doesn't wish to. Did he mean he was holding himself at arm's length for *her* sake? Why didn't the man just say what he meant?

"I understand we raised a healthy sum for the orphans," Amelia said. "The marquis seemed pleased."

Serena nodded absently, imagining how different it would be if Jonah were plucking the jewels from her hair now. He'd gather her hair in one fist and tip back her head so he could ravish her neck and—

"You met a goodly number of new people too, I collect," Amelia prodded, yanking her out of her increasingly naughty musings.

Time to throw her a bone. After all, Amelia hadn't been allowed to go to the ball or even the midnight supper that followed. "Yes, I met the Warringtons and the Coltons. Oh, and that Mr. Alcock you mentioned before." Serena had suffered through a hitching, stumble-footed mazurka with the man. "For a thin fellow he perspires dreadfully."

"I noticed. His handkerchief must have been positively dripping after the reel. I gather Mr. Alcock is an all around unpleasant person off the dance floor as well," Amelia said, then turned to Eleanor once the last of the bejeweled pins was stored safely away. "I'll see to Lady Serena now. You may go."

Eleanor bobbed a reflexive curtsey and nodded sleepily. "Yes, mum, thank you kindly."

Once the door closed behind the maid, Serena

met Amelia's gaze in the mirror. "How do you know about Mr. Alcock's dancing?"

"I was watching from the balcony behind the musicians."

"I still say it wasn't right for you to be excluded. Father should be ashamed of himself."

"Nonsense. I was exactly where I needed to be. Someone had to keep the pianist from drinking himself silly. Up you get." Amelia prompted Serena to stand so she could unhook the long row of seed pearl buttons that marched down her spine. "However, you were not where you needed to be all night."

"Oh?" She'd only fled to the retiring room once and that was when Mr. Alcock's name popped up on her dance card for a second time.

"That waltz with Sir Jonah, Serena." Amelia's voice was tight and Serena knew her lips were pressed into a thin line of censure. "It was…ill-advised."

"It was only a dance."

Amelia finished unbuttoning the gown with more force than was warranted. A couple of the seed pearls plinked on the hardwood. "With a completely ineligible fellow."

"Again. Only a dance. And if I danced only with fellows you and Father deem eligible, I'd be a hopeless wallflower." Serena peeled off the gown, letting the silk slide down her arms and pool on the floor. She closed her eyes and imagined Jonah was doing it. A small fire sparked in her lower belly.

"You know what I mean, Serena. You and Sir Jonah were talking to each other during the waltz far more than the other dancers. What was he saying to you to make you blush so?"

Her eyes popped open. "Was I? I can't think why. Maybe I overexerted myself and you mistook it for a blush."

Amelia raised a skeptical brow and picked up the discarded gown.

"If you must know," Serena said, "we were talking about old sayings. Proverbs and such."

"Well, that sounds harmless enough." Amelia hung the gown up in Serena's wardrobe, smoothing a hand over the silken panels. "He didn't...push himself forward, did he?"

"Did he make passionate love to me on the dance floor with dozens of people looking on? Is that what you're asking?"

"Serena! What an unmaidenly thing to say."

Jonah had made her feel pretty unmaidenly. He made her feel unsettled and dissatisfied and as if something had to happen soon or she'd burst out of her skin. But the stricken look on Amelia's face made her take a deep breath and bite back what she was thinking.

"Nothing untoward happened between Sir Jonah and me on the dance floor. We danced a scandalous dance, I'll admit, but it was over quickly and in full view of the entire company. So how scandalous could it actually be?"

Amelia sighed and gave her a quick hug. "Oh my dear, you really are an innocent."

She helped Serena out of her stays and into her night rail, chattering about plans for lawn bowling, an archery tournament, and a picnic on the grounds for tomorrow. "And if the royal duke's courier arrives in the afternoon as your father expects that he will, there will be an announcement at supper."

A prickle of apprehension shuddered down Serena's spine. "An announcement of what?"

"Your betrothal, of course. The marquis says all the particulars have been agreed to and the solicitors are drawing up the final documents."

Serena's breath hissed over her teeth.

"That's right, my darling girl. It's going to happen." Amelia gave her a longer hug, patting her hair with a free hand. "I can't wait to see the expressions on the faces of those who doubted you would ever become a royal. Mark my words. Every guest who snickered over the fact that the duke did not arrive for the ball or sent you pitying looks this evening will be standing in line to lick the sole of your slipper by tomorrow night."

Serena didn't want that. She didn't want people groveling before her or currying favor. She didn't want to be royal. She knew in a moment of crystalline clarity there was only one thing she wanted in the entire world.

Jonah Sharp.

Twenty-six

Even the most dissolute scoundrel holds himself a gentleman when he honors his word. Nowhere is this more evident than in the sporting life. A Regency buck is a dab hand at whist. He knows a good deal about horseflesh and can sense when a pony is going to run its heart out for a win.

He wouldn't cheat on a wager unless he's prepared for pistols at dawn. But when a gentleman is out of gentlemanly options, sometimes he must wait to see if Providence will roll the dice in his favor.

From Le Dernier Mot,
The Final Word on News That Everyone
Who Is Anyone Should Know

JONAH PACED THE LENGTH OF HIS CHAMBER LIKE A CAGED lion in a menagerie. The urge to slip into the corridor and find his way to Serena's room was so strong, he wished, like Ulysses, he had some faithful friends who'd bind him to the mast to keep from answering her siren's call.

Warrington and Colton, the traitors, were more likely to shove him into Serena's bedchamber and then raise the household so they'd be caught together in that ruinous situation.

Jonah wouldn't do it. He couldn't bring her shame, but the ache of wanting her was fast becoming sharp-edged as a blade.

"Love is damned inconvenient," he muttered.

It also made him suspect he was seeing things. The door to the Africa Room swung softly open and Serena stood framed by the doorway for a flicker. Then she slipped into his candlelit chamber and closed the door behind her with a soft snick of the latch.

It was no imagining. She was real and she was there.

"You shouldn't have come, Serena." He forced the words out. "I can't offer you anything."

She stood still as carved stone, her eyes enormous in the dimness. If his words cut her, she didn't show it, but his chest ached all the same. Sonnet writers had bricks for brains. Love wasn't hearts and flowers and stolen kisses under a full moon. Love tied a fellow's guts in knots. Love hurt. It hurt damned badly, and the more he wounded her, the more pain he felt himself.

"I'm not asking you for anything," she said softly.

He cocked a brow at her. "Aren't you?"

Serena took a few steps toward him. "All right. Yes. I'm asking for you. Just you, Jonah. Just this moment. Just this night." She straightened her spine and lifted her sweetly dimpled chin. Her nipples stood at attention beneath her night rail and thin wrapper. "Can you give me that?"

He moved toward her but stopped before she was within arm's reach. "Let me guess. I've become something to check off your list?"

"No. Something to check off my life. Haven't you ever wanted something—needed someone so badly you don't care what you have to do to get it?"

Yes, damn it, he knew exactly what that felt like. He wanted her, didn't he? Wanted her so badly she was like a sickness in his mind and his blood.

And his heart.

"Amelia says a courier is coming from the Duke of Kent tomorrow. It's evidently been settled. And after that…" Serena's little pointed tongue swept her lower lip. "If I don't have you, Jonah, if for only one night, I'll…regret it the rest of my life."

What if I want more than one night leapt to the tip of his tongue, but he bit it back. He'd promised Amelia Braithwaite he wouldn't speak his heart before Serena gave the royal duke his answer. But he hadn't pledged he wouldn't let his body speak his love for him.

"If we do this," he said slowly, "I can't promise I'll be able to stop with half-measures."

Her eyes flared for a moment as she realized what he was saying. "I won't want you to stop. I want you, Jonah. And I won't settle for half-measures, either."

"If that's the way of it then, I'll take you." Jonah placed a hand at her waist as if they were beginning the waltz again and drew her close. Then he caught her hand and pressed her palm against his chest, willing her to feel the love that made him weak and strong at once. "I've wanted you from the first time I saw you."

"At Boodles?" She blinked at him. "When I was in my disguise as Cousin Rowland?"

It was perfect. The ridiculous image of her in male attire drained all the pent up tension that stretched between them. Jonah shook with suppressed laughter while Serena covered her mouth with her hand. Then he lifted her off her feet and swung her around in a circle.

"That wasn't the first time I saw you."

He'd been watching her for days before that without her knowledge and had roused to her repeatedly. Even so, his body had been more than ready to claim her at Boodles, even in that silly male getup.

And now his heart would let *her* claim *him* in the end.

He meant to hold back, to wait for her to respond, but something feral surged in his blood. He had to obey the urge to kiss her or something inside him would burst.

The laughter stopped in a heartbeat as he ravaged her mouth, drinking in her sweetness. He was drowning in her scent. When she answered his kiss and clutched the lapels of his banyan, pressing her breasts against his chest, blood pounded in his ears. Then the drumbeat moved much lower, to his thick cock, throbbing with life.

Jonah walked her over to the wall and pinned her against it with his body.

Don't be such a dog, he chided himself as he ground his pelvis against hers. He should be gentler, he knew, but he couldn't seem to help it. Serena was giving herself to him. Completely.

He'd take her.

Serena didn't seem to think she was as fragile as he did, though. When he started to ease up, she pulled his head down with a soft groan, urging him to stay.

They took each other's mouths, their tongues

vying for supremacy in a warm wet joust. Serena nipped his lower lip, and his groin ached all the more. She made those desperate little noises at the back of her throat again, the ones that drove him to rutting madness.

His hands roamed over her, claiming each dip and valley, the curve of her back, the plumpness of her bum. He peeled off her wrapper and worked up her night rail. He heard the seam rip as he hurried it over her hips, but he was unable to stop till he'd dragged the flimsy garment over her head.

Jonah paused for a moment, taking in the sight of her. Light from the fire gilded her pale skin with a golden glow. She was like some ethereal being—a fallen angel who'd strayed from glory to tempt him beyond his capacity to resist.

"You're stopping?" she asked, her voice dusky.

"Savoring," he assured her.

Her sigh made her breasts shudder. "Now what?"

"Now, my love…" Surely that wasn't a breach of his promise to Miss Braithwaite. Any rake worth his salt would call the woman in his bed "love" in the heat of passion. "I touch you as a lover should."

With painstaking slowness, he reached out a hand. Starting at the base of her throat where her pulse jumped, he traced his fingertips over her bare skin. She didn't move, though her breath came in hitching gasps.

She was all warm and soft and willing. Oh, the feel of Serena not trying to be in charge for a change.

Jonah paused to dally in every crevice, the crease beneath her slender arm, the delicate skin at the bend of her elbow. His cock urged him to hurry, but he forced himself to take his time.

This night might be all he ever had of her. It would have to last a lifetime.

He ran his fingertip around the outline of her hands, to the deep base of each finger and threaded his way around her knuckles. He taunted the curve beneath each breast. He drew increasingly smaller circles around her navel. His hand dropped lower, and he teased her legs apart.

She draped her arms over his shoulders and gave herself over to him.

His fingers launched a gentle invasion, all the while his gaze never left her face. Jonah watched as desire, pleasure, and need parted her lips and made her eyes go soft and hazy.

When Serena started to untie the belt at the waist of his banyan, he stopped her. "Not yet, love. You first."

"No, Jonah." She pressed her fingertips against his lips. "Once I wed the duke, I expect there'll be plenty of times in my life when I'll be a party to couplings where only one takes pleasure."

Her words were like a door slamming shut in his heart. He didn't know if he felt like dying or hitting something. Preferably the royal duke.

"I don't want it to be that way for you and me." She stood tiptoe to brush her lips across his. "We go together or not at all."

Then she unbelted the banyan and pushed it off his shoulders with excruciating slowness. A breath of night found its way in around the nearby window casement, cooling his feverish skin.

"This lover's touch you speak of," she said, her voice low and sultry, "it must go both ways. After all, if you're not pleased, how can I take pleasure? Now stand still."

There she is. That was the Serena he knew. Even though she was coming to him a virgin, she still wanted to be in command of this adventure. He decided to allow it for now.

Jonah didn't move. He scarcely drew breath as her hands smoothed over him, tickling along his ribs and teasing his nipples into hard knots. Then she cupped his ballocks, rolling the twin orbs between her fingers. He'd never realized he could ache so hard.

She squeezed the heavy muscle in his thighs, then stepped close enough to reach around and run a thumb along the crevice of his buttocks. He was in danger of spending without her even touching his cock once.

"Where the hell did you learn that?"

She bit her lower lip. "I've been studying up. As it turns out, the Wyndebourne library houses a slim memoir of the life and times of a French courtesan... and her arts." Serena cast him a sly grin. "I read it so voraciously, my fluency in French has improved out of all knowing."

She moved closer, then stepped back a pace. Jonah gritted his teeth as her breasts teased him with glancing brushes. Her soft belly pressed against his cock, but Serena carefully avoided touching it with her clever hands. Instead she raked her nails over his ribs and splayed her fingers across his flat belly. When she finally grasped him, it was all he could do not to erupt in her hands.

"Serena, I can't—" he began, then she surprised him by leaping up, hooking her hands behind his neck, and wrapping her legs around his waist.

"Can't what?" she asked with feigned innocence as she wiggled against him, her hot moistness tormenting the tip of his cock.

"Let me guess. This is more from that book on the courtesan's arts?" he asked.

She nodded. "I was always a very good pupil."

"Then let me see if I can add to your education." He covered her mouth with his. All his longing and hope poured into her. The royal duke's bloodless offer for her might come tomorrow, but he'd do everything he could to show her how he loved her tonight.

I love her. Serena Osbourne, maker of lists of forbidden pleasures, unattainable daughter of a haughty marquis. From the cloud of pale hair on her head to the soles of her delicately arched feet, she was all that was lightness and ease. He needed her to knit up the ragged edges of his soul, to fill him with her brand of chaos to replace the dark anarchy that was there now.

If by some miracle he could convince her without a word how much he loved her and make her love him back, he'd spend the rest of his life trying to be worthy of her.

But if he didn't take her right now, there'd be no rest of his life. He'd die on the spot. He pushed her hips down, sliding into her, impaling her slowly on his rock-hard erection. He groaned, awash in the pleasure of her slick, hot flesh. Then he tore through the thin barrier of her purity and she cried out, but not with pain. The gasp that tore from her throat was the feral sound of feminine triumph as she engulfed him completely.

He moved inside her, reveling in her softness, lifting her on and off his full length. Skin on skin, they slid against each other, her head thrown back so he could suck her tender neck. They turned slowly, doing a new sort of waltz, moving to unheard music, keeping rhythm with their shuddering breaths and pounding hearts.

Their bodies joined in perfect concert. Each time Jonah lowered her onto himself, Serena tilted against him, digging her heels into the small of his back, seeking the deepest bonding possible. She kissed his mouth, his cheeks, his closed eyelids. If shared pleasure was their goal, they were nearly there.

Her eyes were hooded as she gazed down at him. She bit her lip and growled in frustration.

"Easy, love," he whispered. "Let me take you there."

He braced his feet and moved more slowly, more deliberately till she began to quake in his arms. But as they moved as one, she didn't look away. He'd never locked gazes at the critical moment with a lover before. Now there was a spark in the depths of her blue eyes, and he saw the exact moment when she teetered for just a blink on the brink of the abyss. Then her insides contracted hard around him as his soul pulsed into her along with his seed.

Jonah couldn't say how long it lasted. It might have been seconds. It might have gone on for hours. Time seemed to dissolve, and everything sizzled in the eternal now. When it was finished, her head settled onto his shoulder and he held her as if she weighed nothing.

Unwilling to part from her, he carried her, still wrapped around his body, over to the waiting bed. He sat down and swung his legs up. Then when she unhooked her ankles, he lay down with Serena draped bonelessly on top of him.

Gradually, the heat of lust cooled. When he slipped from her body, she shifted to settle by his side, laying her head in the crook of his shoulder. Utterly spent, he gazed up at the shadowy mural of an African savanna on the ceiling.

Even if he wasn't restrained by his promise to Miss Braithwaite, there was no need for words. Anything Jonah might say would be redundant. Their bodies had said it all. Surely Serena felt his love enveloping her. His breath had lived in her body and hers in his. They were one soul. With this joining, they were bonded forever.

He'd never be free of her and didn't want to be.

She kissed his neck and snuggled close, relaxing against his body. In a few moments, her even breathing told him she'd escaped into the arms of Morpheus.

Jonah was tempted to follow her, but if he was wrong, if this was the only night he'd have her, he didn't want to waste a moment of it on sleep. He'd let her rest for a bit, and then he'd wake her gently for another go.

Until the stars fled from the sky, Serena was his. It was more than he had a right to ask. More than enough. He wouldn't think beyond the dawn.

Besides, he was pretty sure he could teach her a few things she hadn't learned from that courtesan's book.

Twenty-seven

According to the midwife who attended Lady Caroline Downing during her most recent lying-in, the viscountess was blessed with yet another healthy baby boy. Her husband Lord Downing is reputed to be an affectionate husband who quite dotes on his growing brood. This newest child is the couple's tenth bundle of joy in as many years.

Apparently Lord Downing is extremely affectionate.

From Le Dernier Mot,
The Final Word on News That Everyone
Who Is Anyone Should Know

SERENA WOKE SLOWLY, SWIMMING UP THROUGH LAYERS of oblivion to the realization that a fine male body was spooned around hers and someone's lips were teasing the nape of her neck.

"Jonah," she whispered.

"I'm sorry I woke you."

"I'm not." She turned in his arms so she could face him. Anticipation made it difficult for her to draw breath. Her belly churned as though a whole swarm of fireflies had been released in it. The sensations were mystifying and new, but Serena was ready to give herself up to them with abandon. She was safe with Jonah.

Well, not in some ways, she admitted to herself as she succumbed drowsily to his kisses. She'd given him her maidenhead and they'd not taken any precautions against conceiving.

Of course, if she quickened, she wouldn't be the first bride who delivered her firstborn "prematurely." If Jonah did get her with child, she wondered if the royal duke would denounce her for bringing a cuckoo into his nest. Probably not, since a legitimate child was the main goal of this farce of a marriage and the quicker the better.

The thought of wedding the duke was more repugnant than usual. After being with Jonah, she felt more than a little queasy over the idea that she'd have to be as close to another man, and a complete stranger at that, as she'd been to the fellow who was now nibbling at her ear.

Serena tried to shove the unwelcome thought away. She only wanted to be with Jonah. One night of giving herself to a man who meant something to her, a man she loved, yes, she could admit it to herself even if she couldn't say it to him. That wasn't too much to ask, was it?

The royal duke still loomed menacingly in her mind.

Then Jonah pulled away from her arms and rose from the bed.

"You're leaving me?" she whispered, feeling totally bereft.

"Only for a little." Heedless of his nakedness, he walked across the room to the small commode that held a pitcher and ewer. By the light of the banked fire, Serena admired the strength in his shoulders, the expanse of his back, and the way his lean torso tapered to his tight buttocks. Jonah was as fine a man as she could ever have imagined.

And he was hers, if only for this night.

He dowsed his face with water he'd poured into the ewer. Then he slicked his damp hair back, exposing the tender spot just behind his ear that Serena had discovered she loved to kiss. She climbed out of bed and skittered across the room to stand behind him and nuzzled the hairline at his nape, taking in his man smell. It was a scent she didn't think soap and water could improve.

"Easy, girl," he said as she nipped at his earlobe. "Or you'll have me too randy to think straight."

"What do you need to think about?" Serena sighed as she wrapped her arms around him and laid her cheek between his shoulder blades.

"How to make this night last, mostly," he said, then under his breath he muttered, "I don't want to think beyond that."

Oh, Jonah, give me a reason to say no to the duke.

He wet a cloth and turned to face her. "You went to sleep so quickly, I didn't have a chance to do this earlier."

"Do what?"

He knelt before her. "Spread your legs."

She obeyed and with extreme gentleness he used the cloth to clean away the dried red streaks on her inner thighs. There hadn't been much blood, but enough that she was glad he'd thought of it. Serena shivered.

"That water's cold."

He replaced the cloth in the ewer and toweled her dry. "My hands are warm. Would you rather have them?"

"You can put your hands anywhere you like."

"Remember you said that." Then he began stroking her ticklish ribs.

Serena loosed a giggle before she could catch herself. Jonah clapped one of his big hands over her mouth while he replaced the fingers tormenting her ribs with his tongue. Between his warm breath and the way his mouth smoothed over her skin, all thoughts of laughter fled from her mind.

She felt all achy and curiously heavy inside.

When he knelt before her again and covered her sex with his mouth, she began chanting his name without realizing she did so. Then when he'd reduced her to shaky-kneed weakness, he stood, captured her, and pinned her, arms stretched over her head against the smooth mahogany paneling. The coolness at her back was a pleasant respite from the heat building inside her.

He pressed his hard length against her. A flash of warmth between her legs answered his slow knock. His tongue invaded her mouth, and she welcomed the raid.

He pinioned her wrists together in one of his large hands and gave the other one freedom to explore. There were roughened calluses at the base of each of his fingers. They set her skin tingling.

She strained against his grip, trying to free her hands so she could touch him. "Let me…please, Jonah…I want to…" The man made her weak as water.

"Patience, love," he whispered. "You've heard that hunger makes the best sauce, haven't you?"

She nodded into his kiss. *Love. He called me love.*

"Well, desire prolonged makes the best loving," he explained when he came up for air again.

"Is that so?" She managed to pull free and strolled around him, running her fingertips along his lean waist. "Maybe you'd like a taste of your own sauce."

"I didn't know you could cook."

"I can do lots of things you don't know about," she said. "Now stand still."

He came to attention and she tormented him with her nearness. She brushed her breasts on his flesh with glancing touches. He bent his head to kiss her, but she stopped him with a hand to his chest.

"Patience, love," she mimicked. It was as close as she dared to a declaration of her feelings until he made a clearer one of his own.

She circled him again, admiring the fine contour of his spine and the slight indentations above his buttocks. Those twin globes were dusted with fine hairs that glowed in the firelight. She trailed a lazy finger around his hip bones and slid her hand over the length of his maleness in a teasing pass. A muscle ticked in his cheek when she stood on tiptoe to nibble at his neck. Every muscle in his body was tensed with the effort of holding himself still for her. It gave Serena a sense of more power than she'd ever felt.

How could even a royal duchess feel more?

"Can I move now, Serena?" he asked between clenched teeth.

"I'll be terribly disappointed if you don't."

Jonah swept her up and held her as if she was light as a basket of feathers.

He kissed her closed eyes, the apples of her cheeks, the column of her neck. Her insides went soft and warm and almost drowsy, surrendering to the sweetness of his mouth.

Somehow she became aware that he was lowering her to the bed again. She'd been so lost in the wonder of his kisses, she hadn't felt him walking with her across the room.

Serena leaned back against the plumped pillows. The linens were cool and delicious, smooth under her palms. Her newly awakened senses delighted in everything she touched and everything that touched her.

Jonah started with her lips and then began to kiss her all over, moving steadily down past the indentation at the base of her throat, between the hollows of her breasts, on down her body and legs to the soles of her feet and then back up. When he reached her mouth again, Serena felt more tinglingly alive than anybody had a right to feel.

In the years to come, how can I do without him?

"You make me feel so loved," she said as he lowered himself to her. *Why doesn't he say it?* She ran one hand absently through his hair, enjoying the clean feel of it. Jonah kissed down her neck to suckle her breast. "Isn't there something you'd like to say to me?"

Jonah raised his head, his face screwed into a frown. "You want to talk now?"

"No, not exactly. I just want you to…" The truth hit her in a blinding rush. "You don't love me."

"Did I say that?"

"No, you haven't said anything."

"Too many words can spoil a moment."

Serena bit her lip, unsure what to say. "And too few can ruin it."

Jonah stretched out beside her, dallying with the neat triangle of curls that covered her sex. "I told you when you came to me that I can offer you nothing. That hasn't changed."

Despite the tingling pleasure he gave her, she grasped his hand to still it. "You mean to stand by and watch while I wed the royal duke then?"

He narrowed his eyes at her. "If that's your choice."

Serena sat up. "Don't you realize when you care about someone you can't stand by and watch while they make a mistake?"

He dropped a quick kiss on her belly. "So you do think wedding Kent would be a mistake."

"Don't you?"

"What I think is of no consequence. I'm not the one marrying him."

Serena made a growling sound in the back of her throat. "I wouldn't stand by and do nothing if you were about to do something that might ruin your life."

"I'm in no danger of doing that."

"Yes, you were. Or at least, I thought you were when you were trying to find that fellow in Portsmouth." The words tumbled out of her mouth before she considered the consequences of them. "You know who I mean, that Sergeant Leatherby."

"How do you know his name?"

"That's not important." She couldn't admit she'd opened his mail and eavesdropped on his conversation with Lord Rhys and Lord Nathaniel at the old castle.

Jonah's expression went suddenly hard. "What did you do?"

"Once I knew who you were looking for, I thought you were trying to find him because the Triad had ordered him killed. I knew how much your work for them weighed on you, so...so I ordered Mr. Honeywood to find him before you did and send him away."

"So you're the one who paid for his passage to Boston."

The steel in his tone chilled her, but she nodded. If they had nothing else between them, at least they'd have the truth.

He sat up straight and raked a hand through his hair. "Do you have any idea what damage your meddling has done?"

Meddling! She was only trying to help the man. "I might have a glimmer if you'd just say what's on your mind once in a while. Believe me, I only thought to spare you, Jonah. If you'd told me why you were looking for him, that you needed his help..." She bunched the bed linens in her clenched fists. "You see, too few words really can ruin things."

"You want words? You may not when you hear what I have to say now." Jonah rose from the bed and began pacing. "Here's why we needed Leatherby. Just before the Battle of Waterloo, Warrington, Colton, and I led a failed assault near the village of Maubeuge. We led our men into an ambush and only a handful survived."

The look of abject misery on his face made her want to crawl not just beneath the covers, but the bed itself.

"There was an inquiry. While it demonstrated that the scouting reports we received were false, we couldn't prove we hadn't colluded with the French somehow. Sergeant Leatherby has information that will exonerate me and my friends. If we'd been able to find Leatherby and compel his testimony on our behalf, I wouldn't have to…"

She tucked the sheets under her armpits and rose to her knees. "To what?"

"Fortescue Alcock threatened to see me brought up on charges of treason. I'd have fought the accusation, but even the suggestion of a scandal that horrific would destroy my family's good name. My father and brother would be tainted by my disgrace. The only way Alcock would let the dead in France stay buried there is if I agreed to do his bidding."

Amelia had said the MP was an unpleasant man. She didn't know the half of it. "What does he want you to do?"

"He doesn't want you to wed the royal duke, and I'm supposed to stop you."

"How do you propose to do that?" She hoped her use of the word "propose" wasn't too on the nose, but the man hadn't caught any of her more subtle hints.

"He wants me to ruin you."

"But you wouldn't."

"Look around, love. I already have."

"Oh, God." She felt the blood drain from her head, and her vision tunneled for a moment. Jonah didn't love her after all. He'd only seduced her to save his own family.

Somehow, she forced herself out of the bed and retrieved her discarded night rail and wrapper.

She felt wooden, like a child's discarded toy, as if her arms and legs were controlled by someone else as she put on her clothing without a glance in Jonah's direction.

"Serena, that's how it started with you and me, but now I can't go through with it. You're only ruined if you're caught here," he said softly. "No matter what Alcock does to me and mine, I promise silence about what has passed between us."

Silence. That just about summed up the man when it came to matters of the heart.

She still didn't dare look at him. Her heart might leap out of her chest if she did. "For how long?"

"Forever. It'll be as if it never happened."

As if it never happened. She felt dead inside. Hollow. How was it possible that she continued to breathe? "Then none of this meant anything to you."

"How can you think that?" He stood before her, naked and magnificent and with an intense expression that dared her to read his mind and heart.

But he wasn't saying any of the words she needed so desperately to hear.

"Do you love me?" she asked in a whisper. She hated herself for asking, but she had to know.

Jonah's chin dropped to his chest. Serena counted ten beats of her heart before he raised his eyes to meet hers. The misery in them matched the sinking feeling in her own belly.

"Whether I love you or not makes no difference. You must choose your own path, Serena. You always have. But if you decide to wed the duke, don't imagine there will be any more of us." His face hardened into an unreadable mask. "I've no wish to be the pet of a royal duchess."

Serena felt as if her mare had kicked her in the gut. She should have remembered that Jonah was a rake. How could she have imagined that he loved her? Something inside her had died, and she felt close to joining it.

Then she remembered who she was.

She was Lady Serena Osbourne, daughter of the house of Wyndleton, and if she accepted the Duke of Kent's suit, she might well become the mother of a future monarch. She straightened her spine and walked out of Jonah's bedchamber without a backward glance.

Twenty-eight

The Hymen Race Terrific has pounded along for nearly three months now. Some of the fillies are tiring, but for one, at least, the finish line is looming large on the horizon. Word has reached our ears that an offer for Lady S. may well be forthcoming from a certain royal duke.

One hopes Sir J.S., who's been rusticating in the country as part of the house party at the Wyndleton estate, has saved his blunt. He could be called upon to settle the wager into which he entered with Rowland Osbourne concerning the latter's lovely cousin. Of course, the lady is not directly named in the wager ledger at Boodles, but it doesn't take a gypsy to read these particular tea leaves.

Or should one say "coffee grounds"?

From Le Dernier Mot,
The Final Word on News That Everyone
Who Is Anyone Should Know

"HURRY, SERENA," AMELIA URGED AS THEY MOVED swiftly down the wainscoted corridor toward the marquis's study. "Your father is waiting."

"Do you know something you're not telling me, Amelia?"

The older woman blinked at her. "Only that the duke's courier arrived shortly after breakfast after riding all night, and Lord Wyndleton has been closeted in his study since that time."

"Then you don't know for certain whether you're trying to rush a future royal duchess or not," Serena said wryly.

"Oh." Amelia clapped a hand to her mouth and slowed her pace. "Forgive me, my lady."

"Oh, for heaven's sake, I was only joking," Serena said. "Since when do you and I stand on ceremony?"

"We may well have to begin to very soon if the offer is what we hope."

"You mean what my father hopes."

Her usually mild features stricken with a look of concern, Amelia stopped her with a hand to her forearm. "You want this too. At least, you used to. You were full of plans for the education and molding of the character of the future monarch of England. What's happened? Has that Sir Jonah said—"

"Jonah has nothing to do with this." Serena sighed. "Believe me, the man has no opinion at all about whether I marry Kent."

"Good. I mean, this is none of his business in any case." They walked on, but Amelia stopped her again just outside the door to her father's inner sanctum. "I wish there'd been time to apply a touch of rouge to your cheeks. You don't look at all well, dear. Are you ill?"

Serena was sick at heart, but she couldn't confide in

Amelia. It was a hurt she had to bear by herself. Once she'd made her way back to her bedchamber after leaving Jonah, Serena had wept till she had no more tears and then, dry-eyed, she watched the sun rise. It made no sense that the rest of the world continued to turn when hers had been so completely upended, but since the people around her persisted in the fantasy that life went on, she had no choice but to indulge their whims.

"I'm fine," Serena assured her. "I simply haven't been getting much sleep." That at least had the ring of truth.

Amelia rapped softly on the door to the marquis's study.

"Come," her father's voice sounded through the heavy oak.

Stiffly, she entered the room and crossed to greet Lord Wyndleton. Her father came around his massive desk and took both her hands. Serena experienced a sense of unreality, as if she were dreaming and would wake presently or as if her spirit had somehow floated up to the ceiling and she was watching herself from outside her own body. Surely it was someone else who was about to receive a proposal of marriage from a royal duke.

"My darling girl." He raised Serena's knuckles to his lips. When Amelia made to go, he stopped her with an upraised hand. "No, stay, Miss Braithwaite. You've played such an important role in my daughter's life. I want you to be present for this momentous occasion."

Both the marquis and Amelia beamed at her.

Serena realized she was expected to say something and was mildly surprised when a coherent sentence formed on her lips. "I understand you have news."

"And not just any news. *The* news." Her father's face couldn't have been more radiant, and Amelia gasped with joy. "My allies in the House of Lords have prevailed and His Royal Highness has finally agreed to take an English bride."

Serena fought to keep her shoulders from sagging. Not only was she blessed with a loveless match, she was facing a reluctant bridegroom who'd had to be strong-armed into choosing her to boot. "How very…flattering."

"Indeed!" her father exclaimed, totally missing the irony in her tone. He moved around to the other side of his desk and picked up a piece of foolscap. "I've taken the liberty of drafting a letter of acceptance for you, my dear. All that's needed is your signature, and plans for the royal nuptials can begin."

Serena took the letter from his hand and pretended to read it, but she couldn't seem to make her eyes focus. A few words leaped out at her. She'd be entitled to style herself "Her Royal Highness." An extravagant dowry was named, which her future husband would control. If the rumors about the royal duke's debts were true, the funds still wouldn't be enough to make him totally solvent.

This probably pleased her father since it rendered the duke still beholden to the House of Lords, upon whom he would continue to depend for his income. Her father was fond of saying "He who holds the purse holds the power."

"Of course, there are more details to be agreed upon, but you needn't concern yourself with those," her father said as he settled onto his throne-like chair with the air of a pasha dispensing favors. "Since the royal duke is much your senior, in addition to your dowry, I wish to convey a trust upon you which will support you independently should he predecease you."

"That's very generous, Father," she said, her mouth suddenly dry. Serena had known for months in an abstract sort of way that a match with the royal duke was a possibility.

In the same way I know it's possible for a meteorite to fall to earth and land on my head.

Now her father was talking about dowries and trusts and predeceasing husbands. Oh, it all sounded so very final.

Why couldn't it have been a meteorite?

Serena's knees gave, but she covered her weakness by sinking into one of the chairs before her father's desk. "May I see the preliminary agreement?"

Her father's brow beetled, but he handed over an oilskin packet which contained a thick sheaf of papers. Serena pulled them out and leafed through them. Written by a royal scribe's overly elaborate hand and all festooned with curlicues to make them seem celebratory, they were still horribly official-looking.

Serena laid the packet on her lap. The weight of it made her feel as if she were about to sink into the floor. She chose her next words carefully. "While I'm sensible of the honor bestowed upon me, Father, you have always counseled me to be circumspect about serious decisions."

"Decisions? What is there to decide?" A blotch of red marred her father's neck just above his cravat and began to creep upward to his tightly locked jaw. "You only need sign your name to this letter and you're on your way to becoming the mother of a future sovereign of the realm."

Serena steepled her fingers in her lap and studied them with absorption to avoid her father's eyes. "Might I have some time to read through the documents?"

"You don't need to read them. Good God, girl, do you have any idea how I've moved heaven and earth to make this happen?" As he rose slowly to his feet, the volume of his voice rose as well. "The arm twisting, the concessions I've given, the favors I've called in—"

"My lord."

Serena's head snapped up at the sound of Amelia's voice. She'd never interrupted the marquis before. How did she dare do it now when he was in such high choler?

"I put it to you that Serena's request is a reasonable one. This is a momentous occasion and one that might daunt a stouter heart than your daughter possesses." Amelia came forward and placed a hand on Serena's shoulder. "Why don't you allow her until teatime to read the documents and consider the matter?"

Her father's jaw worked furiously for a moment, and Serena wondered why Amelia didn't cower under his fierce scowl. Then he drew himself up to his full height and tugged down his waistcoat. "Very well. Consider the matter. Consider it carefully, and while you're considering, be certain to consider the fealty a daughter owes her father."

Each time he said "consider" it sounded more and more like a curse. Serena decided to make good her escape. Hugging the oilskin packet to her chest, she stood, dropped a curtsey, and forced herself to walk away sedately.

She really wanted to flee like a hare from the hounds.

❧

Fortescue Alcock had been standing with his ear to the keyhole, but the damned door was solid English oak and he'd only been able to hear one word in three. Now he barely had time to duck into a nearby curtained alcove to avoid detection by Lady Serena as she bolted from Lord Wyndleton's study.

He peered through the slit in the rich damask in time to spy the royal insignia blazing on the thick packet Lady Serena carried. If the Duke of Kent were turning his eyes to the princess on the Continent, he wouldn't have sent so much blasted paperwork to this English miss.

Damnation! Sharp had failed. Lady Serena's honor was still fully intact and unless Alcock was much mistaken, she was in possession of a formal proposal from the royal.

In his eavesdropping, he'd pieced together enough to gather that the lady wasn't entirely enamored by the idea of the match. The angry voice of the marquis spilling out into the hallway now seemed to confirm his suspicions.

He crept out to listen again.

The more conciliatory tones of the one-time governess didn't carry as well as Lord Wyndleton's, but she seemed to be taking her employer to task. Alcock didn't have time to puzzle out that social oddity, but filed the information away for future use. He was more anxious to keep Lady Serena from making a formal acceptance of the duke's suit.

Alcock stole down the hall and back to the more public portions of the great house. Once he returned to London, he'd begin proceedings to bring Sir Jonah Sharp up on charges of treason for his role in the Maubeuge disaster. Sharp would have no defense. Alcock had a long list of people willing to perjure themselves on his say-so, many of them bit players on Drury Lane. Politicians and judges always loved good theatre.

He'd leave Warrington and Colton out of it since they'd at least had the goodness to marry the virgins he assigned to them to spoil, though personally he'd have preferred the scandal of having the ladies publicly ruined.

Never let a good scandal go wasted. That was one of his favorite political mottoes.

His plan to thwart the royal duke's courtship wasn't lost yet. Alcock pulled his pocket watch out and checked the time. If Lady Serena kept to her usual schedule, she'd go riding in half an hour.

He smiled as he remembered another favorite motto.

If you want something done well, do it yourself.

Twenty-nine

There seems to be a rash of our young London dandies and their chosen ladies thumbing their noses at tradition. They refuse to wait for the banns to be read for three consecutive Sundays. Some even eschew paying for a special license so they can hurry along their nuptials, haring off for a wedding over an anvil at Gretna Green.

Is it, we wonder, because fathers of marriageable girls often intimidate the would-be bridegrooms so much, they don't dare step forward to ask for the lady's hand like a gentleman? Of course, if the fellow is unable to beard the old lion in his den, shouldn't a sensible young lady ask herself if it's worth leaving the pride for a suitor with no teeth of his own?

From Le Dernier Mot,
The Final Word on News That Everyone
Who Is Anyone Should Know

"LEONARD, YOU MUSTN'T TRY TO FORCE THE GIRL," Amelia said, her usually sweet face now a mask of determination. "Serena has never responded well to the stick."

"What better carrot could I offer than the chance to wear a crown?" Honestly, if he lived to be a hundred he'd never understand the female of the species.

"There's something she wants even more." Amelia sank into the chair his daughter had just vacated. "Your approval."

The marquis paced before the fire. "All she has to do is sign the letter accepting the duke's suit and she'll have it."

"Dearest, she ought to have it no matter what she decides," Amelia said in that infuriatingly conciliatory tone that meant she felt she possessed the high ground in their argument. It never failed to grate on his last nerve. Especially since it meant she was probably right. "Don't you see, husband? Love with conditions is not love. And Serena needs yours most desperately."

He stifled the urge to stomp his feet in frustration. "This is preposterous. How can she doubt that I love her? Haven't I arranged the best match in Christendom for her?"

"She may not see it that way."

"What other way is there to see it?"

With the grace that had first drawn his eye to her after his wife died, Amelia rose and came over to put her arms around him. "Serena wants what we have. She wants a love match."

He drew her close and buried his nose in the juncture of her neck and shoulder. She smelled so good. It was impossible to keep up spirited discussion, much less an argument, with a woman who smelled like springtime. He sighed. "Then there's no hope she'll see reason."

"I didn't say that." Amelia kissed his cheek. "She hasn't said no to the duke. So long as she hasn't made a definite decision and set her feet, we have reason to believe that she'll come around to your side."

He bent and kissed her. "At least I know *you're* on my side."

She smiled up at him. "Never doubt it, Leonard."

He'd have covered her mouth with his again, but someone interrupted by pounding on the door as if they were demanding entrance to an alehouse that was closed for business. Amelia wiggled out of his arms and skittered across the room as the door opened without waiting for his permission.

Sir Jonah Sharp strode into the study. "My lord, I'll have a word with you."

Leonard had meant to summon Sharp later, but now he narrowed his eyes at the upstart baronet who'd interrupted a perfectly good stolen moment with Amelia. He'd miss the clandestine aspect of their marriage once it became common knowledge, but for now, he had business to attend.

"This is fortuitous, Sir Jonah. I have a few words for you as well. Will you kindly leave us, Miss Braithwaite?"

❦

Once Amelia glided from the room, Lord Wyndleton's expression turned icy.

"Someone should have warned you that I don't suffer fools gladly, Sharp," the marquis said as he took his seat behind the ornate desk. "And barging into my study uninvited is by definition foolish."

"I'm not here to curry favor." Jonah had little time

for fools either. When he was planning this little inter-
view, he decided his best course of action was to keep
the marquis off balance. Blustering his way into the
lord's presence seemed a good start. "I'm merely here
to serve notice that I intend to marry your daughter."

Wyndleton's eyes blazed. "Out of the question."

"You're mistaken, your lordship, if you think I'm
asking your permission."

Lord Wyndleton's Adam's apple bobbed furiously.
"You insolent puppy. How dare you—"

"I dare because I love your daughter, and I mean to
make her mine if she'll have me."

"If she'll have you," he repeated. "Have you
spoken to Serena of this ridiculous notion?"

"No. I'm waiting to see if she turns down the Duke
of Kent first. I understand his courier has arrived."

The marquis confirmed it with a curt nod.

"Has she accepted his offer?" The marquis's mouth
twitched, and Jonah read irritation there. "So she
hasn't then. When will she give you her decision?"

Lord Wyndleton's fingers drummed a frustrated
tattoo on the top of his desk. "We should know by
teatime."

Jonah cocked his head at the man who routinely
destroyed his political enemies in the House of Lords
but appeared totally stymied by his own daughter.
"You haven't tried to force her, have you?"

Some of the vinegar went out of the older man's
expression. "No. Why haven't you asked her to
marry you?"

"For the same reason you haven't imposed your
will on her. She's not like other women. She's…"

Jonah waved a hand as if he could pull the right word out of the air to describe the unorthodox woman who'd so tangled up his heart he'd never be free. But words failed him. He dropped his hand back to his side. "I love her, but she needs to be free to make her own choice."

Even if it's not me.

If he asked her now, she might accept. But later, when she considered the crown she'd given up, she could well resent Jonah. He wouldn't take that chance. He could only hope she loved him enough not to be dazzled by a royal offer.

The marquis glared at him, as if his intent stare would ferret out the secrets of Jonah's soul. "You should know, Sharp," he finally said, "that I will not grant my daughter a dowry if she marries beneath her."

"She'll be marrying beneath her no matter who she chooses, so that doesn't signify. I don't want your money. I only want Serena." Jonah bunched his fingers into fists. "I can provide for her abundantly. You may rest easy on that score."

One of the marquis's brows arched. The lord's system of informants was reputedly so efficient, he could probably estimate Jonah's yearly income to the nearest shilling. It wasn't a prince's living, but he was independently wealthy enough to treat Serena like royalty without financial help from her father.

"Are you sure you haven't spoken to my daughter of your intentions? She has no idea?"

"No. I couldn't speak to her because I gave my word I wouldn't."

"To whom?"

"To your wife."

The marquis's eyes went hard as the gray granite of the nearby castle ruins. "Do not presume you may use whatever you think you know to harm those I care about."

"If I feel bound to honor my word to Miss Braithwaite, how can you imagine I'd bring her harm?"

Some of the grit went out of his expression. "No, I suppose you wouldn't. That's something they told me about you. Women and children were sacrosanct."

Now it was Jonah's turn to feel off balance. Only one group of people would have known about Jonah's strictures regarding the treatment of the fair sex and children. Lord Wyndleton raised a hand to indicate that Jonah should sit. Jonah sank into the chair opposite the marquis's desk.

"What you are about to hear must never leave this room," Lord Wyndleton said.

Jonah nodded his assent.

"For some time now you have been in the employ of the Triad. For many reasons, the identity of your employers has remained a mystery to you. However, as you may have surmised, I make up one third of that body of His Majesty's most loyal supporters. One of the members died unexpectedly, and I was chosen to replace him. I have only been part of the group for the last fortnight, but I have been thoroughly briefed on all our operatives."

"Then you know I have not taken a commission from the Triad for some time."

Lord Wyndleton shrugged. "I have one now I feel certain you'll accept."

"I intend to marry your daughter, sir. I can no longer act as your assassin, however noble your motives for ordering the elimination of certain persons may be."

"Hear me out." The marquis raised an imperious hand. "When you were serving in France, you led your men in a battle near the village of Maubeuge. It was a disastrous defeat, and you and some of the other officers were blamed. There was even a whiff of treason hovering about your names. I made it my business to learn the particulars."

The marquis steepled his hands on the desk before him and gazed coolly at Jonah. "My factors tell me that someone made sure you received faulty reconnaissance information."

Jonah released the breath he'd been holding. Finally, someone in authority believed him and his friends innocent.

"We had identified a Sgt. Leatherby who was willing to testify to that," Jonah said. "Unfortunately, he has taken ship for Boston."

Lord Wyndleton waved a hand. "It is of no consequence. Why settle for the testimony of a common foot soldier when a peer of the realm is on your side? We have identified the person responsible for delivering the flawed reports to you prior to the battle. It was Fortescue Alcock."

Jonah gripped the arms of the chair hard. "Hundreds of men died needlessly. Why would he do such a thing?"

"Just as members of the Triad take the long view on such matters, Mr. Alcock has his own plans. No doubt he thought having three capable young men such as you, Warrington, and Colton under his thumb was worth sacrificing all those lives." The marquis took a key from his waistcoat pocket and opened a locked desk drawer. He took out a much folded piece of parchment. "We learned of Alcock's plot to end the line of the House of Hanover by thwarting the royal dukes in their quest for brides."

"Then you've also learned that he assigned me to your daughter. I was supposed to seduce and ruin her." Jonah leaned forward. "Instead, I fell in love with her. I'd sooner cut out my own heart than harm her."

If she accepted the duke's suit, cutting out his heart would probably hurt less.

"Your attachment to Lady Serena is not the topic under discussion at present. However," Lord Wyndleton said grudgingly, "I am disposed to believe you." The marquis handed the paper to Jonah, which both named the man to be removed and absolved the assassin of any guilt in the act so far as the law of the land was concerned. "This is your final assignment for us. Fortescue Alcock must be eliminated. The succession of kings is in God's hands, not a measly Member of Parliament's."

Jonah thought the marquis risked a few lightning bolts by ordering an execution while at the same time calling on the Almighty's aid in arranging the royal succession. But this was one assignment he couldn't pass up. Mr. Alcock had made Jonah's friends' lives miserable. He put Jonah into a situation where he had to choose between his family's welfare and the woman he loved. And most of all, the blood of all the men who died at Maubeuge were on Fortescue Alcock's skeletal hands. Jonah pocketed the order.

"Consider it done, sir."

"Now about my daughter—" The marquis was interrupted by rapid banging on the door. "Come, confound it!"

Mr. Honeywood stepped inside the study, wringing his hands and hanging his head sheepishly. "Begging your pardon, my lord, but there's someone asking to see—"

"Not now, Honeywood. Can't you see I'm busy?"

The butler tugged at his collar. "The caller isn't wishing to speak to you, my lord. They're here for Sir Jonah."

Jonah said nothing. Until the marquis gave him leave, good manners dictated that he not respond.

"It's about the Lady Serena," Honeywood said with a ragged edge to his voice that almost sounded like hysteria.

Good manners be damned.

Jonah rose to his feet and gave the marquis a curt nod. "I will return when I've fulfilled your commission." Then he started toward the door.

"Sir Jonah."

He stopped and turned back to face Serena's father.

"You gave your word on another matter to someone else. I consider that pledge as made to me as well."

"As do I." No matter how tempted he was, he couldn't speak his heart to Serena till she made her decision regarding the duke's suit. As much as it rankled his soul, it was the only way to be sure she would be happy with her choice. He didn't want to be simply another option for her.

He wanted to be her only option.

Once the study door closed behind him, Mr. Honeywood urged him to haste. "His lordship is exceedingly liberal in his policies, but even he might take umbrage at this sort of person turning up at his kitchen door."

"Who's asking to see me?" Jonah said as he strode after the scurrying butler.

"A gypsy woman. She says her name is Nadya, and she refuses to leave the premises until she speaks to—and I quote—the tall man who knows horseflesh better than people. Since you've been inspecting his lordship's herd, I assumed…"

Jonah lengthened his stride. After Serena's visit to the gypsy woman, she was different. He could only assume the woman had said something to unnerve her, and there were few enough souls in the world who could do that.

Jonah plowed through the manor house's extensive kitchen and found Nadya sitting on the small stoop outside the back door. Eyes closed, her brown face was tipped upward to soak up the pale March sun.

"You wish to speak to me," he said.

Her dark eyes fluttered open. "Ah. The horseman. Good. I have seen something."

Jonah frowned down at her. She must have been skulking about spying on the people at Wyndebourne. Honeywood was right. The marquis would not take kindly to such goings on.

"What have you seen?"

"Not with my eyes, you understand." The woman rose and began to walk away from the imposing manor house. Jonah was forced to follow after signaling to Honeywood to remain where he was by the back door. "This thing I have seen in the Hall of Dreams. Not once, but three times, so it is confirmed."

"How much will it cost me?" Gypsies were always willing to tell people whatever they wished to hear and charged them royally for the privilege.

"Because it touches a lady's safety, I will tell you now, and later you can decide what my words are worth."

"Serena's safety, you mean?"

"Assuredly. Have I not said so?"

Not really, but Jonah didn't see the profit in arguing with her. "Go on and I'll deal fairly with you."

The woman shot him a wry grin. "If I did not believe you would, I would not offer you my help." Her smile faded. "In my visions, I see the lady. She is in a place she loves and feels safe, but she is not. There is one there who will do her harm."

"Who is it?"

She shook her head, setting her dark curls jiggling. "One who is unknown to me, but in the Hall of Dreams, I sensed he is well known to you. This person has already dealt you a grievous blow, you and your friends."

"Alcock."

"It may be," Nadya said. "The spirits, they do not trouble to tell me his name. Only the condition of his heart, which is black as a moonless night."

Then between one step and the next, the gypsy woman collapsed in a shuddering heap to the ground.

Her back arched. Her eyes rolled back into her head, leaving only the whites showing, and her mouth was drawn in the rictus of a silent scream.

Jonah knelt beside her but was at a loss for what to do to help her. Fortunately, after only a few heartbeats, she stopped convulsing and closed her eyes. Nadya drew a deep breath and snaked up a bony hand to grasp the front of his shirt. Her eyes flew open wide.

"Now. It is happening now. You must go to her."

"Where?"

"In the place where she feels safe." The woman struggled back to her feet. Whatever toll the fit she suffered exacted from her, at least she seemed able to shake off its effects quickly. "The place where she played as a child."

The castle ruins. With all the crumbling stones and the desolation of the place, there were any number of ways Alcock could arrange for Serena to have an accident there.

"Fly," Nadya urged, and Jonah took to his heels.

Thirty

In a surprising turnabout, it has come to our ears that an emissary from a certain royal duke has been dispatched to the Continent as well as one to a peer of the realm's country house. What the significance of this could be, we are at a loss to explain.

Could it be the duke feels the need to hedge his bets and offer for both of the ladies to whom he's been known to direct his attention? Such a thing ought to be unheard of, but to our knowledge there's never been an opportunity to put one's progeny on the throne like this before, either.

We wait on pins for the outcome.

From Le Dernier Mot,
The Final Word on News That Everyone
Who Is Anyone Should Know

SERENA HOBBLED HER MARE IN THE SHALLOW GRASSY depression that used to be the castle moat and left her to graze. Then she wandered through the bones of the old ruin, placing a hand on the stones here and there as if that might enable her to hear its ponderous thoughts. Surely something that had stood as long as these gray granite slabs must contain some wisdom from prior generations of Osbournes.

She was in desperate need of it.

All she need do to please her father was agree to the duke's offer. Unlike her list of forbidden pleasures, which now seemed like a distant lark, an ascent into royalty would be a different sort of adventure, one in which she had no control of either her person or her actions. The only strawberry in that repressive situation was that there was every chance she would become the mother of a future sovereign.

But she'd have no life of her own, no free choices at all.

Of course, she'd made rather a muddle of her life by making her own choices. Serena ran her list of pleasures through her mind. They'd been diverting and mildly exciting, but none of them had given her lasting joy. A few had even turned out to be rather unpleasant.

Even the last one, the one she'd never had the courage to commit to paper—*Item eight: Lie with a man for no other reason than because I want to*—had failed her in the end.

One night of loving with Jonah would never be enough.

But he didn't give any indication he wanted to have her in his bed on a permanent basis. He'd never even said he loved her, much less offered her marriage.

The idea of a loveless match, however glittering by the world's standards, was abhorrent. If she didn't wed the duke, she'd have only the long march of days as a spinster to look forward to, along with the added burden of knowing she'd disappointed her father beyond remedy.

She climbed the stone stairs to the top of the curtain wall slowly, as if her legs were leaden. The wind freshened when she stepped alongside the stone parapet. Maybe it would send her fresh thoughts.

Instead it must have covered another person's quiet tread. She didn't hear Mr. Alcock's advance until he was within ten feet of her.

"Oh." She put a hand to her chest when she caught sight of him, mildly alarmed. "You gave me a start."

"My apologies, milady," he said, his words rolling out in that oily cadence only politicians can manage. "It seems I've interrupted your musings. I suppose you do have a good bit to ponder since word about Wyndebourne is that you have received a proposal from the royal duke."

"You should know better than to listen to rumor." All Jonah's warnings about the man and how he wished to stop her from just such a match flooded back into her.

"Rumor is mother's milk to one such as I," he said, spreading his hands in an attempt at a self-deprecating gesture designed to put her at ease. It failed miserably. Every fiber of her being was on high alert. "For argument's sake, suppose you did receive such an offer. What would be your answer?"

"I'd hardly tell you before I told my father."

"So you haven't given an answer then."

She edged away from him a step or two, but he followed. "This is none of your business."

"On the contrary, whether or not the House of Hanover continues its reign over our land is the business of every forward-thinking Englishman," Alcock said with such vehemence that spittle bubbled at the corner of his mouth. "The Hanoverians have squandered the wealth and prestige of our nation."

Fear shuddered through her. If Alcock was wild enough to speak so openly of treason, the man might be capable of anything. She needed to mollify him somehow.

"If it makes you feel any better, sir, I have decided to turn down an offer from the royal duke...should one be forthcoming, of course."

She hadn't actually made the decision till the words spilled from her lips, but now that they hovered in the air, she knew it was the right thing to do. She loved Jonah Sharp, whether or not he loved her back. She couldn't marry anyone but him, not even a prince.

And if Jonah never asked her, she'd simply die alone.

"Well, now," Mr. Alcock said, "isn't that convenient? You've told me exactly what I want to hear. If you'd been born a man, I'd say you had a future in politics, my lady."

She continued to back away from him, but there were a few places on the narrow walkway where the stone had fallen away, and she didn't dare move quickly. "I've told you the truth."

"That's as may be, but I find I cannot rely upon merely your word. You might change your mind. Women are prone to doing that in my experience." He leaped forward, closing the distance between them in a heartbeat. The fellow was quicker and stronger than he looked. He snatched her close in an iron grasp. "Now if Sharp had only lived up to his bargain, you'd be sadder but wiser with your reputation in ruins, but at least you'd still be alive." He made a tsking sound. "However, now you won't be."

Then he punched her in the face. Stars reeled behind her eyes, and her vision narrowed to a long dark tunnel before winking out completely.

❧

By a trick of acoustics, Jonah heard snippets of voices coming from the ruin long before he broke out of the surrounding trees. He couldn't see Serena on the curtain wall, so he dismounted and moved closer to the gray stone on foot.

"What are you going to do?" Jonah heard her asking.

"Oh, it's not what I'm going to do. It's what you will," Alcock said. "Distraught over your choice, you have decided to end it all, just like Judas, in a headlong plunge from these ramparts."

His heart pounding like a cannon volley, Jonah crept up the stone steps. He'd faced a French cavalry charge. He'd been in countless duels that might have gone either way, but he'd never known this gut-strangling knot of fear before. If anything happened to Serena…

"I'd never do something so silly, however distraught I might be. My family knows me better than that. No one will be fooled." Serena's voice was forced but even.

God love her, she's trying to talk a man out of murdering her.

"They'll believe it when they find you hanging

here. They'll be too wild with grief to question it. With any luck, your father will blame himself and follow suit." Alcock loosed a simpering giggle. "Once your young cousin Roland succeeds Lord Wyndleton, he'll be nothing to face down in the House of Lords. You must take heart that your death will help speed the end of the Tories. Possibly even of the monarchy itself."

"You made a mistake, you know. You shouldn't have hit me," Serena said. "I can feel the bruise starting already. If I'm supposed to have hanged myself, how will you explain the bruise?"

Alcock had struck her. By God, he was going to pay dearly for that.

"What a sheltered life you've lived, milady," Alcock said. "Most hanged persons don't die instantly, you see. Your family will undoubtedly believe you dashed your face upon the stone of the castle wall in your final struggles."

"People who hang themselves don't generally bind their own hands and feet," she said, an edge of desperation creeping into her tone.

"Never fear, milady. Once you stop thrashing, I'll cut your bonds."

Damn the man, he had an answer for everything. Jonah inched up the steps and peered onto the parapet. Alcock was kneeling beside Serena's prone figure, tying another knot to keep her arms and legs still. She'd put up a fight, but she was no match for a man's strength.

No matter. Alcock was no match for him. This was one killing that would trouble Jonah's conscience not a bit. He thought about using his horse pistol, but the report of a round might draw unwanted attention to the area, and it would be best for the Triad if Alcock's body wasn't discovered for some time.

Jonah decided to use his hands. It was brutish. Primal. And in this case, he expected it to be supremely satisfying.

He rushed from his place of concealment, roaring in rage. Alcock was too surprised to mount any sort of defense as Jonah grabbed him, lifted him over the parapet, and gave him a toss.

But at the last second, the MP grasped Jonah's arm and held on with a grip like a bulldog's bite. Jonah was nearly dragged over the crenellated edge along with him.

Jonah's chest slammed against the unforgiving stone, forcing all the breath from his lungs. His arm was practically yanked out of its socket.

"Don't let me go!" Alcock wailed.

"You fool. I'm not even trying to hold you." Jonah's only concern now was that when the man finally did take the long drop, it wouldn't be far enough to do him in immediately.

"Jonah, pull him back up," Serena said softly.

"Stay out of this, Serena. I'm under orders."

"The Triad?"

He nodded and gave Alcock a vigorous shake, but he wouldn't let go. The man kept trying to scrabble his heels against the castle wall and clamber up Jonah's aching arm, but he couldn't seem to gain any purchase with his slick-soled boots.

"Fortescue Alcock is a traitor to the Crown, and

as such, he deserves no mercy," Jonah said through clenched teeth. "He'd have given none to you."

"There's got to be another way." Her voice called to a small part of his heart, the part that loathed taking a life, even one as deserving of death as Alcock. "Not for his sake, Jonah. For yours."

He wiggled out of his jacket and tied a sleeve through an iron ring embedded in the castle's stone. Alcock continued to screech for help.

"Pray that the wool is of high quality," he said, glaring down at the man dangling from the other sleeve. Alcock spouted threats and pleading, but still managed to hang on with white-lipped determination.

Jonah knelt beside Serena and untied her bonds. Then he pulled her into his arms and inhaled her warmth clear to his toes. Suddenly it didn't matter if she accepted the duke's suit. If she was only safe, he'd ask for no more.

Serena, however, had plenty to ask of him. "Don't kill him, Jonah." She cupped his face with both hands. "Don't you see? If you do, you'll never be free. You weren't made for this."

Somewhere inside him there was still a young ensign who'd ridden off to war with clean hands and a heart full of love for king and country. He'd never be that innocent again, but he longed for a small slice of it with all his soul.

"No matter what you've done in the past," she went on, "you can change things now. Truly. It starts here."

"Why, Serena?" He fingered the purpling bruise on her cheek. His insides burned with rage for the man who was still screaming his head off as he hung suspended between life and a painful death on the rocky scree at the base of the castle wall. "Why do you want me to spare that piece of offal?"

"Because mercy blesses the one who gives it more than the one who receives," she said. "Because I want to see you whole. Please. I love you, Jonah."

She loved him. It washed over him like a benediction, lighting all the dark corners of his heart and chasing away the old ghosts. It didn't matter that he'd be disobeying a direct order from the Triad—one from her father, even. There was nothing he wouldn't do for her. Now or at any time.

Their mouths met in a kiss of fervent desperation. When they finally parted, Serena whispered, "Will you spare him for me?"

Jonah rested his forehead against hers. "As long as I breathe, I'm yours to command."

"Good." A smile broke over her face, though it was a little crooked since the bruised side didn't lift as much. "That'll come in handy once we're married."

"No doubt." Jonah dropped a kiss on the tip of her nose, scarcely daring to believe his ears. Somehow, without having to put together the right words, something he'd never been overly good at, he'd managed to steal a woman away from a prince. Then he picked up the piece of rope that Alcock had already fashioned into a noose and loosened the loop.

"Slip this over your head and under your arms," he ordered Alcock after he flopped the rope over the side of the parapet. Jonah braced his feet as the man complied. Once he hauled the MP back up, Alcock

collapsed on the gray stone in a sniveling heap. A foul
smell wafted from him and Jonah realized the man had
voided both his bladder and his bowels in terror.

"What…are you going to do with me?" Alcock
finally said between gasping breaths.

"A good question since the fact remains that you're
a traitor not only to the Crown, but also to the men
who fought at Maubeuge."

Alcock's eyes went wide. "You know about that?"

Jonah nodded grimly. "So I can't simply let you go
as if nothing has happened."

The Triad used its assassins to quash those who
were a danger to the Crown without arousing public
outcry. Alcock might be brought justice through a
trial and finally hanged as an example. But such cases
of treason were difficult to prove and would stir up
unrest among those who were tired of the monarchy.
Alcock could become a rallying point for dissatisfac-
tion, a martyr to his cause.

Serena rose shakily to her feet and pleaded with
her eyes. Jonah couldn't simply dispose of him and he
couldn't bind him over to the law either.

Below the castle ramparts, Warrington and Colton
came riding into view. Jonah had ordered Honeywood
to send them after him when he set off in pursuit of
Serena. His friends were too late to help with her
rescue, but a new idea took shape in Jonah's mind.

After their search for Leatherby, Warrington and
Colton knew their way around the Portsmouth docks,
which ships were berthed there and where they were
headed. Surely one was bound for Botany Bay soon.

"Thank Lady Serena for your miserable life,

Alcock," he said. With any luck at all, it would be completely miserable. After all, a former Member of Parliament who was forced to take ship for Australia's penal colony in britches stained with his own shite wouldn't be on a pleasure cruise.

Thirty-one

Heads are shaking over the surprising disappearance of Mr. Fortescue Alcock, Esq., noted Member of Parliament and leader of a particularly unpleasant faction of Whigs. However, few are registering displeasure over the gentleman's unexplained absence. Most notable in the "happy-to-see-him-gone" column is his wife.

Mrs. Alcock has been spotted at soirees and entertainments all over Town. She has reportedly sought advice from a solicitor regarding how long she must wait before her husband may be declared legally dead. Whatever the man's sins and wherever he may be atoning for them now, it appears he was not over-blessed with conjugal bliss.

And speaking of all things conjugal, one leg of the Hymen Race Terrific is officially over. This coming May, Prince Edward, the Duke of Kent, will wed Princess Victoria Mary Louisa of Saxe-Coburg-Saalfeld at Amorbach in Bavaria. We suspect, with resigned distaste, that the ceremony will be conducted in German.

From Le Dernier Mot,
The Final Word on News That Everyone
Who Is Anyone Should Know

"AH, WELCOME BACK, MR. OSBOURNE." THE DOORMAN at Boodles scraped a low bow. "I see you've shaved your mustache."

Serena merely nodded and handed the man her topper. Jonah stomped across the threshold behind her. The early April day felt more like the first of March. A brisk wind followed them in.

"Seat us someplace near the fire, if you please," Jonah said to the porter, then dropped his voice so only Serena could hear him. "It's colder than a witch's tits outside."

"If you know anything about anyone else's tits, witch or otherwise, I'll break your arm," Serena whispered behind her hand as they followed the servant to the same seats they'd occupied a little more than a month earlier.

"Duly noted, wife." Jonah chuckled as he settled into the comfortable wing chair and ordered coffee for them, making sure to request extra cream and three sugar lumps for Serena's cup. Then he signaled for Mr. Filbee to bring out the wager book.

"If you check there, Mr. Filbee, you'll see that my companion and I entered into a wager concerning a certain young lady. The outcome of the bet has been determined, and Osbourne is here to pay."

Serena took out a money pouch and counted out one hundred pounds into Jonah's waiting palm. Then they both signed the ledger indicating that the debt was settled to mutual satisfaction. With any luck, cousin Rowland would never know he'd ever entered into and lost a bet with ten to one stakes with Serena's new husband.

Once Mr. Filbee left them, she leaned forward.

"'This is really very silly. That was your own money I counted out to you."

Jonah gave her an affronted look. "A debt of honor is never silly."

Serena crossed her legs. This time she was wearing a pair of drawers beneath the masculine garb that took the itch out of her wool trousers. She took a sip of the creamy coffee and sighed. It was just the way she liked it. Why couldn't all her forays into forbidden pleasures have been like this? "You should have at least let me pawn my jewels to repay you."

"The day I let you sell any of your gewgaws is the day I turn up my toes."

Serena smiled into her cup. She and Jonah had married by special license only a few days earlier. Her father had been upset at first by her decision not to accept the royal duke. However, when he learned how Jonah had saved her life at the old castle ruins and disposed of Alcock by shipping him to Australia under threat of immediate death if he ever showed his face in England again, Lord Wyndleton came around.

Especially after Amelia goaded him into admitting that he and she had been secretly married for some years. Serena was delighted because it meant she would continue to have Amelia in her life forever. And Amelia was such a good tempering influence on the marquis. Serena even thought her mother would have approved of her father's choice.

"Now, my dear Osbourne," Jonah said after he finished his stout black coffee, "can I ply you with some Orange Fool?"

"Oh, I'm sorry, sir, but I couldn't help over-hearing," the nearby footman said. "Orange Fool is still not on the menu. Cook refuses to reinstate it until we discover the identities of the culprits who upset that vat of cream earlier this month."

"Pity," Serena said, pitching her voice as low as she could. "It's a pleasure I was looking forward to."

Once the footman moved out of earshot, Jonah rummaged in his pocket and came up with a crisply folded sheet of foolscap. "Speaking of pleasures, I've come up with a new list for you."

"Oh, really?"

"Yes, really. Read them and see if they don't sound like adventures worthy of the name."

Serena unfolded paper slowly. "This is something I generally prefer to do myself, you know."

"Perhaps, but I'll wager there are things on that list a lady would never dream of."

She ran her gaze over a list of ever more decadent and enticing sensual adventures. Her eyes widened and heat pooled between her legs. "Is number four even anatomically possible?"

Jonah gave her the wickedly rakish smile she loved. "There's only one way to find out. As soon as we've finished our coffee, let's head home to give it a go."

Serena upended her cup and drained it in one long gulp. Then she swiped her hand in a parody of masculine manners and stood, eager to be gone. "Now we've only one decision to make."

"What's that?"

"Do we go back out the front door or escape through the kitchen again?"

"Since we can't count on a vat of cream to cover our exit this time, I recommend the front door." Jonah finished his coffee and rose, his gaze sizzling down at her. "But if you check item seven on that list, you'll see a rather inventive use for cream."

"Better than Orange Fool?" she asked as he collected their hats from the doorman.

"I promise."

"Then take me home right now, Jonah Sharp, or you'll never live down having 'Rowland' Osbourne kiss you right on the lips before God and all the gentlemen at Boodles."

Jonah grinned down at her. "If it means I get a kiss from you, Serena, I don't give a flying fig."

Authors' Note

After the death of their niece, Princess Charlotte, the unmarried sons of King George III scrambled to wed in order to present their father with a legitimate grand-child and insure the continuation of the Hanoverian line. The Dukes of Clarence, Cambridge, and Kent went a-courting and that race to the altar forms the historical underpinnings for our Royal Rakes series.

Prince Edward, the Duke of Kent, is the royal suitor featured in *Between a Rake and a Hard Place*, and in many ways, he certainly was a hard fellow. His early years as a military man were stained with one disaster after another. When he was made Governor of Gibraltar, his harsh discipline fomented a mutiny which required him to leave in disgrace and never return.

He gave no evidence of softness in his personal life either. Kent had numerous mistresses, some of whom bore him children. He took the wife of a baron as his mistress for twenty-eight years and kept house with her in Quebec. The lady was forced to retire to a convent when he decided, at the age of fifty, to marry a younger woman in order to beget an heir to his father's throne.

On May 29, 1818, the Duke of Kent married Princess Victoria of Saxe-Coburg-Saalfeld. A year later, Princess Alexandrina Victoria was born. But Kent did not have long to rejoice in his offspring. He preceded his father King George III in death in 1820, after succumbing to pneumonia.

However, Kent did win the race for the crown. His daughter ascended to the throne as Queen Victoria at the tender age of eighteen in 1837. She reigned for sixty-three years, the longest of any female ruler, and ushered in an era which still bears her name.

We hope you enjoyed *Between a Rake and a Hard Place*. If you missed the other two books in the series, be sure to look for *Waking Up with a Rake* and *One Night with a Rake*.

Happy Reading,
Connie & Mia

Acknowledgments

No book springs to life as the result of one person's efforts. Or even two people. Mia and Connie would like to thank their editor, Leah Hultenschmidt, and agent, Natasha Kern, for pairing them up to write the Royal Rakes series. Leah and Natasha were first to recognize the value in bringing the two of them together. Working as a team has been good for both writers. Thanks, Leah and Natasha!

Then there are the tireless folk at Sourcebooks who lovingly poured themselves into *Between a Rake and a Hard Place*. Special thanks go to Nicole Komasinski, who designed the wonderful cover; Danielle Jackson and the rest of the marketing department for making sure the world learns about this final book in the series; Pamela Guerrieri, who did the copyedits; Rachel Edwards, the production editor; and Cat Clyne, the editorial assistant who pulled it all together. You're very much appreciated.

We'd be remiss if we didn't thank our critique partner, Ashlyn Chase, and our beloved beta-reader, Marcy Weinbeck. Without the encouragement of these two special women, this book would never have been written.

And last, but never least, Connie and Mia want to thank YOU, dear reader. Without you and your imagination, it's only ink on a page.